When Morning Comes Again

JUNE MASTERS BACHER

HARVEST HOUSE PUBLISHERS
Eugene, Oregon 97402

Scripture quotations are taken from the King James Version of the Bible.

WHEN MORNING COMES AGAIN

Copyright © 1988 by Harvest House Publishers
Eugene, Oregon 97402

Bacher, June Masters.
    When morning comes again / June Masters Bacher.
        p.   cm.
    Summary: Courtney's Christian faith sustains her as failing silver mines, fire, and the kidnapping of her baby girl threaten her family in their valley on the Washington State frontier.
    ISBN 0-89081-694-8
    [1. Frontier and pioneer life—Washington (State)—Fiction. 2. Washington (State)—Fiction. 3. Christian life—Fiction.]
    I. Title.
PS3552.A257W47   1988
813'.54—dc19
[Fic]   88-7650
                                                                     CIP
                                                                      AC

Printed in the United States of America.

Dedicated to
three
FATHER-AND-SON LOVES
who
bless my life:
George and Bryce Bacher,
Bob Hawkins and Bob, Jr.,
and
The Master and His Son!

Contents

Prologue

IN RETROSPECT...

Justice! The word rang out like a bell, dulling all other sound. *Justice.* Harshly, the unuttered cry hung over a list of the vanquished printed on a single pine board until proper headstones could be erected. Those responsible would come to justice in this new land. All else was secondary, even temporary, obscured by layers of night in the mind of Courtney Desmond.

"Vengeance is mine, saith the Lord," somebody quoted.

Vengeance? Not vengeance. *Justice!*

Gone were the paintings of the past in their heavy, ornate frames. Gone was the long table of love around which the family prayed. Gone were—no, *no*, she could not face that! It was enough to know that in place of it all was blackened rubble. Never mind the night riders, whoever they were. She, mistress of the Mansion, had let it happen. She would pay forever. But for others— *justice!*

Shaking off the supporting arm around her, "Don't pity *me*—pity *them!*" Courtney said.

In retrospect, it was all a beautiful dream. A beautiful dream in which Arabella Kennedy Lovelace had lived to see a classic drama played out, its action neither comedy nor tragedy. Life had been more of a gentle sadness, a candle giving off a bright light while acutely aware that it was burning low....

"I will make it right," Courtney whispered of the drama Cousin Bella would never see end....

I remember running over the hills just at dawn one summer morning and, pausing to rest in the silent woods, saw, through an arch of trees, the sun rise over river, hill, and wide green meadows as I never saw it before.

Something born of the lovely hour, a happy mood, and the unfolding aspirations of a child's soul seemed to bring me very close to God. . . .

—Louisa May Alcott

"...forgive, if you have ought against any; that your Father also which is in heaven may forgive your trespasses."

—Mark 11:25

CHAPTER 1
End of an Era

❦

The air was minted with spring. Courtney, climbing the little hill to gaze down on the quiet Columbia River Valley, inhaled deeply to fill her lungs with the morning freshness and to shake off a feeling of apprehension Cousin Bella's earlier words had hung around her heart.

"I have an announcement to make," the queenly mistress of Mansion-in-the-Wild had said matter-of-factly when the family finished breakfast, "so I should like everyone present at dinner. It will affect you all—as it marks the end of an era."

Courtney sank into the warm sweetness of the grass, letting the tall blades close over the pointed toes of her high-topped shoes. The fullness of the long walking skirt billowed out, catching the wind like a sail and then lay still as the wind swept upward to tease the new needles of the Douglas fir trees above her head.

April. Courtney loved its newness, its hope, its resurrection, and its tender green precociousness. Not unlike Cousin Bella, she mused with a smile. The fourth month and the woman who peculiarly was a distant paternal relative to Courtney and a maternal aunt to Clint (but closer to both husband and wife than bloodline dictated) were so predictably *un*predictable. Always about Arabella Kennedy Lovelace there was a hint of spring—a tantalizing promise without disclosure, a grand entrance and then a hasty retreat, in her manner.

Dear Cousin Bella. How she had endeared herself to the frightened 16-year-old half-woman, half-child

Courtney had been when her own mother bundled her away from the East Coast to the West. Stilling her fears. Drying her tears. Approving (no, *fostering* it really) the marriage between her two "children." Loving the offspring that blessed that marriage as if they were her grandchildren. And teaching her that God, in His infinite wisdom, would lead them through the unbelievably tragic chapters representing their lives here on the frontier. And God had done just that—in His mysterious way.

Mysterious. Thought of the word spun Courtney's mind back to the questions at hand. Cousin Bella was a no-nonsense woman, a devout believer that the Lord would hold her accountable for every idle word. Secrecy, yes, but no trickery. What the beloved matriarch had to say tonight was exactly as she had said—*important.* If it had to do with the Kennedy Mines, Clint would have told her.

But why speculate? Why not enjoy the stolen moment on this very gentle day? She parted the grasses and looked upward prayerfully at a sky watered between skim-milk blue and pale sweeps of cloud. It was a sacred moment—this moment alone with God. It had nothing to do with her husband with whom she fell more in love every day—or their precious children—or the extended family. And yet, it had *everything* to do with them. They all blended into one through God's love.

The rays of the sun grew warmer. She must return to the Mansion. The children undoubtedly had found new ways of tormenting Mandy and Mrs. Rueben. Courtney raised her head reluctantly, feeling in so many ways still a child herself. Momentarily the child in her nature watched the wind come again and wondered why the human eye was unable to see it. One could only watch as it laid the grasses aside in long silvery swaths and feel its presence as it passed. How like life's changes—great or small. With any degree of sensitivity, one could feel them coming, watch the signs. Surely she had known for some time that the winds of change were blowing....

Leaf-light, she sprang up to let the wind play in her long, dark hair which the grasses had loosed. The sword ferns tattled, swaying slightly to reveal silky curds of elder blossoms, murmurous with bees. Donolar would love hearing of the "bee-loud glade" even though the amber-furred creatures would have flown away. Below the ferns lay a thicket of vines starred with wild white roses, her brother's favorite flower. He would have tonight's centerpiece arranged for the dining table, but Donolar would welcome more—like the child he was. His garden, the envy of all women in the settlement, furnished more than enough. But Courtney gathered some of the white stars for the prodigal joy of gathering.

Apron filled, she paused, something deep inside begging that she hold the shining, fragile moment cupped in her hands. There it was again—the knowing that somehow things were destined to change. The winds were resting and, in the woodsy silence, there came the gentle whir of wings and she was surrounded by a cloud of small yellow butterflies. What was it Donolar said about a swarm of the wee insects? Good luck or bad? How foolish....

Yet, Courtney Desmond knew that, indeed, the end of an era had come.

CHAPTER 2
Surrender of the Keys

Arabella Kennedy Lovelace had changed little, Courtney reflected, watching her cousin preside over the long dining table. Oh, the white in her heavy braids was now predominate over the black. And yes, the older woman was thinner—perhaps more pale. But the compelling charm remained, the upright posture of her angular body lending an air of quiet authority. The unquestionable matriarch and Courtney herself were the only throwbacks to the "dark side" of the Glamora clan. Clint took after the Kennedys, his aunt said. And Courtney's siblings were cast in their mother's dresden beauty—yes, even the men, her twin brothers. Efraim, the lawyer with the brilliant mind, and Donolar with his wide, innocent, agate eyes that, though without expression, saw life as a poem without end.

And now a new generation. Yes, the children also were too beautiful to be true...Jordan and Jonda—looking deceptively like six-year-old angels—as lovely as their fair mother whose life had ended so tragically...as well as Clint and Courtney's roly-poly two-year-old, Kennedy.

"Brother Jim, proceed with the prayer."

Cousin Bella's command cut short the rambling thoughts and allowed Courtney no time to take roll by casting eyes discreetly the length and breadth of the great linen-covered table. She dared not look up now although she needed the security.

And then it was there. Clint had taken her small hand

between his without a ripple of the silence cloth. Nothing the relatives had to say could matter now.

The reverend gentleman, a star boarder of sorts, usually plodded through his prayers pleading God's mercy on the "saints gathered here" and His wrath on what Eastern newspapers occasionally finding their way to this frontier called "organized crime," as well as "disorganized crime" in this new land. Nervous perspiration would bead his cheeks as he fervently pounded fist against palm. After all, here he was, one man challenging the devil to enter the ring, hoping for a lasting victory—the odds roughly matching those of the miners getting rich.

Tonight, however, though the ex-prize-fighter's jaw was set, he postponed mention of an exhibition match. "Just know we're in the competition, Lord, and we'll never give up—even when we're temporarily on the mat—for we know the rewards You've promised! Now bless this bread about to be broken and these words about to be spoken—"

The chorus of *Amens* was broken by Jordan.

"You forgot to say, 'in Jesus' name.' "

"Did." Jonda's head of golden curls bobbed up and down in affirmation.

"Mind your manners, you two!" Cousin Bella said briskly.

Jordan nodded gravely. "Yes, Auntie Bella. I said it *for* him."

The best treatment for such a spirited child was to ignore him, according to Arabella Lovelace's philosophy. "If you are ready to carve the ham hocks, George Washington?" she asked her husband.

With a twinkle in his merry eyes, Doc George picked up the carving knife, honed the cutting edge, and—with the precision of his practice—sliced the hickory-smoked ham into rings. Courtney, sitting diagonally from the country doctor, watched with as much fascination as the twins. Such a stouthearted soul. Whatever crosses the Santa-faced George Washington Lovelace had to bear, he bore comfortably. Whatever would the valley do without his teasing bedside manner, his horse with tireless legs? What would *Cousin Bella* do? Their marriage was a source of inspiration in these often-troubled environs.

"Ahhh, dandelion greens—early for them, or is it wild mustard?" Cousin Bella's tone was one of praise, bringing a wide, white-toothed smile to the cook's dark face.

"Ah dun hafta tell y'all it's some uv bof, wid lamb's-quarters mixt in—sum'pin holy-like 'bout dem greens lak de blood uv de lamb—"

Jordan's blue eyes widened. Quickly, Courtney withdrew her hand from Clint's and put a silencing finger to her lips to stop his flow of words. The timing was right. Mrs. Rueben set a steaming bowl of succotash on the table and then a mold of butter.

"Sourdough biscuits?" Doc George's tone was hopeful.

"Naw suh, cracklin' bread dis time," Mandy said with pride, causing the German housekeeper to look at her in scorn. And Courtney was sure that a look of malicious pleasure crossed Mrs. Rueben's face at Jordan's reprimand.

"*You* broke the bread!" he said of the golden-brown squares Mandy had cut.

"Jordan," Clint's voice was low but authoritative as he buttered a piece of bread, "this looks delicious. How about eating instead of talking—*for the rest of the meal*?"

"He talks and talks and—" Jonda championed, favoring her uncle with an angelic look. Clint promptly stuffed her mouth full of buttered bread. Jordan's periwinkle eyes turned black with triumph, but both children began to chew obediently. Wheedling would get them nowhere.

Later Courtney was to remember each of those little details, trying to sort out which, if any of the clan, held the reins completely. Always it had seemed like a family affair, everything decided by council. She had liked the arrangement. Everybody had. Or so she supposed. It was a comforting feeling, reassuring. It was so peaceful here. *Home.* Home and the only real family she had ever known. Courtney loved every fertile inch of the new land her mother had called a wilderness. Between the heavy brocade drapes Courtney could see even now a narrow band of new wheat stretched away to the horizon, losing its shape in the shadows of the towering timber. As yet the mines would not be dusted with summer or rutted by the winter cold. She tore her eyes away.

Everyone was talking at once. Which was strange. Usually, when there was a matter to be reckoned with, there was a formal silence bordering on the ridiculous. Tonight, however, there was a carnival-like atmosphere. Doc George announced that a new judge had come to town. He seemed right smart—at least, he had a lot of books.

"He has a drawl that smacks of Georgia—thick as sludge. Even at that, he pauses between sentences—"

The others laughed at his joke and Brother Jim said the good man probably came in with the new wagon train. "Man callin' himself Cheyenne brought them through—a disreputable-looking slouch whose talk goes faster than a freight train. But when I tried invitin' him to church, he had to cup his hand to his ear to hear. The men up the street a piece heard my invite. Maybe now they'll come in his stead."

The conversation turned to the mines. Courtney only half-heard Clint's report—something to the effect that the silver veins were harder to find now ... still 30 men to every woman ... but looking for overnight riches and ...

Courtney's dark eyes drifted from one face to the next. Donolar, unusually quiet, concentrated on his food. Clint (Could he be 30?) was boyishly animated as he spoke of the Kennedy Mines, his jawline still firm and strong. The Lovelaces appeared to listen, Doc George's head inclined to one side and his wife nodding at points, yet sending little mysterious messages to one another. The twins' heads were nodding, tummies filled and eyes heavy with sleep. They should be tucked in like the rosy baby. But, while two *was* a bit young for joining the family, Cousin Bella granted, six was not. Nursery? Nonsense! Children, like adults, needed family life—and that included all members. Dear Cousin Bella. Courtney wondered if another such household would include the bird-like, sober-faced Mrs. Rueben and the massive black woman with the musical laugh and disposition that defied ruffling (except where her rival, Mrs. Rueben, was concerned). It was the Lord's table, Arabella Lovelace said, and didn't He say, "Let the little ones come unto me"?

There was a sudden stillness. Mandy, Courtney recalled, had served brown betty (using dried apples)— dear Mandy, so gifted, capable of creating a banquet from dishearteningly sparse makings when seasons demanded it. Nobody had picked up a spoon when Cousin Bella asked for a moment of silent prayer, something which had never happened before. Then when the grandfather clock struck seven, she said: "Amen! May I present the new mistress of Mansion-in-the-Wild? Please stand, Courtney, and take the keys."

CHAPTER 3
Counterpane Talk

Long-lashed eyes were closed in exhaustion before the twins' heads touched their respective pillows. They had had a busy day—roughly one-half as busy as Mandy and Mrs. Rueben's. The two women, talking in a duet, gave hair-raising accounts of a game the children invented called "Spider." Jonda Spider and Jordan Spider wove a giant web of "the madam's" red knitting yarn, suspending it from ceiling to floor (yessum, shure 'nuf). Poor Mrs. Rueben was the first "fly" to be caught. Mandy's attempt to rescue the German-spouting housekeeper, succeeded only in bringing down the wrath upon herself. So now the two were not speaking again. Not that they didn't find fault—with their eyes! No'm, dat wuz'n all, the cook explained while rolling dark eyes heavenward so far that only the whites showed. No sooner wuz Miz Arabella's yawn rewounded, when de "fallen angels" up'n giv' po' Mouser uh bath in de chamber pot (here Mrs. Rueben's eyes narrowed in disdain, indicating that *if* she were speaking, her native tongue provided a more appropriate term than the American euphemism). Summary: Cat, housekeeper, and cook had their fur rubbed the wrong way.

"It's a wonder to me how children live to grow up," Clint, still stunned by the evening, whispered as their heads met over Kenney's cradle.

"It's more a miracle how *parents* survive," Courtney replied as she checked the baby's forehead and, finding it moist, folded down one of his bunny-rabbit quilts.

Back in their own room, with the children's doors ajar, Courtney wordlessly set to work turning back the heavy coverlet on the giant bed dominating the room. Carefully, as if something depended on it, she removed the oversized bolster and replaced it with duck-down pillows.

"Is it true that this poster bed dates back 200 years—?"

"At least. The pinecones carved at the tip of each post are for supporting a canopy, shipped from Rotterdam as Aunt Bella said—say, why all the preoccupation with this bed?"

Courtney was spared an answer. Clint had leaned over her and, taking her thin shoulders firmly in his grasp, spun her to face him. To look up...up...up into his penetrating blue eyes—no, blue *lakes* in which she could drown. Courtney forced herself to look away.

"I'm very tired, Clint. Let's turn out the light and go to bed."

"Back to that bed again!" His voice was low—low and filled with laughter and love, as if she had extended an invitation. "By the way, congratulations, Mrs. Desmond, mistress of the Mansion!" He was drawing her closer.

"The light, Clint."

He obliged, turning the wick low, then cupping his hands around the chimney as he blew out the flickering blaze. They undressed in the cool darkness and felt their way into bed. There, Clint immediately pulled her to him. He must have sensed something unyielding in her body, this wonderful man who understood her better than she understood herself, for even though he drew her still closer, his embrace was more tender, more understanding.

They lay still beneath the counterpane Clint had pulled from the scroll into which Courtney had rolled it. How often they had journeyed to the stars like this. But tonight there were no stars. A misty layer of clouds had shut out their twinkle and the thin sailboat moon had anchored below the horizon.

Courtney tried in vain to summon courage to speak. But what could she say that would unknot the tension inside her, dispel her allover weariness, erase her fears of the unknown?

Then, mercifully, Clint's gentle kiss, where her long hair parted in the middle and fanned darkly over both pillows, mutely assured her that she need not say anything at all. Oh Clint . . . her beloved . . . her own. . . .

Courtney snuggled closer. Feeling the smooth stones that were the muscles of his arms. Knowing that in the stronghold of his love no harm could come. And yet—

"Feeling in need of some counterpane talk, my darling?"

Counterpane talk. Troubles, some people said, should never be settled at the table or in bed. But "some people" did not include them. This was their shallop for rowing gently and tenderly together to a little island of privacy. And each exploration brought to them new discoveries about each other. Soon the words would come.

Keeping his left arm beneath her head, Clint wound a strand of her hair around his right forefinger. "Something tells me that my little madonna was not ready to accept her rightful throne."

"Throne! Oh Clint, you make it sound worse."

"But I'm right?" He twisted the strand tighter.

"Ouch! Yes, you're right. It's too soon—I—we—I'm not ready."

"How long would it take?"

"I'm sorry. I'm worried."

"Don't be."

"Which?"

"Either! You'll do it with grace and charm. Everybody loves you, Courtney. You know that."

Courtney relaxed against him, feeling a warm surge of pure joy course from her fingertips to her very soul. Of course they loved her. As she loved them. Why then—?

Clint gave her hair a playful yank.

"Stop that, you—" she began.

"—wonderful man," he finished for her. "Tell me about it or I'll pull harder!"

They giggled then and went into a little clinch. When Courtney could catch her breath, she felt her heartbeat quieting—even a delicious languor although the questions lay ahead.

"I guess," she said slowly, "that I never felt the house belonged to me. I was first a stranger—then I belonged to *it*."

"That's the way it is with old houses, I guess," Clint answered as if he had pondered the propriety of houses. "They take on a personality of their own. But think of the generations it has sheltered, going back to 'White Eagle'—our common ancestor."

Dr. Joseph McLoughlin! "That's what scares me," Courtney whispered. "It's awesome. I was so frightened when I came here...Indians...storms...Cousin Bella ...even her arrangements to have us meet..."

"You're sorry?"

"Oh Clint, you know better than that! But I was so hurt, so insecure. Not ready to grow up, bury the past, be *me*. Not ready for marriage—a home—children—and now all the insecurities are back—I need time."

"Not time, darling—*God!* Where do you think *He* will be? Right here watching over you and me, our 12 children, and our grandchildren—"

The old house sighed and settled down for the night.

CHAPTER 4
To Shine Away
the Shadows

❧

Courtney had supposed that she had only her own fears and misgivings about her new role to conquer. She was mistaken.

One would suppose that the ancient house would run itself, considering that everybody knew exactly what was expected. Only they didn't! The first morning was sheer bedlam. Clint had lighted a fire in their bedroom and left for the mines without awakening her. Courtney, usually an early riser, overslept. Exhausted from the excitement of the night before, the twins overslept, too.

It was Kenney's call that awakened her. "*Mom*-my!" Wan' Mommy—"

Even as she reached for a light robe and hurried to the cradle, hoping Jonda and Jordan had not awakened, Courtney had a sense that something was wrong. Picking the baby up and holding him close, she listened. And then she realized that it was not the noise but lack of it that was disturbing. Not a sound. Except for an occasional creaking groan of the great house, its bones complaining of another day.

Stuffing Kenney into a pair of yellow rompers, Courtney talked low and soothingly, "There, you look like a daffodil. Now, darling, you may crawl on Mommy and Daddy's big bed."

He rewarded her with a dimpled smile. Such a good child. And *so* beautiful! Courtney kissed a cluster of curls that fringed his forehead and playfully pretended to toss him to the beamed ceiling before lowering him gently to the bed. He played happily as she made haste to dress. The first item of clothing her fingers touched as she opened the wardrobe was a blue-striped pinafore. The while brilliantine Peter Pan waist would be best as it buttoned down the front and she felt a need to rush. Hurriedly, she brushed her hair and scooped a mildly protesting Kenney into her arms.

Halfway down the stairs, she stopped to gasp at the scene below. Standing at attention like tin soldiers were Mandy, Mrs. Rueben, and Donolar. Arabella Kennedy Lovelace was seated regally, wearing her black-and-white again without a touch of color. The first rays of the rising sun slanted through the windows of the sun room, robbing the foursome of substance. Transforming the dearly familiar faces to shadows—shadows of strangers. *What on earth—?*

"Good morning, Courtney."

Cousin Bella's voice told her nothing. The former mistress of the Mansion nodded a signal to the other members of the household. Donolar (near breaking Courtney's heart in his effort to please) babbled something unintelligible. " 'Mawnin,' Miz Courtney." (*Miz Courtney* when Mandy always addressed her as "Courtney hon"?) And Mrs. Rueben reverted back to her native tongue (another insult to Mandy who had taught her some English with a Southern accent during a brief cease-fire period after a summer revival). "*Gut morgan, Frau Court-nee.*"

"Cookie—wanna cookie." Kenney, the darling of them all, broke the tension. The cook's and housekeeper's faces softened, but they dared not break rank. It was Donolar who sprang forward.

"Come to Uncle Donny, Kenney. I have cookies and fresh honey at Innisfree. The butterflies will welcome you, and we will put a wee-tiny bit of coffee in your milk—"

Courtney lifted her eyes to the needlepoint sampler above Cousin Bella's head: CHILDREN SHALL NOT DRINK COFFEE OR TEA. But if Cousin Bella heard, she made no protest. "Come on down, Courtney," she said.

Courtney, feeling a little foolish, left the landing and joined the group, aware that something was missing. Oh yes, Cousin Bella's morning tea. "Shall I steep you some tea?" she asked without thinking.

"How you delegate responsibilities here will be entirely up to you after this meeting. But for now, we are here to talk—not work."

"Preparing tea is hardly work—" Courtney protested weakly, realizing too late that she was putting her beloved Mandy in an unfavorable light.

No matter. Arabella Lovelace had other matters on her mind. And she went straight to the point.

"I love Mansion-in-the-Wild, Courtney. I have tried to be a good steward so that my descendants could have a tradition to carry on. My forebears did that for me."

Courtney could only nod. They had been over this before.

"It is the cause in life God assigned to me—and I would lay down my life for it. I suppose anyone failing to appreciate such a heritage could do irreparable harm."

"I suppose so—" Courtney murmured, hardly knowing what was expected of her.

Arabella Lovelace sighed. "Of course," she said as if talking to herself, "one does not marry for love of a house."

The great fortress-like house (which, indeed, it had been at one time) had captured Courtney's imagination when she caught sight of its shrouded gray towers her first night in the Columbia Territory setting...the towering timber...grassy hillocks below snow-peaked mountains...verdant summers, softened by misty rains... smoky-blue autumns with their abundant harvests...the pristine winters when sparkling streams were tongue-tied by frosts . . . and the wild, sweet beauty of spring. But the *house* she had always stood in awe of—except for the stout old apple tree by her bedroom window.

Love it? Courtney was not sure. But one thing was certain. She loved those within it! Not one day passed without her praising God for His goodness in bringing her here to be a member of the most wonderful family in the world. So yes, since the house was such a part of them, she had developed a certain affection for Mansion-in-the-Wild. And since it was obviously her duty to keep the guarded traditions, with God's help, she would try.

Cousin Bella continued to talk almost dreamily. "It's a large estate—homestead land, virgin timber, rich soil—spreading out over many acres. Large, yes, even for today. It requires a lot of care. It is difficult to blaze new trails, as our ancestors knew and those who continue to come West are finding out. Sometimes the old, familiar roads feel more comfortable. But, my dear," she turned knowing eyes on Courtney, "you are a girl of great courage—and much more strength than you give yourself credit for. Take the untrodden trail—pitted with holes though it may be—and find your treasure there."

The speech should have been made last evening. Instead, there had been gaiety. That it was made at all, then, meant that Cousin Bella, as always, sensed her hesitation. But why the formality?

This was ridiculous. Poor Mandy and Mrs. Rueben were still standing at attention. Donolar had split kindling and laid fires the night before, but nobody had lighted them. Breakfast-time, always early, had come and gone. Yet there was no food. It would be comical were it less touching.

"Should we all sit down now?" Courtney's question was gentle.

The older woman stiffened. "First, I wish to inform the staff that Mrs. Desmond is now in charge. I shall expect her to receive the same excellent service they have given me."

"Yessum," Mandy replied, obviously striving for dignity. And Mrs. Rueben muttered something akin to "*Ach—pretty soon now weel I do mit de work.*" The two cast appealing looks at one another. The thinly veiled expressions said that each would have to depend upon the other for support in this uncertain future. Heretofore they had been "family." Were they now servants?

Without warning, a laugh began deep inside Courtney and spilled over. Aware that the other three women were looking at her with curiosity, she laughed harder, wiping her eyes with a wisp of a handkerchief—and feeling absolutely wonderful.

"Oh, dear Cousin Bella, you mean well—and I love you with all my heart. But how could you entertain the idea that our relationship would change? I—I—why, I could no more run this house without your advice than I could issue orders to these wonderful women who know more than I do. Is there any reason why things must change?"

Without waiting for an answer, Mandy's heavy, warm arms were about her. "Mah baby, mah baby," she crooned. "Ah dun shudda knowed wuz'n nothin' a-gonna change. See, what I dun tole y'all, Miz Rueben?"

"Of course, things *will* change," Cousin Bella said, motioning Courtney to a wicker chair across the marble-topped table from herself. Mandy and Mrs. Rueben, awaiting no further dismissal, bustled to the kitchen. Smells of brewing coffee and frying bacon wafted into the sun room, mingling with snatches of Mandy's mellow humming. And Courtney could have vowed that the German housekeeper joined her.

"—as well they should," Cousin Bella picked up the conversation. Courtney had known all along that this was a part of the plan, had she not? A dream, really, in which the older woman saw herself extended? Carrying on tradition, yes, but more? Giving the old house what she could not: youth . . . children? Courtney kept nodding as Cousin Bella talked on. "The silver very well may play out in the mines, but you and Clint are land-rich. One could hardly call this a potter's field! Just remember to be penny-wise with money and pound-foolish with love. I wish," her tone became wistful, "that I could offer you more privacy, say that George Washington and I would—" her voice broke.

"*Leave?*" Courtney reached out to grasp the blue-veined hand across the table, tears springing to her eyes. "Why, this house would stop breathing without you! It is home—and you are its family—and ours!"

Arabella drew a quivering breath, but her voice was stout when she spoke: "Then dry your eyes. God bless you for the laughter you have brought."

* * *

The rest of the week was unsettling. The episode with Cousin Bella, Mandy, and Mrs. Rueben hardly prepared Courtney for what was to follow. Thank goodness, Cousin Bella volunteered to make it clear to Doc George and Brother Jim that their presence was not only welcome, but a necessity, to look after both body and soul of the clan. But it had not occurred to Courtney that Donolar would harbor fears. Strangers the lad (*man*—she corrected herself—and her senior) was afraid of, but her? Courtney, the sister he adored?

Donolar continued playing with the children and pampering his rose garden, but he no longer brought roses to her room or summoned her with the call of a quail just to share something the butterflies had foretold. In fact, he avoided her.

It had to be the twins who spelled out the problem. "Uncle Donny says he may have to leave and never come back 'cause his name is Kennedy and yours is Desmond and ours—"

"Wait—not so fast, Jordan. This is Uncle Donny's home and his name is Kennedy because he chose it. Once we both were named Glamora; but, you see, when I married Daddy—"

The name had slipped out unconsciously. Courtney was loosening the soil in a potted geranium and almost lost her balance when both Jordan and Jonda gave whoops of joy and all but leaped astride her bent-over back. "Daddy! You called Uncle Clint *Daddy*—so you won't send us away!"

"Won't." Jonda echoed her brother.

Dropping the trowel, Courtney bent to draw the children to her. "Did the butterflies tell you this? Oh my darlings, never in a million years—and that includes Uncle Donny—"

Donolar appeared from nowhere. "Oh, thank you—what do I call you now? It might be improper—"

"Donolar, darling, I am your *sister*, Courtney, who loves you."

The three skipped out, leaving Courtney baffled. But only momentarily. Why, it was a conspiracy those three planned. She laughed aloud.

* * *

A sort of revelation came as she mounted the stairs to freshen up. The house—with all its ells, turrets, lofts, and garrets—belonged to another century. But it had no quarrel with her. It might even welcome an airing of the unused wings which she must someday explore again. They, too, might welcome the lightness of laughter.

So running a household translated into more than feeding the occupants (although Courtney was pleased that Mandy was teaching her the culinary arts), beating the carpets, and applying castor oil to the leaves of the rubber plant. It meant keeping alive a certain spirit that met the emotional needs. And maybe that was harder. She must blossom out—for others. What was it her father had said so long ago? She had almost forgotten. But now—

Courtney turned her steps toward the shadowy library, pausing in front of her ancestral lineup. The austere faces of her grandfathers no longer threatened or intimidated. But her father, "Big Gabe" Glamora, whom Courtney had loved so dearly and lost as a small child, still looked at her with dark eyes so like her own that she felt she was seeing inside herself. "Never fear being different, dear baby of mine. 'Tis better to be too shy than not shy enough, yes, 'tis. The shy suffer pain, but those lacking, inflict it."

Mother and Vanessa, he meant. Yes, he had suffered ... as had she ... but they had never inflicted pain on others.

Her eyes were still misty as she looked at "Another Spring," her childhood sweetheart's farewell gift. How beautiful the autumn leaves were—as lovely as April's bloom. Lance's critics said that he painted right over the world's dark phases ... a "full moon" artist, they said. But Courtney knew it was faith with which he lighted the dark canvas.

Of course! "We talk about *having* faith, Lord, *having* inner peace as if it were something to own. Let me *live* in it, Lord, and *walk* by it. Only then can I shine the shadows away."

CHAPTER 5
Sacred Ground

🍃

Efraim came the week following. Giving his sister an affectionate hug, he congratulated her on her new title. But Courtney was aware that his intelligent "Bellevue-side" eyes studied her closely. Was she happy? Was she at peace? Dear Efraim. How would she have survived their mother's indifference without him? She, a little girl lost, had clung to his improbable promises. Efraim had the capacity of spinning dreams for her—and more. When he finished law school, the two of them would seek a new life in the Oregon Territory (which included Washington then)... an alien world, in a sense, but filled with challenges and opportunities... virgin timber... mountains hiding their heads in the clouds in secret watch of fertile valleys... and rivers, clear, pure, unpolluted by industry, watering the inland and providing a playground for leaping salmon, before rushing on to the ocean. Flowers? Why, little sister, the land flamed with color... snowdrops... daisies... rhododendrons and azaleas.

"Oh Efraim," she would breathe, young ears hearing the water's soft surging, eager nostrils filling with the sap-scented breath of the forests. Maybe her childish enthusiasm inspired him, because here they were two decades later, both with mates they loved dearly. Their marriages and surrender of their lives to the Lord only strengthened the bond between brother and sister.

"That's a faraway smile. Care to explain it, darling?"

An explanation might make no sense, but Efraim would understand. "Faraway, yes—I was thinking how once upon a time you built me a cage for catching and holding dreams."

Her mood was contagious. "We were quite a pair. Remember the excited letter you wrote saying you had captured and frozen the moon for me in Mrs. Thorpe's pewter washbasin until I came home from school?"

"Oh, Nanny was cross with me because I hid the basin to keep the reflection safe—yes, of course I remember!"

"And you were so crushed when your treasure melted, I had to tell you it was no fault of yours, that the moon had changed phases—"

Both were laughing heartily when Cousin Bella entered the sun room where they were standing. She motioned them to chairs. How long had she been using a cane? But Arabella Lovelace's face did not invite questions.

"Best be seated just in case people *can* die of laughter—although the Good Book tells us that a merry heart doeth good like a medicine."

"Perhaps we should refrain from making mention of that in Doc George's presence," Efraim said lightly, taking the cane and laying it on the drop-leaf table before seating himself.

"It's no secret." The voice, like the speaker, seemed to come from nowhere. Donolar had entered like a colored shadow. "He reads Proverbs—and that is Proverbs 15:13."

"Thank you, Donolar," Cousin Bella said politely. Then, turning her attention back to Efraim, she said, "It seemed wise to include your brother."

So far the talk made no sense. Listening intently, Courtney failed to hear Mandy ask if she should bring coffee.

"Courtney," Cousin Bella prompted, "you are in charge."

Courtney jumped. "Why—er, yes—I mean I guess so," she stammered and was surprised when Mandy set the silver service before her.

Courtney poured with shaking fingers. She was mistress here. Why did she feel like a stranger? An intruder?

"You brought the papers, Efraim?" Cousin Bella's voice was matter-of-fact as she accepted her cup, seeming to ignore that it contained coffee instead of her morning tea.

In wordless response to Cousin Bella, Efraim pushed aside Donolar's bouquet and began to spread out all sorts of documents and maps. "That was a big order—deeds, correspondence, agreements, licenses, virtually every conceivable kind of legal document. Besides, I have my office shelves, file cabinets, and flattop desk heaped until other documents are spilling onto the floor. Poor Roberta—"

"Good that you chose a lady lawyer for a wife, Efraim," Cousin Bella approved. "Donolar, dear, perhaps we should move your sweetbriar."

"*Eglantine*," Donolar spoke for the first time to correct. "Its beauty is lauded in William Shakespeare's plays—one day Courtney and I will finish our book, the journal she writes to God in . . . she tells Him everything, so the twins have to be careful . . . and we will add my own . . . about all the strange things that have happened . . . like we were living a beautiful dream—with feet always over death's doorsill till butterflies—"

"Yes, you know how to leaven the pain, Donolar." Cousin Bella's words diverted the boy (*man*, Courtney corrected herself again). She had seen her brother's writing. A patchwork of incidents, miniature tales filled with an army of characters, ruminations, asides, and ramblings like his talk. But he had managed to capture *something*. Supposing, just supposing, the two of them pooled their talents and told the story—preserving the genuine spirit of close-knit pioneers who listened to each other, running comfortably over one another's threshold, mansion or tumbledown cabin, but holding onto the salt-of-the-earth settlers and the "salty sorts" as well. The querulous...rebellious...fatalistic...stubborn—and Brother Jim's downright "evildoers." And the Indians, of course. Hadn't both adversaries taken each other's measure like Cara did for her sewing projects and over the years developed a sort of grudging accommodation with each other? Not friends, but not strangers either. Yes, they could tighten the narrative spine for a book and leave a history which, laughing through its tears, brought others to God.

Courtney pulled herself back into the present with an effort. "I have brought all you asked for, Cousin Bella, although some of it could have waited—" Efraim was saying.

"We live on the thin edge of life here." Arabella Kennedy's mouth was set in a determined line as she reached for a folder. Quickly, her fingers explored the pages without comment except for little *um-hmmmms* of satisfaction. When she closed the folder, her nod gave blanket approval.

"You'd better read this, Courtney," Efraim said.

"You tell me. I know nothing of the *to wittens*."

He laughed. "That is the meaning."

"What?"

"To *know*. But, briefly, this document specifies that you and Clint and your offspring are sole heirs of the estate—owners, as a matter of fact—except for Innisfree. That belongs to Donolar—"

But Donolar heard no more. With a childish whoop of delight and babbling unintelligibly, he darted from the room to tell the twins.

"As such," Efraim went on, ignoring their brother's exit, "you are free to make changes and here are some suggestions for remodeling and redecorating. The previous owner—"

"Cousin Bella?"

"Yes darling—legal talk. Cousin Bella had me note neglected areas and suggests that, in case you wish to preserve the old embroidered hangings, they need repair. However, you are free to redecorate."

"Of course I won't redecorate!"

The idea was preposterous—as disturbing as the thought of some archeologist desecrating the pyramids! Mansion-in-the-Wild must be preserved with its rich, mellow wood, colored rugs glowing against polished floors, and its multipaned windows—like compound eyes—keeping watch day and night.

"As for tapestries, I—I am no needlewoman, but (brightening) Cara can help us! And as for the bedrooms—"

Here Courtney paused and shuddered. Then, forgetting that their cousin was present, she looked into her brother's face. "I was remembering our mother's bedroom—"

Pink. Allover pink. Carpets. Ruffled curtains. Even the bedjacket trimmed with pink swansdown. *Sugary.* "No changes," she repeated.

"I am glad you view this house with respect, Courtney. Read on, Efraim." Cousin Bella's command failed to cover the tremor of emotion in her voice.

Dear Cousin Bella. She would die for this house and its sacred traditions, she had said. Well, she wouldn't have to!

It was sacred ground.

CHAPTER 6
Dreaming Ahead

Courtney was still seated between twin towers of folders, slender shoulders pushed forward in concentration, when Clint entered undetected. Catching her completely by surprise, he covered her face with his hands, long fingers splaying over her eyes, the little fingers tickling beneath her chin.

"Clint!" Courtney gave a little squeal of delight as he pulled her up gently and cradled her head tenderly against the scratchiness of his heavy work shirt. "I've been sitting here for hours—oh, the rhetoric of all this!" She spoke against his chest.

Her husband leaned down to kiss the part in her hair. "I know, darling. Aunt Bella has spent a lifetime getting her house in order. It's touching how she struggles to make sure of our happiness—"

"Oh Clint, my dearest, I would be happy with you anywhere—just you and me alone in a cabin in the woods—"

Clint's head jerked erect. Pretending shock, he blinked as if she had slapped his face. "It seems to me that my wife is overlooking something," he told the ceiling. "There's a matter of 12 children. A *cabin?*"

"A very *large* cabin," she murmured. And then, forgetting her resolution to wait for exactly the right moment, Courtney blurted out, "You see, number four is on the way!"

This time shock was not feigned. "You mean—you mean—how do you know?"

Courtney snuggled closer. "Just a bit of queasiness—Doc George says it will be in November, about Thanksgiving."

"You told the doctor before *me*?"

"Silly! You do not tell doctors. They know such things."

A little beside himself, Clint gestured grandly. "Sit down this minute where you can be comfortable."

Courtney smothered a laugh. On *that*? The wooden settle Donolar had made? But to Clint it was the most exorbitantly expensive rococo revival chair ever imported.

Over Clint's objections, Courtney went back to the folders. The two of them must go over the materials together, Efraim had said on departure, see if they had questions. Cousin Bella was napping before dinner. And yes, the children were with Donolar. Now, to business—

It was hard getting Clint to concentrate. It was equally hard to concentrate herself, feeling her husband's eyes—blue lakes of fire—burning through her body and right inside her heart.

"You knew, of course, that Cousin Bella turned over all mining interests to you, Clint?"

"Yes, my love."

"Clint, be nice. Help me with this. Efraim mentioned reforming the company—selling more shares."

That captured his attention. "Shares?" Clint's voice held a note of puzzlement. "The miners are shareholders. And even they—"

"Yes?" Something in his voice made her uneasy.

"Nothing to worry about—at least, at the moment. I have a feeling, however, that Aunt Bella is unaware that the main vein has played out. We may have to go to ore."

"Is ore less precious than silver?"

"Less market for it—and less of it." The crease between his eyes deepened. So Clint had waited as she had waited to discuss the matters so vital to them. Well, no matter. She was relieved.

Clint was examining other folders. "Your brother has done a commendable job with these. Everything is spelled out." He began thumbing through the higher of the two piles. Courtney knew by the light in his face when he located the object of his search.

"A school! It is what she has always planned—Kennedy School. The name is so precious to my aunt. But it is the school that I care about—a school for our dozen—"

Clint reached out to her, then dropped his arms—something else having caught his eye. "Look—oh Courtney, *look*—the answer to the prayers of the valley. A church, a larger one—and a cemetery. Oh, it's all here—praise be to God for this wonderful woman who is my aunt. It all began with her dream for us."

There were tears in his eyes as he grasped her hands, closed his lids, and began an inaudible prayer. Courtney joined him with her own silent prayer, the cup in her heart overflowing:

> *Oh Lord, my God, there are no words in any language with which I can thank You enough. The blessings are just too bountiful. But Lord, You understand me. You know that love is my life—that my joy demands no material things. So Thy will be done. Amen.*

For, even then, Courtney knew that dreams do not always come true.

CHAPTER 7
Cara's Caring—
and Concerns

❦

It was the kind of morning that makes one feel at peace with the world. Courtney paused on the bridge spanning the stream which divided to create a near-mote around the "Isle of Innisfree." Donolar's garden flamed with color in the lazy warmth of the May-morning sun. The mountain range formed a shimmering backcloth. Like problems which beset her only a month ago, the mountains were reduced in height by distance. *Peace*, a lovely word.

Reluctantly, she walked on toward the Laughtens' cabin. Grounds of the homestead were neat and well-kept and pleasant barnyard sounds mingled with the drone of bees from the tangled mass of flowers in the yard. Windows were dressed with starched curtains.

Cara, her plain face made beautiful by a smile that shone like the pots and kettles on the old wood stove, greeted Courtney warmly. "Oh, Miz—I mean, Courtney—it's real good seein' you. John told me 'bout yore bein' mistress of that great big house an' we want you to be knowin' how proud we are—you and the bossman bein' such fine folks and all."

Courtney thanked Cara and accepted the rawhide-bottomed chair she offered. Yes, juice would be nice. The day was unseasonably warm. Cara hoped it would not wilt her early garden "considerin' what the bossman said."

"What did Clint say, Cara?" Courtney kept her question casual as she accepted the glass of grape juice. "Thank you—my, this feels nice and cool."

"We let it down in the well—pour it in a bucket, you know. The little 'uns like it. Sure hope we don't be runnin' low—" Cara, realizing what she had said, colored.

Courtney pretended to take no notice. Running low on *anything* would create a problem for the family—seven, she believed.

"Fruit crops will be on again before you know it, Cara. Now (setting her empty glass on a three-legged stool which served as a nightstand) you were saying—"

Cara deliberated as if wondering how to broach the subject—or wondering if, indeed, she should have spoken at all.

"It is all right, Cara. You may confide in me."

"I keep forgittin' that—you bein' such a fine lady 'n all—but he, the bossman, thinks we may be in trouble at the mines—that the silver may just be playin' out. The pickin' 'n diggin's gittin' harder. Once the shovels hit solid clay—oh now, I've done upset you—"

"Maybe we are being premature, Cara. I know a little about mining. These things happen. Sometimes miners reach a layer of cement gravel and scoria—hardpan, you know. It is not unusual to abandon a mine—pan further upstream. True, the mine is no real bonanza—but darling, please stop worrying. Let our men do that!"

Cara dropped her head like a scolded child. Courtney reached for her hand and was about to apologize or explain when she felt the telltale bulge beneath the loose, drop-yoked garment Cara wore.

"Cara! Another baby—how wonderful!"

"Yes—ain't it?" Cara's voice was quiet and Courtney thought she detected an odd note. "John's—er, surprised, I'm guessin'."

"So was Clint!" Courtney blurted out.

The two women embraced warmly. But Courtney wondered if their tears were for the same purpose. They chatted then, pondering as women have pondered through the ages, how their other children would receive the news and how many garments from previous layettes they could put to good use. The subject turned to Cousin Bella, whose pallor and use of "that walkin' stick" concerned Cara.

"Right nice you can be takin' on her work, but with you in a family way 'n all, Courtney—"

"You sound like Clint," Courtney laughed. "I will be fine. But it is about the big house that I have come. We want to do some renovating—mostly repairing—tapestries, drapes, and slipcovers. I am all thumbs with needlework. Would you be willing to take on the job?"

Cara's face lighted up. "Oh, I'd be lovin' that—'ceptin' I got no yarn or embroiderin' thread—" she paused uncomfortably.

"There are closets of all that at the Mansion. I would pay you, of course." Courtney made a point of sounding firm on the matter.

Color flooded Cara's face. "I don't want—after all you've went 'n done for me 'n John—"

"Nonsense! You have done *much* more for me, Cara. Just knowing you is a joy. We will have a wonderful time. But there *will* be pay."

Courtney's thoughts were disturbed as she retraced her footsteps to the Mansion. Were the Laughtens in need? She must talk to Clint. But for now the noon sun was relaxing, slightly soporific. And she was so tired.

CHAPTER 8
"Clanimals"

Once a week Courtney recorded in her journal, keeping little notes in between. Her feelings and deepest thoughts went into her writing. After all, it was between her and God. Sometimes the pages told of the goings-on in the busy household. At others, there were short-paragraph prayers in explanation of why the sentences were fragmented. "Running this big house is a greater task than I expected, I guess, Lord, as I know You knew. I can tell by Your frequent references to the home and family.... Why do I tell You what *Your* Book says? It just makes me feel better, I guess, knowing You understand...."

The old comradeship resumed between herself and Cara as they decided which pieces should be redone to preserve their natural beauty. There was more than Courtney had planned as she decided on new bindings for quilts with such intricate patterns that they were destined to become heirlooms. Then there were unfinished pieces she was sure had an interesting history. However, Cousin Bella had caught cold and Doc George ordered her to bed. These things *could* be contagious, he said. His ancient *Homeopathic Medical Book* hinted at the possibility while doctors fresh out of Jefferson Medical College got their noses out of kilter over the matter. Not that they knew everything just because they came from that worthy institution. Some of their ideas were as old as the first Studebaker wagon, all fuss and feathers all of them—young doctors without enough fuzz for shaving. But the *Kansas Weekly Herald* was featuring some articles (by older doctors, mind you) which went back to sounder ideas. Colds just could be contagious. Here he paused for breath, having gone full circle.

"Forgive me, my child, for rambling on."

"You are concerned about Cousin Bella."

"Yes," Dr. George Washington Lovelace said tiredly, running a dimpled hand through his cloud of white hair as he glanced about. "You two are doing wonders here. I will report to Arabella as she ordered some vetch tea." He turned to leave the drawing room where Courtney and Cara were working but halted at the door. "Say, should you run across an old violin—could be in the east tower—"

"It will be a long time before we climb that high at the rate we are going," Courtney laughed. "But you can be sure we will look. Give my love to Cousin Bella."

"Count on it! Then, there's a sheaf of papers—old ledgers, some material on ottering, that kind of thing."

His footsteps died away. "Have you—uh—did you ask the bossman 'bout the mines? Not that I oughta be askin'." Cara bit a thread, her hand shaking as she tried to run it through the eye of her needle.

"I promised you that our talk was confidential, Cara, and I plan to keep it so. I had hoped to speak of the mines in general, but there never seems to be time alone."

And then he is vague, she wanted to add. But that would only add to Cara's concerns.

At that very moment Jordan and Jonda burst in, eyes aglow. On their heels was Donolar. Although his face was expressionless, there was secrecy in his manner.

"We have something to show you—something *very* special—Donolar says we may be rich 'cause we've made a discovery—" Jordan's eyes were brilliant stars and his breath came in ragged gasps.

"Have! Me first this once." And, with a toss of yellow curls and lift of a dimpled chin, the little girl shoved ahead of her brother for the first time, bringing her hands from behind her.

Face crimson with anger, Jordan hurled himself forward, his elbow striking Jonda's ribs. "Rude—you're rude—and you'll get no dividends. Move *now*—lest I rip thee asunder!"

It was Courtney, of course, who ran between them ("ripping them asunder," she laughingly recounted to Clint later—Donolar's language certainly had rubbed off on the two).

"Be seated, both of you. Not together. You over here, Jordan. Behavior such as this means that neither of you reports until I hear from Donolar." Courtney spoke with studied firmness.

Subdued, they looked like Rafael's cherubs. And Courtney told herself for the millionth time that there should be a national coronation day set aside for mothers. They should be awarded diamond-tipped crowns.

Donolar, in his moment of glory, began unloading his pockets of treasures and spread them on the cabbage-rose carpet. What the two women saw made them gasp. Animals of such profile and proportion they would have challenged Adam and Eve to come up with a name!

"What on earth—?" Cara's needlepoint fell from her lap, peacocks trailing iridescent plumage about her feet.

"Clanimals," Donolar said proudly.

"*Clanimals?*" Courtney could imagine these creatures with upturned tails, flat heads, and irregular ears scratching, pinching, pushing—devouring the world. How on earth had the three welded them together—and from *what*?

"Clanimals," Donolar was explaining patiently, "are animals molded from clay. We created them different from all other species (*That was for sure!*) then used the sun for an oven to bake them. The beautiful colors we made from wild plants like the Indians make dye—but first, you have to know where to find this special clay."

"Where *did* you find it, Donolar?" Courtney's voice shook a little.

His answer came as no surprise. "At the mine. Are we not all rich now?"

* * *

"What does it mean, Clint?" Courtney asked as they surveyed the menagerie left proudly for inspection.

"That we have ourselves some Michelangelos—you know, sculptors of characters from an undiscovered planet that spring forward with superhuman strength." Head against his chest, Courtney was unable to see his face. But his voice sounded strained. *Let him open up to me, Lord.*

"Did it—come from the mine—the clay?" she whispered.

"I didn't want to burden you, darling. You have your hands full."

"What concerns you concerns me. Tell me. We are partners."

Clint drew her to him fiercely. "Any idea how much I love you?"

"Some, yes—judging by my own feelings. I love you because of your faith in God and yourself and the rightness of your course, your determination in spite of setbacks, misfortune, and failures, and how you take life's unfairness and injustices in stride and press on like the apostle Paul."

"Oh, my precious darling! It is easy to put a ceiling on ambition with you at my side—my partner in battle—my crown of achievement—"

They had met halfway. Clint shared his plan. Together they could make it work. Together they could make the valley, even yet, into the yielder of bountiful harvests—such as God intended.

CHAPTER 9
Changes

❧

Eastern newspapers were doing their work well. They continued to paint the frontier in exaggerated colors. Lured by adventure, emigrants pushed westward in a never-ending quest for a better life. More families staked out land, most of which went under the plow. More trains were running now, feeding passengers and freight to the western shores. Money was not as plentiful as the "Go West, young man!" recommendations promised. But most of the newcomers stayed for the simple reason that they had insufficient funds for returning home. Wheat profits soared, but growing wheat took time. And the mines were "holdin' up their milk like some stubborn cow," as the old-timers put it. Coastal cities grew violent.

These conditions men discussed mostly in cloakroom get-togethers. Women worried about their men—and their children.

At the Kennedy Mines, Clint's plan had swung into action. The good and the bad of it. It was no longer a secret that the future had lost some of its promising glow. Tony Bronson, who manned the Company Store, said housewives and some of their "hen husbands" complained more and more about the shortage of salt and spice—it being pickling time. And, of course, Deacon Higginbotham "jest sets close by th' cracker barrel spreadin' scare tales, fer th' world lack a grinnin' skull!" The proprietor scratched his big, round head.

Mrs. Rueben stood stiffly *en tableau* at Mandy's report. After all, what could one expect when that "other woman" shopped? Mandy, instinctively aware of the housekeeper's hostile gaze, looked back at her with disdain. " 'Course dem whut's in right minds 'stead uv bein' soft-pated ninnies ud know Mistah Clint'd be fixin' thangs." She set the armful of crudely wrapped parcels of staples "in the bulk" onto the cooktable with a meaningful plop! "Mistah Efraim he wuz theah, too. Ain't nothin' a-goin' wrong."

And it was from Efraim that Courtney received her first progress report.

Efraim came just as the sun was starting down, seeking refuge behind towers of clouds, their windows darkened, that zigzagged along the horizon. The two of them watched in awe from the front gallery of the Mansion while the fiery ball sank, dragging long, black carpets, lined in what one could only describe as bloodred, behind it. There was something eerie about it—something that made Courtney a little sick. But then, so many things did these days.

"I was with Clint again today," Efraim began and then stopped. "Say, I am interrupting the six o'clock dinner hour."

Courtney took his hat. "I am afraid hours are less regular since I became mistress. The men keep irregular hours—and Cousin Bella pays little attention. It is hard to tell whether she has lost interest, hesitates to interfere, or if—well frankly, Efraim, I am concerned over the state of her health. The cold hangs on. Shall we go to the library?" Courtney led the way, then pointed to a chair.

"Things are changing all over," Efraim said thoughtfully as he pulled his trouser legs up to accommodate his knees for sitting. "Wave after wave of immigrants. Two sawmills have been built just outside the Kennedy holdings. Which," he frowned, "is good in a way. Although I hate to see the timber go, there is a desperate need for employment. Strange thing about the economy. When prosperity is in full flower, it is impossible to find help. But when there is a surplus of manpower—no jobs—"

"I understand. You are saying that Kennedy Mines can no longer support those in its employ." It was hard to say the words.

"Something like that. But that man of yours is no quitter, God bless him. Some of the men want their shares in cash—"

"But I thought shares meant a percentage of the profit!"

Efraim nodded. "However, I am looking into it all—just in case, well, the mines close or—"

"Oh Efraim, no! Never, *never*! They are Clint's life—and (tears choked her voice to a whisper) it would kill Cousin Bella."

Efraim laid a gentle hand on her shoulder. "Darling, I said *in case*, nothing more. The good news is that Clint ordered the men up the gulch and—are you ready for this? They got past the clay and into black dirt. Not much, mind you—"

"Pay dirt," she whispered, causing her brother to laugh. "My little sister is learning the language of the land! So I will tell you in the same tongue that a few of the men are going at it hammer and claw!"

"The others?"

"They walked off—mumbling. That is why I must be prepared."

Courtney made no mention of other facets of her husband's plans.

CHAPTER 10
The Test of True Love

Signs of Courtney's pregnancy were showing. July was airless and heavy so corseting was out of the question. Cara, farther into her pregnancy, went into "confinement," in accordance with custom. Courtney had no such plans. If the latest Desmond entered the world in church, what better place? Except that Cousin Bella would miss out on the excitement if her cold persisted.

The morning sickness had passed, so Donolar's profusion of roses throughout the crowded confines of Church-in-the-Wildwood no longer made Courtney ill— just comfortably sleepy. A condition for which Brother Jim had an effective cure. One was unlikely to doze off during his castigating sermons. And on this particular day, he was at his loudest if not his best. When the chorus of *yes-yes* came in response to his usual is-it-well-with-thee question, the giant man pounded the rickety pulpit with such force one wondered if it would survive the blow.

"Nay, nay!" he shouted. "You walk in darkness, little children. The whole shebang of you are inflicted with blindness like the Syrian army, Saul of Tarsus, the men of Sodom. Your hearts are blinded and John warned against this state of sin!"

The congregation quailed, knowing there was more to come, when their spiritual leader paused to gulp down a glass of water, hiccup, and mop his flushed face before resuming. Courtney had grown accustomed to Brother Jim's handling of the Lord's work. Nevertheless, it was good to have Clint squeeze her hand reassuringly. And one look into his face told her that he knew what was coming next.

Oh, how good to have this man You gave me by my side, Lord, her heart whispered. *Absence does not make the heart grow fonder. He was never absent from my heart, my mind, my soul during his blindness . . . separation is the canny culprit . . .*

And that, of course, was what Brother Jim was saying. *Separation from God . . .*

"Take a look around you and stop playing dead—else you *will* be! Why, we're sprawling every direction in a regular brawlers' paradise, where shootin' is the rule instead of the exception! Holdups—another just last night! Decent folks are scared out of their wits by the greedy carrion! And not a doctor left at the fort. As soon as the pickin's grew short here, they headed for the richer veins, not with pickaxes and crowbars but with lancets and stethoscopes, that's what—where they could grow fat bandaging up battered skulls after barroom fights. Parasites, all of 'em—and we, brothers and sisters, are worse for being blind to the needs—"

Images flashed into Courtney's mind, a nightmarish mosaic pieced together by what Efraim, Clint, and Doc George had told her guardedly. A once-wooded area devoid of trees . . . all that was beautiful trampled underfoot by an overpopulation of escaped convicts, horse thieves, and gamblers, with gaudy women-of-the-night gesturing from the unglassed windows of something called a brothel . . . sanitary facilities nonexistent . . . while filth and lust hung over the unholy place like a plague.

Maybe she was going to be sick, after all. And certainly things were not proceeding according to plan—not Clint's plan, anyway.

A red-whiskered man wearing a suit several sizes too small leaped to his feet just ahead of Courtney and Clint.

His diction, clear and concise, was out of keeping with his appearance.

"The pathetic situation is evident to all with one iota," he said in a low growl. "But what's the good of harping on it—particularly in the presence of ladies? Now if you have a solution?"

"Yeah," a man's voice jeered from the back, "we all feel like we been pulled through uh pipe. How come you go brayin' on like that less'n you kin prove yore words? Ain't none uv us in this here church house what was reelin' round in Digger's Saloon las' night. We wuz home with our wimmen 'n kids—eh, fellers?"

There was a restless shuffling of feet as a murmur of agreement mixed with fear ran through the congregation. Folks did not cross Brother Jim. What with him bein' "priestly," mightn't a wrath from On High rain down fire and brimstone? Spared that, there'd be earthly punishment. That fighter-preacherman knowed ever' rule of the ring—and busted 'em all. Any boxer who'd offer takin' on th' devil bare-fisted was bound on flagrant fouls—hittin' a man who was downed, kickin', buttin' an' deliberately usin' them kidney punches and rabbit blows. Th' saintly man could eliminate any opponent with upper-cuttin' words, too—right in th' solar plexus...

How right they were. Brother Jim jerked his head back as if avoiding a straight-arm punch then faced his challengers, clearly exhilarated by the contest. "You hear that, Satan? I woke 'em up! All right, men, I accept the challenge. Stand up, you sparring partners who spent last night in Sin City suckin' up firewater!"

Nothing like this had ever happened. And in that tense moment, Courtney felt a surge of gratitude that Donolar had taken the children in search of wild lupine and thistles for the caterpillars. Glad, too, that Doc George had ignored Cousin Bella's protests and remained at the Mansion with her. Inside, lips moved in silent prayer.

A sudden commotion outside the window tore everybody's attention from the battle of words within the church. Three drunken men in filthy, sweat-soaked overalls reeled by. Watery eyes made an effort to focus on the spectators and lustily one of the party began to sing, "I'm jest a pore—wayfarin' stran-ger . . . a trav-'lin' through thiss-s-s—wor-ld—o' woe—"

The singer stopped and would have fallen except for the two staggering partners who grasped him on either shoulder with peals of raucous laughter. Friendly attachment kept them all upright.

Behind them a regiment of drunken trappers in odoriferous buckskins and tattered coon hats clomped, rubber-legged. One stumbled, cursed, and took a swing at the poacher closest to him. Cheering filled the air as the other men tried to egg on a fistfight. But hilarity suffered instant death. The initial punch threw the aggressor against another and there he clung for support, head bowed, retching violently. Friction forgotten, the congregation prayed audibly now.

Courtney fought off waves of nausea. "The children—" she whispered against Clint's comforting shoulder. "What—"

Then everything happened at once. Donolar, carrying the baby and followed closely by the twins, burst into the church. Kenney was wailing from excitement. The other three were screaming in fear which had nothing to do with the scene outside the window.

"Indians! Indians! They're attacking!" Jordan screeched. "Is—are!" Jonda echoed. "Indians . . . *Indians* . . ."

"Indians!" The congregation took up the frenzied cry.

"*Injuns!*" The men outside the window sobered instantly and Brother Jim told worshipers for years afterwards that the drunken men actually set fire to the woods in their hasty retreat. Or maybe the trail of smoke *did* come from brimstone. The Lord could be mighty mysterious.

Brother Jim could hardly restrain himself. That he wanted to whoop for joy showed first in his eyes then in the slow smile which stretched the width of his full-moon face.

"Fear not, little flock," he said soothingly. "I've a feeling the Lord's timing was just right. Our red brothers and the fearsome troublemakers have scared each other away, probably still be runnin' come tomorrow morning. *Now*," Brother Jim's chest swelled with pleasure, loosening a button on his vest Courtney noted as she and Clint snuggled the children close, "do you recognize the need? Can there be left even *one* Doubting Thomas?"

When there was silence, Brother Jim lowered his voice. "I can go back to bein' a New Testament preacher then. For what's goin' to save that miserable mass of pottage? Love, God's love and ours. Let me assure you that there's a way to change those barns into tabernacles. Now, we've escaped the wrath of God today. Sooo, the test of true love is what we do with the sacrifice made for us—how we spread the good news." He paused. But nobody, including Courtney, was prepared for his next words. They were simply, "Brother Efraim!"

Efraim was here? So much had happened this day that nothing should surprise her. But her brother? Yes, he was striding forward. And in simple language, he explained Arabella Lovelace's generous gift.

There were tears. There were hymns. There were prayers—and more volunteers to build the grand church than could be put to work. More room. Prayers answered. A dream come true. A test passed. But was evil stemmed? Courtney wondered. . . .

CHAPTER 11
A Woman's Destiny

❧

Courtney was interrogating Donolar and the twins when Roberta arrived unexpectedly at the Mansion the next day. Smart as always in her English tweed riding skirt, Roberta was riding a magnificent roan, Courtney noted from the corner of her eye. A new horse?

Oh, how wonderful to see her beloved sister-in-law— or was she a sister? But let Mrs. Rueben meet her at the door. The matter at hand must be settled. It was incredible that she and Clint had been robbed of time to get to the bottom of the "Indian attack" alarm that Donolar, Jordan, and Jonda had sounded in church. True, the outcome had been a happy one, but that was no excuse. If they were making this up...

"Now," she continued where she had left off, "did you or did you not see Indians—and please speak one at a time. Donolar?"

The agate eyes looked vague. "This is Indian land— all of it. Maybe the land is angry and wrinkled its face to make mountains—maybe it was once a church, all of it, then the butterflies found it. But butterfly moments fly away—and maybe the Indian buck looked in at the window because he does not like buildings for churches— it's all sacred ground—"

Would that I did not have to interrupt his beautiful flow of poetic thought, Lord, Courtney's heart whispered. But aloud she said as quietly as her quickened heartbeat allowed, "He looked *inside*?"

The twins could no longer restrain themselves. He *did* look. Yes, he did. And there were other Indians in the grove behind the church, sort of crouched down like they were looking for footprints and "talking funny." All of them kept pointing at the church and they were about to burn it for sure—

"Now, we do not know that," Courtney protested with some uncertainty, wondering just what they *did* know. "It is always best to tell exactly what you *saw* instead of what you thought—you *did* see Indians?"

The three heads bobbed in unison. And Jordan's eyes widened with that special look of piety Courtney recognized as a ploy to put him in the good graces of all, above and below. "Jesus would be sad and might cry if we told stories—and you and Daddy would, so we'd cry, too!"

"That is right," Courtney said a little weakly. This one surely had a way of switching roles with her. Were all mothers so bewildered?

"Auntie Ro!" The trial ended without the defendants being dismissed when the three caught sight of Roberta coming upstairs.

It took some doing to rescue a laughing Roberta. The sack of peppermints helped. When the trio left to divide the candies in thirds under the old apple tree, the two young wives embraced.

"They adore you—so do I—and it has been far too long!" Courtney burst out in one breath.

"I know, I know," Roberta answered, still clinging. "I had forgotten how smart they all are. Efraim says Donolar knows as much Indian history as he himself knows, and Efraim is having to dig into the matter. So much has come up, disputes over claims—one having overlapped an Indian burial ground—"

Courtney drew back. Even before asking, somehow she knew.

"On our land—the Kennedy estate?"

"The same."

"But—but—" Courtney, stunned, floundered foolishly. "I—I thought they—Indians—here were buried in their war canoes in *treetops*."

Roberta, seating herself without invitation, shivered. "Some Indians were—right in that dark, old grove of cottonwood—and the bows are pointed west down the Columbia—that's why the winds moan." Her voice dropped to a ghostly whisper. "Oh Courtney, I'm upsetting you because it disturbed me that—that—"

Courtney, feeling queasy again, sank onto the edge of the poster bed. "What, Ro—tell me—what is it?"

"The surveyors cut through the trees and—oh Courtney, it was ghastly. Some of the remains are still there—skeletons sitting upright facing west—"

"Does Cousin Bella know?"

"Efraim thinks you should decide whether to make mention of the find. He will discuss it with Clint after checking all the terms set down when the reservation was set aside. Donolar has a point, you know—we all belong here. It's a shared history—everybody pushing West. We're the Western world. And the Indians are a part of us." Roberta smiled and then quipped, "Let's not fret our visit away about our ancestors who couldn't keep their Berings Strait!"

Courtney relaxed with a laugh, meeting Roberta's amber-spoked eyes for the first time. Had her lovely eyes, her best feature, lost a bit of their sparkle? Her skin, some of its glow? Love had made Roberta beautiful and now, except for the polished-oak of her hair, she looked plain, pallid, actually ill.

As if sensing Courtney's examination, Roberta turned the talk to other matters. "Have you heard from our shared parents?" she asked lightly. "Had a letter postmarked 'Paris'?"

Courtney had not. It made for such a strange relationship, they agreed, that Roberta's father should marry

Courtney, Donolar, and Efraim's mother. They were sisters and sisters-in-law.

A laugh bubbled from Courtney's lips. "Why, Roberta dear, you married your own brother! Try and figure the relationship of our children when—"

Roberta was saved from answering by the soft padding of baby footsteps and Kenney, rosy with sleep, toddled in. But her face was aflame as she caught the roly-poly, blue-flannel, wiggly warmth of the baby in her arms, burying her face in his fine, gold curls.

"Umm-m-m, you smell like talcum, you precious creature," and, tracing the button nose, she held him closer.

Kenney, ever the good-natured darling, obliged with a giggle. Then, frightened by Roberta's almost desperate squeeze, he held dimpled fists out to Courtney. As she leaned to take him, she heard Roberta gasp. "Courtney— you—you are—uh—"

"The word is pregnant!" Courtney said with saucy pride. "Another look-alike, I guess. Cousin Bella says we could tie a string on the foot of all three and forget which one wore the bow!"

But Roberta was not laughing. She was weeping!

"Roberta, what is it, darling? Something I said?" Courtney longed to hold her beloved friend in her arms, comfort her, console. But she turned Kenney's eyes away instead. With him, weeping was contagious.

"Do you want to tell me?" When Roberta cried harder, Courtney tried teasing. "Come, come, Ro—you know you are too tender of heart to leave the door locked on any poor little skeletons in your closet."

It was a wrong thing to say.

"It's so easy for you to treat the matter lightly!" Roberta's voice was sharp with pain. "So easy. And there's Cara who can afford no more children and undoubtedly wishes medical science would come up with something to stop reproduction—and yet she goes on having babies.

I envy you both—I *covet* your children. God forgive me, I do!"

Courtney's heart turned over inside her, but she bit her tongue to hold back comment. *Let it all out, dear Roberta,* her heart willed.

Roberta went on talking in a stream of conscience, but her voice was losing some of its bitterness. "I am so filled with maternal love that I stopped to watch and weep over a white-faced cow and her newborn calf on my way over—"

Kenney's chubby legs pumped up and down in a little dance of frustration at being held still too long. "Wanna pway—don' cwy—" little Kenney whimpered.

"Oh sweetheart, Auntie Ro's so sorry." Roberta tried a quick recovery. Wonderful thing about children, they never questioned. But Courtney saw that the twist of remorse lingered on Roberta's face. "Here—I brought you something."

The baby squealed with delight, accepted the bright rubber ball, and took a few steps toward his favorite play-corner. Then, remembering, he toddled back. "Hugga neck," he lisped and, after the hurried embrace, went into his private little world of play.

The moist kiss brought fresh tears to Roberta's eyes. Without words, Courtney patted a place beside her on the bed. Tall, angular Roberta sat down somewhat awkwardly. The lovely radiance Efraim's love had brought to her face was gone. Courtney waited for her dear friend to curl into a knees-to-chin position the two of them used at "girl-talk" time. But this was no girl sitting arm's length away. It was a woman torn apart emotionally.

And then the tense moment of silence passed. Roberta, like a magician whose sleight of hand has failed, began pulling sentence fragments from her bag of confusion.

"I—we—nothing is right anymore. Oh, Efraim says it is, but a woman knows... I mean, he hardly touches me...after all our dreams. I—I want to run—any-where—as long as there are no fulfilled women—smug mothers—but I can't run away from myself.... Oh Courtney—I'm *barren!*"

Courtney longed to reach to her but dared not. "Two years is too soon to decide."

Fury was dwindling to something between resigna-tion and defeat. Roberta's voice was dead when she spoke. "I have the doctor's word. Actually, I had it a long time ago but refused to believe it until now. Otherwise, I would never have married Efraim."

"There have been revolutionary changes."

"Some things do not change. The condition is due to my childhood bout with a strange malady—something called 'red-eye fever' which I contracted in San Fran-cisco. I can never bear a son. With Efraim the Glamora line stops—since Donolar—you understand—?"

Yes and no. So this was why Roberta had been avoiding her. If she was giving her husband the same treatment—

"Do you honestly think Efraim would reject you be-cause of this situation?" Courtney asked softly.

"A man has a right to put away a barren wife. The Bible gave him that," Roberta said, her voice so sad Courtney could have wept.

"We are no longer under the old Mosaic law," Courtney pointed out. "And even so, having a *right* does not make it compulsory."

"But he is noble—and I could never bear the pain of knowing that he stays out of duty. Why would he want me? An empty shell—"

"You are his wife!" Courtney's voice was firm and sure now. Reaching out, she took her sister-in-law by the shoulders and shook her gently. "You disappoint me, Ro. I have a higher opinion of my brother. Crude as this sounds, do you think he married you for *breeding?*"

The question was a shocker as Courtney had hoped. In fact, it blew Roberta to bits. She rallied and rubbed her eyes as if she had awakened from a bad dream. "You are an angel—"

Not an angel. Just a person who understood, having dreamed sweetly and waiting...and waiting...and *waiting*. Only to lose two precious babies whose squeals of mirth she would never hear, whose plump bottoms would never bumpty-bump down the carpeted stairs, worn a little thin by preceding generations of scooting offspring...and the dreams slowly fading. Until God took over!

"He bought me the roan to make me feel better!" Roberta burst out.

"And yet you think he is about to 'put you away'? Oh, Ro—"

Roberta's eyes lighted up and then darkened again. "But why doesn't God hear my prayers? What's left when prayer fails?"

"God is sometimes baffling," Courtney admitted, "but darling, prayer *never* fails for God is *always* listening. We women must hold tight to faith. Someway, somehow, He will see that we fulfill our destiny."

This time the light stayed in Roberta's eyes. Temporarily.

CHAPTER 12
Mysterious Guest

🍂

Courtney longed to talk over Efraim and Roberta's problem with Clint. But, although the family was all assembled at dinner the evening following Roberta's visit, the subject was far removed from marital relationships and replenishing the earth.

She did have an opportunity to make mention to Cousin Bella, however, although their time alone was brief. Mrs. Rueben, who was undisputedly the neatest housekeeper west of the Mississippi, broke the news to Courtney that *Frau*—Miz, should say—Arabella was desiring to be down to dinner since company was coming, without breaking the rhythm of her dusting, shaking draperies, then dusting again. If Miz Desmond— Courtney, should say—thought it be foolishness, should she maybe be upstairs discouraging the good woman? Mandy, undisturbed by either the guest or Cousin Bella's announcement, sang her golden-throated hymns loudly enough to be heard "down heah" and "Up theah." A fact that caused the housekeeper to beat and dust with increased vigor. Courtney promised to check.

Cousin Bella was sitting erectly before the long mirror of her recently rubbed-down fruitwood dresser, all three swell-top drawers unlocked and open for convenience as she reached for the items to complete her toilette. Although the long gray-black hair hung about her face, already she was attired in a dressy black taffeta silk, the waist of which was trimmed with lace over folds of pale blue set off by embroidered French knots. A little late to suggest that she skip the scheduled appearance.

Courtney could only gasp, "Cousin Bella, you look wonderful!"

"Come in, my dear," Arabella Lovelace said warmly. "It was only the sniffles, hardly enough to make an invalid of me. George Washington is undoubtedly the finest physician around, although he tends to coddle his patients."

Dear Cousin Bella. Never welcoming sympathy, but opening her heart to love.

"You are entitled to some coddling," Courtney smiled affectionately. Then, noting the telltale pallor of Cousin Bella's fine-grained skin, she said, "Please—may I do your hair?"

"You will find the brush and combs in the upper-right drawer."

Surprised and pleased, Courtney reached for the ebony hairbrush with 11 rows of soft Russian bristles. It should be kind to the scalp.

But Cousin Bella protested. "The one in the box, please. George Washington wants me to try Dr. Scott's electro-brush—recommended for headache and neuralgia. And the tortoiseshell-back comb—"

"It was good to see Roberta," Cousin Bella said as Courtney brushed and braided. "I am very fond of the girl, but she seemed preoccupied. She praised the work Cara has done then spoke vaguely of what she would like in a home—if things were different."

Pinning the heavy braids into a coronet, Courtney secured the high comb in back. *She suspects*, Courtney thought. *She knows.*

"There! Your hair looks lovely. How does your scalp feel?"

"Combed. What's wrong with Roberta, Courtney, other than being unable to have children?"

"That *is* the problem. Ending of the Glamora blood-line."

"Nonsense." The word was a near-snort. "The Glamora blood flows in all our veins. But," Cousin Bella spoke more slowly, "who am I to deny that there is a certain pride in carrying on a *name*? God has answered my prayers so completely that it frightens me at points. We have to learn patience when He does not behave like a magician, pulling a needed answer from a hat. Some of our prayers fall on the wrong side of God's will. The timing of His will is a great mystery. My goodness, when I remember how I tried to outline everything step-by-step, forgetting how incomplete and imperfect the human mind is—why, Courtney, my prayers are an embarrassment!"

"I know—how well I know. We have to learn to appreciate surprises. At least, I did."

"As did I. If you will hand me my shawl—"

Courtney wrapped the fringed, white-wool scarf about the thin shoulders, allowing her hand to linger there in a caress. Cousin Bella reached to touch her hands, their dark eyes meeting in the mirror.

"How I grieved, Courtney—oh, how I grieved—for my lost love and our lost youth, George Washington's and mine. I wanted this house filled with children's laughter. I wanted swings in the apple tree. I even wanted children crying in the night and George Washington and me lifting them, soothing them, banishing their fears with a kiss and a prayer." She sighed deeply. "And now I have it all 'acceptable and perfect.' "

Courtney felt happiness bubble up inside her. It translated into a joyous laugh. "We are sentimental sillies, are we not? I am still dreaming of you and me seeing the children setting off to school with lunch baskets bulging...as adolescents trying to outwit us...falling in and out of love...and all the time loving and being loved. All this is denied Roberta."

"So far," said Cousin Bella.

* * *

The Mansion was filled with the rich aroma of parching coffee beans when Clint brought the guest. Dr. Henry Freeman (with a degree in anthropology) was a small man who wore half-spectacles below pale eyes that changed expressions from jovial to solemn. His teeth were too white and evenly aligned to be his own. But there was a frank openness about him that Courtney liked immediately and her liking for him grew as the evening wore on.

First, he appreciated the smell of the coffee beans (and that won Mandy's heart). He admired the details of the great house: the mellow woods, fine tapestries, and paintings. He complimented the children's manners, which saved the evening. With memories like theirs, their busy tongues were stilled during dinner—even when Dr. Freeman's dentures clacked as he gnawed corn off the cob. And the greatest plus in his favor was the attention he paid to Donolar.

"Ah, roses—my favorite blossom," he said of the centerpiece of sword fern and rosebuds. "My compliments to you, young man."

Donolar thanked the guest (Courtney still wondered if Dr. Freeman had a mission or was one of the countless people who were always welcomed here). Then Donolar added, "Roses express love. Pink symbolizes grace—which we have not yet said."

Brother Jim, who apparently was acquainted with Dr. Freeman, turned and said, "Hank, will you ask the blessing?"

The prayer was brief. Donolar resumed his oral treatment of roses. A deeper shade of pink expressed gratitude . . . white conveyed innocence . . . yellow, joy . . . and,

"Rosebuds say, 'You are young and beautiful and I love you still.' Those are for Courtney, my sister."

Dr. Freeman wiped matchstick fingers with his napkin and clapped his hands. "Bravo!" he said.

Courtney felt a flush rise from her neck to her cheeks when the clapping spread to the four corners of the long, linen-skirted table. But her embarrassment ended abruptly when she realized that this undoubtedly was the first applause Donolar had ever known. How gracious the man was!

"It's true, you know—you are and I do!" Clint whispered from the corner of his mouth as the applause slowed to a stop.

"Are you acquainted with the mysteries of the Stinking Rose, Donolar?" Seeing the puzzlement in the wide eyes, Henry Freeman tactfully turned his question to Doc George. "Is it still a cure-all?"

Doc George chuckled. "For those who are believers in my homeopathic prescriptions, yes—everything from baldness to snakebites—and (his grin spread wider into that fat-cheeked 'Santa smile') great for 'the vapors.' "

The two men laughed heartily, leaving the others to guess—with a fair degree of accuracy.

Garlic! Of all the odd turns for a conversation to take. Brother Jim said that some otherwise perfectly sane people hung braids of the stinking rose in their homes to ward off evil spirits. Its history dated back to prophets and philosophers, Cousin Bella stated, saying they touted the pungent herb as affording a certain mystique. A relative of the onion...yes, food of the first pioneers ...the camas...a discovery of the Indians.

There was dead silence—stemming, Courtney was sure, from the last word. Did that explain Dr. Freeman's presence? She shivered.

CHAPTER 13
The Disappearing Cemetery

❧

"Mandy, will you see that Cousin Bella gets to bed? The children are settled in and there is something I must do." Courtney spoke softly.

The grandfather clock struck 11. The men had been gone for hours and they were to have been right back, bringing a sample of their grisly finds from the grove of cottonwoods. The archeologist was to examine—*ugh!*— a skull. He was qualified, Doc George said, to determine whether the remains in the tree branches were bona fide skeletons or if the whole thing was a hoax. Henry Freeman would somehow be able to tell the difference between the bones of a red man and those of a white. It was morbid—but this was no time to be thin-skinned, no time to yield to fear. But they had been gone so long. Something must have gone wrong.

Mandy's eyes were white saucers. "Y'all ain't a-gonna go t' dat—dat *graveyard!*" The last word was whispered in horror.

"No scolding please, Mandy. I will take Donolar—"

"Dat boy'll be scarder'n me—now, Courtney hon, y'all dun knowed dat doctah man don' need no hep—'n Doc George he sez ridin's bad—"

Dear Mandy. She must be one of God's favorites. Courtney hugged the massive goodness of her close. "You make us some of that famous coffee our guest so enjoyed and," Courtney continued with sudden inspiration, "not a word to Mrs. Rueben. You are in command."

Mandy's ebony face creased in delight at the conspiracy. "Ain't a-gonna tell dat meddlin' woman nothin'. Iffen she comes inspectin' mah bizness, hit's a-gonna be wors'n de Civil Wah wuz!"

Yes, one caustic or ill-chosen word was sufficient for a full-scale verbal brawl. A fact Mandy verified. "Ah ain't agin' hair pullin'." And with a growl, she tightened the red bandana around her head.

Minutes later, Donolar was saddling Peaches. Without a word, he helped Courtney up and mounted in front of her on the little mare. Away they sprinted, letting Peaches have her head, while Courtney held tightly to her brother. Through the pale shafts of light from a sliver of moon, Courtney could see Peaches' mane flying, her eyes bright with spirit, and nostrils flared as they sucked in the clean, crisp night air. She was running as lightly as a colt as her hoofs clopped across a bridge leading to forbidden territory. Forbidden to Courtney, at least. But it was obviously a well-beaten path for Peaches who was allowed to graze the entire estate. Clint, however, had discouraged Courtney's taking this direction, saying one never knew who or what could lurk in the broad expanse of leggy trees woven together by brambles and undergrowth. Its lushness suggested a spring or high-level water table. But no water was needed, so the land was undeveloped.

The mare slowed and Courtney felt Donolar tremble. He ruffled Peaches' mane. "Good girl," he murmured. Then, babbling something unintelligible, he pointed ahead. Courtney gritted her teeth to keep them from chattering. For there, bobbing like evil eyes, were lanterns shifting from tree to tree as if seeking prey. *Oh please, Lord, let it be Clint—and the others*, Courtney prayed as she and Donolar quickly dismounted.

Courtney stopped in mid-prayer, alerted to some danger. Donolar, sensing her fear, stood motionless. Strain her ears as she would, there was no sound—just a feeling that someone was close by. Clint had told her that the Indians were quelled, that she need have no fear. Nevertheless, her hand instinctively touched her hair and she squatted, pulling Donolar down beside her. Were the Indians back to honor their ancestors? Harmless? Why, then, did her mind conjure visions of an entire tribe searching the woods for her? Once upon a time, so history told her, young bucks stole white women. She could see them—some painted hideously, others bearing scars of battle—all advancing with spread-apart knees slightly bent, sweating chests thrust forward, feathered tomahawks in hand.

For the first time in her life, Courtney Desmond, to whom violence was a stranger, wished with all her heart for a weapon of defense. She wondered then if Clint, Doc George, Brother Jim, and Dr. Freeman were armed. It occurred to her then that Indians did not attack at night.

"Be very quiet, darling," she whispered to Donolar. "No movement—"

And there she stopped. For, although the stalking scalp-hunters had to be a figment of her mind, the sound of footsteps in the brush just beyond the ravine was not. Overhead an owl hooted as if to alert the forest of her invasion. But what sent the tremor up her spine was the outline of a man, too large and clumsy to be an Indian. He had to walk slowly because of the tremendous box or sack—it was too dark to tell—he carried above his head. In the split second he lumbered toward them, Courtney wished the ground would open up and swallow her and Donolar. An earthquake would be welcome.

Then, miraculously, the great hulk turned, dropped on his bloated belly, and crawled through the briars— pushing the object ahead. Soon there was silence again. *They had survived!*

And suddenly the house of Courtney's mind was in

order. She was no longer afraid now that she had faced what could have been death. Who was to say? In a methodical, orderly fashion, she began putting together as accurate a description as possible. Information which might be helpful when this was over. She had met a crisis without panic—a vital part of being mistress of Mansion-in-the-Wild.

It was Donolar who spotted Clint. He was leading the way out of the dense cottonwood grove. The lantern swinging high overhead illuminated his dearly familiar features, and a kind of giddiness overtook Courtney. She was an emigrant...meeting up with a wagon train ...and she was falling head over heels for the wagon master. There would be no questions, no scoldings, no recriminations of any kind. She would simply fall into his arms.

And she did.

There was little talk on the way home. Once there, all the men talked at once. But the real message each had was, "The cemetery, if ever one existed, was gone—not a sign of a canoe or human remains—"

Brother Jim alone had spotted the man Courtney saw. Big as a bear, he said. Forearms bigger around than four-by-sixes. And a chest the size of the bran barrel in which Mandy stored the hams and bacon. He was pushing something—just could've been a canoe. Courtney confirmed his story in less-descriptive language. And Donolar, bless him, had stopped shivering and said lucidly: " 'What lies behind us and what lies before us are small matters when compared to what lies within us,' said Emerson. And my sister was very brave—so much within, she makes me so!"

Before Courtney could react, Cousin Bella entered the kitchen where a smiling Mandy was serving coffee and oversized ginger cookies.

"Arabella!" Doc George seated her gallantly. She thanked him absently and said she was not surprised at the fruitlessness of the search. Nothing added up, she said, if they accepted surveyors' reports as being on the level. The men nodded as she stirred her coffee.

"Tree burial is uncommon in these parts. 'The Happy Hunting Ground,' Columbia Indians' concept of heaven, can be reached only by departure from Memaloose Island, 'The Island of the Dead.' "

"In the river—near the gorge?" Dr. Freeman asked with interest.

"Correct. Look closely and you will find low, hut-like structures that served as waiting stations. They are ancient. Now most bury their dead in a small plot behind the mission. Interesting history—"

Interesting, yes. Life, as they described it, had been so simple then, Courtney thought fleetingly. The red men were worshipers of nature and nature was overpowering here, even now. Snow peaks standing tall along the Cascade Ridge . . . woods stretching away, past the tumbling waterfalls, scaling the mountains to join the snow line. Here the gods sent warm storms in from the ocean and cold storms through the gorge to make a beautiful weather pattern. It was easy to understand how the Indians came to believe that all nature—rocks, birds, and beasts—spelled out the "spirit," of which the coyote was king. Totem poles told the story of how the king met their needs—bringing fire to cook bread made of tree moss, pine nuts, seeds, and bark.

"They were without science," the anthropologist said, draining his cup. "They never invented the wheel or learned to control the lever, but they knew more of nature than we—and were just as human."

"We took away their gods," Donolar said without inflection.

"But we introduced them to Another, our Universal Father!"

Silence fell after Brother Jim's declaration. Interesting as the conversation was, it had skirted the issue. *What became of the cemetery?* Time alone would tell.

CHAPTER 14
The Old and the New

The weeks following were busy ones. Dr. Freeman advised members of the household to refrain from making mention of the strange happenings to outsiders. "It would only alarm the valley as well as impede our investigation." And, promising to get to the bottom of the matter, he returned to town.

Clint extracted a promise from Courtney (with very little effort) that she would go nowhere near the setting. "I have never scolded you properly, you know," he said with the beginnings of a tender embrace. Laughingly, he stooped to kiss the part of her hair instead. "I will be glad when I can reach around you again."

Courtney giggled. "And I, sir, will be glad when I can see my toes!" Not that she minded much—when Clint said she had never looked lovelier.

That was in August, the night before Clint announced that it was time to make some changes and adaptations at the mines—as well as at the Mansion, providing, of course, that they met with Courtney's approval. Whatever he did would be right, her eyes signaled.

"What would you say to Roberta's moving in—at least for a time? Efraim may be away—here, in fact—sort of in and out—"

Courtney felt herself stiffen. "Is there trouble, Clint—between her and my brother?"

"You know he is too much of a gentleman to discuss his private affairs even if a problem existed. Say—what gave you that idea anyway?"

Courtney told him. Clint tended to brush it aside. "Efraim has enough problems without Roberta's giving imagination free rein. And it *is* her imagination, darling. It's a sound marriage. He adores her. His preoccupation is with business. There were problems, as you know, with suits and countersuits over Indian rights and claims—even before this senseless thing in the grove. Now there are more—"

"Are you afraid, Clint?" Courtney's voice was a whisper.

"Afraid? No—but cautious. I would feel better if Roberta were here with you. You have to be lonely with Cara no longer able to come—?"

It was true. Cara's baby had three-month colic and required one parent or the other walking the floor 24 hours a day. Still—there seemed more to the suggestion. She waited for Clint to go on.

He did. "The fact of the matter is, Courtney, we are running out of cash and silver at approximately the same rate. I have been waiting for an opportunity to tell you that Efraim offered to go in with me—get a loan." He sounded so tired. Courtney longed to run her fingers through his hair, massage his neck where the sun-bronzed hair curled upward when the humidity was high. But she refrained. (She could feel tension seep from her own scalp, slowly dripping down her spine like liquid from a bottle.) "With a little help, we can eke out enough to pay a skeleton crew—some have left, you know—and put the others to work, with pay, on the church and school," Clint planned on.

"But they volunteered!"

"I know, sweetheart, but they—the ones who stayed—have families to feed. Cousin Bella's arrangement provides for the materials and I can manage the rest. This was our plan, remember, before running low."

"You are wonderful," Courtney whispered with tears in her voice. "And I know God thinks so, too. I think I am going to cry—oh Clint, anything you want to do—*anything*—is fine."

Clint drew her to him, forgetting the baby between them. "That's one of the million things I love about you!" He was laughing, but she sensed tears in his blue, blue eyes. "You have the uncommon wisdom, the amazing judgment, the good taste combined with knowledge, and what the locals call 'horse sense' to know you married a wise man!"

As usual, he had put her heart at rest. Could Roberta be wrong about the change in Efraim? It occurred to Courtney suddenly that she should share Hannah's story with her sister-in-law. What was it her husband, Elkanah, had said? "Why weepest thou. . . . Am not I better to thee than ten sons?" Roberta had missed Brother Jim's sermon on the First Book of Samuel. Did she know the miracle of the baby Samuel's birth? Yes, it would be nice to have Roberta here . . . good for Cousin Bella, who enjoyed company but was not up to entertaining . . . and good as an added means of security, Courtney admitted to herself. For in her heart she knew that no cemetery, or facsimile thereof, could simply disappear in thin air. Oh, the men tended to dismiss the incident lightly. That was just it—*lightly*. Men, bless them, could be so transparent. Women had been giving birth since time began. Why must they be so overprotective? She felt so good physically that she could deliver this one in the blackberry patch and go right back to picking the purple fruits which were at their peak for Mandy's jelly. But the mine was another matter.

*   *   *

The men of the church met to examine plans Efraim had drawn up for the new one. Best they get started at once before harvest time and then the rains. Cyrus

Stringfellow said they were welcome to camp in his melon patch, "them what comes a long ways from home." Course now, they'd be working only betwixt jobs they could find here and there. What with the mine not producin'—well, the good Lord would have to be providin' somehow. Yes, them was grand ideas the parson had—wantin' what was it, a "molten sea of ten cubits" and all them gold instruments ... tongs ... spoons ... and cherubims like Solomon's temple? But, declared Ahab the smithy, grand as them ideas be, he could forge some mighty fine articles without waiting for such grandeur. Yep, sure could, Tony Bronson who operated the Company Store, agreed. Why now, he'd carve out window sashes with his pocket knife if money got scarcer than 'twas.

That was before Clint made an appearance. And then Efraim.

It was Brother Jim who broke the news to Cousin Bella and Courtney. Hatless, coatless, his shirttail out, and waving his arms exultantly—obviously having left the meeting early—he galloped out of the woods.

"It's here, here—it came through!" he shouted breathlessly as he leaped from his horse and sailed onto the gallery without seeming to touch a doorstep. "Some brick arrived—and Efraim—"

He stopped then, mopping his red face and casting a guilty look at Courtney behind the great blue bandana. Maybe he wasn't supposed to make mention of a loan in Miss Arabella's presence. "Efraim shared the plans," he finished weakly.

"Did Efraim get the loan?" Cousin Bella's voice was clipped.

Brother Jim's mouth dropped on its hinges. "You knew?" Surprise mingled with relief.

"Of course I knew! Trying to run a mine without capital would be like trying to organize a week without a

Sabbath. And I wish you to know that I have no time for riddles. Just be as forthright here in my parlor as you are in the pulpit. A cold and senility are not one and the same. I hope the men went to work before the ink was dry on the contract." Arabella Lovelace paused and looked out the east window. "I can almost see the foundation of the brick buildings from here. It's to be beautiful, you hear?"

Brother Jim kissed his palm and patted a Bible on the marble-topped table. "*Impressive?* That church is going to be the bestseller for religion this side of the Continental Divide. There'll be something for everybody, a pulpit fit for a king, comfortable pews, a pump—that's right, our own pump—so folks can stop totin' fruit jars of water for their children, and watering troughs for those poor horses and mules that have been bone-dry during preaching, poor critters. Oh, a belfry, too, with a cupola. It'll be impressive, all right—about like 50 pounds of black powder explodin'—boom!—hittin' the rich and the low-lifes alike—a real ding-whister, er, pardon, ladies. It'll be the making of civilization here. And the school now—" On and on he thundered.

"Brother Jim..." Arabella Lovelace interrupted at last.

"Yes, ma'am?"

"How much? How much did that tight-fisted Isaac Jacobson dole out from the bank?"

Brother Jim's smile shortened as he named the amount.

Cousin Bella's face clouded. "That paltry sum? He should know me better than that. Of course he has a mind-and-a-half of his own, but he knows I stand up and claw—not that I have to anymore—"

But the release from pressure she tried to reflect sounded affected. She had surrendered all to her beloved successors. Unbegrudgingly. And with her heart. But the land was still in her bloodstream, Courtney knew, and always would be. The great lady would make no mention. There was no need. She might as well be marching down the boardwalks of the city to the beat of a tom-tom and carrying a banner: MISTRESS OF MANSION-IN-THE-WILD. But time had stolen it away. *Oh Cousin Bella, I will guard it as kings guard treasures ... not because of my love for the land ... but yours ...*

Time would come for Courtney to recall that vow—with deep sorrow.

But for now, Brother Jim was speaking again. "Don't you go worrying, Miss Arabella. Clint will keep the men's time balanced between the building and the mining. There's a need for that school and church and you can rest assured the Lord will be lending a hand. That small vein of silver up-creek, weakling though it is, is bound to be paying its own freight in nothing flat."

Cousin Bella agreed, but her voice lacked conviction. "There is need for more cash-on-hand—a mortgage would have helped, I guess."

"He—the Jacobson fellow—offered—" began Brother Jim.

"Oh he did, did he? Yes, he would. He would love sinking those gold teeth into this property!"

Brother Jim looked smug. "Clint laughed in his face."

A look of pride crossed the older woman's countenance. "It's in the right hands—my family's and the Lord's. My cane, please."

*   *   *

September flooded the fields with liquid bronze. Another season blending the old with the new. Courtney welcomed a turn of the calendar. Summer's sun had been full-force and tempers just as fierce. In the fields. In the mine. Among the builders. And, reportedly, in the impermanent clutter of shacks erected by emigrants continuing to arrive in quest of gold. Someday, she supposed, the settlement would straddle the river in confusion. Well, they were preparing to deal with it—weren't they?

CHAPTER 15
A Man's Pride

❦

October brought a burst of glory—and Roberta. She moved in to "help when the baby comes," she said . . . then "because the town is dangerous for a woman." Not a vacation exactly, but—well, maybe she and Efraim needed a vacation in the sense of being apart from one another. "I'm no wife—just a reminder of failure."

Courtney, helping Roberta with her bags, wondered what there was to say. Her heart bled for Roberta. Did she resent the fact that life continued to scatter gold coins for her and Clint?

"Don't lift that!" Roberta's voice was razor-edged. "I'm sorry. The heat, I guess," she murmured, loosening a hairpin and removing her brown felt poke bonnet.

Obediently, Courtney set down the lightweight bag. The heat had nothing to do with Roberta's obsession. And trying to convince her of Efraim's love would do no good whatsoever. She yearned to believe it was true while clinging to the doubts buried deep from an insecure childhood.

One day, Lord, we will work this out, You and I, Courtney promised. And aloud she said, "You high-fashion ladies will just have to pay the penalty, Ro. Nobody outside a *Godey's Lady's Book* would venture out in this heat wearing wool! Tell me about the city. It has been so long ago that I was there."

Another indirect reference to her pregnancy had slipped out. Courtney resolved to be more careful and was glad when, as they turned upstairs, Roberta took another direction in answering—eager, it seemed, to back up her statement about the evils of the place.

"Brother Jim's right. It is absolute pandemonium—bad enough in the daytime and impossible at night. Even the most indulgent of the decent residents would testify to the fact that the windows rattle six miles in every direction."

"Can the law do nothing?" Courtney asked. They had paused at the landing to breathe before making the turn for the rest of the climb. Courtney noted from the corner of her eye that Donolar, spotting Roberta's horse, had entered and was looking at the baggage with a questioning face. She motioned for him to bring it and he nodded as if sharing a conspiracy.

"—and the judge Doc George told you about is staying. It is good that a new marshal and two deputies to assist are hired. I drew up contracts—"

"Yes, very good," Courtney answered, having heard only part.

"There are fewer murders since the judge took to hanging—oh Courtney, I'm sorry—"

Courtney stopped on the next-to-the-top step and drew a deep breath. "Ro," she said slowly, hoping that she could choose her words well, "must we go on weighing words like this? We never have before, and now we handle one another like spun glass."

"Which way?"

Courtney sighed and pointed to the east wing. She had failed to get through. Well, let Roberta try and dodge this one!

"This is the suite you and Efraim will occupy," Courtney said matter-of-factly. "Furniture is topsy-turvy in the other rooms where Cara and I left off when her baby came."

"You—we—I—he—" Roberta was sputtering helplessly. "I told you that your brother won't be coming here—and we—"

"You did?" Courtney asked innocently. "I have no memory of that. My, it is close in here. Let's get some windows open."

Donolar deposited the bags and wordlessly helped Courtney with the windows then silently stole away. Bars of sunlight slid in to bring vibrant spirit to the Georgian-period furnishings, dancing from the Sheraton armchairs near the great fireplace to the Hepplewhite desk, and pausing on a circular-framed painting entitled "The Cattle on a Thousand Hills."

Roberta stood, lips parted, in the center of the great room. To bridge the awkward moment, Courtney chatted about the imposing furnishings. "Actually, this was a sort of drawing room, a part of the original McLoughlin mansion. Can you imagine what a stir such neoclassical facade would have created way back then?"

Surprisingly, Roberta closed her eyes and then opened them as if reliving some memory in her affluent, but loveless childhood. "Charming..." she murmured almost inaudibly as she moved from one item of furniture to another, tracing each with the tip of her index finger. "If the Go-Backs could see what can be accomplished with time—"

"Go-Backs?"

"A name thought up by the Stayers-On—you know, those who stick to their bush here while neighbors go back where home is."

Sticking to your bush could be applied to your marriage vows, too, dear Roberta, for better or for worse, Courtney longed to point out. But she remained silent. Self-doubt had become malignant in Roberta's mind, its cells uniting with poor-little-rich-girl recollections and spreading to doubt in her husband's love. Mere words, however wise and inspired, were an ineffective balm. Only God could heal her heart—and then, only if she opened its door to Him.

Roberta was looking with interest at a fanlight crowning a heavy door leading onto a balcony.

"It even has vines leading up a trellis," Courtney said airily, "you know, like in *Romeo and Juliet*." Seeing Roberta flinch, Courtney shifted the emphasis. "We have to keep a sharp eye on Donolar and the twins. They are forever trying to act out that scene."

When Roberta turned, Courtney took her elbow. "Come see the master bedroom since we moved the packing barrels. Oh, what treasures we found! We are still looking for Doc George's old violin and some papers—see, have you ever seen anything more magnificent than this Brazilian-walnut bed?"

"You can put away your fishing pole, dear heart," Roberta said sadly. "Your brother and I no longer share a bed."

Courtney felt a sudden surge of impatience. "My brother! My word, Roberta—do you no longer refer to Efraim as your husband?"

Roberta began wadding her brown-flecked skirt in a manner remindful of her behavior when overshadowed by the lawyer-father who wanted a son. Once again, she slumped forward, allowing loosened hair to cover her face and her voice reverted to the apologetic whisper. "We do not live as husband and wife—in a true sense."

"Why?"

The blunt question threw Roberta off guard. "I— don't think—"

"That seems to be the case all right! Not that *thinking* would resolve matters. For goodness sake, Ro, don't the two of you ever *talk*?"

Roberta, her back to Courtney, deposited her bag on the bed and murmured something about their being apart so much . . . his impatience with her concerns, indifference really . . . forgetting that she had a body and heart as well as a mind. She continued to do the legal work even now, but—

Courtney wondered which of them had changed sleeping arrangements. She, too, spent countless nights in bed alone and lonely. But those hours apart had given her a new perspective. Clint's dedication to work no longer stood between them. The land and the mines had been his aunt's life. Now they were his and a woman followed her husband's chosen vocation. Whether he was right or wrong was beside the point. He *believed* in his work and felt that it was as much a calling as Brother Jim's to the pulpit. God had given man dominion over the land. If only—*if only* Roberta would review her commitment, accept that life did not have to be either or, and talk matters out.

She sighed, then sighed again. After all, there was only so much even the mistress of the house could do. And she had done that. Clint had said Efraim would be "in and out." He was going to share that suite with his wife or be embarrassed.

Clint was unable to get home overnight now. He was working 24-hour shifts, catnapping only, in an effort to spend days building and nights working the ever dwindling mine. But tonight he used his catnapping time to make a hurried trip to the Mansion, creeping up the stairs like a fugitive, just to check on Courtney. Propped on an elbow, he lay on top of the covers beside Courtney, and caught her up on his progress, then listened attentively to her report on Roberta. "You-know-where holds no fury like a woman scorned, so why didn't she shout it out instead of changing beds? After all, a man has his pride—*you* are mine, my pride and joy," was his good-bye whisper.

CHAPTER 16
News and Views

❦

Roberta settled in. Cousin Bella was delighted. After all, the family was growing, she said, ignoring Roberta's flinching. She had always loved the girl—modest, sweet, and blessed with an exceptionally keen mind except where matters of love were concerned. It was good that a fine young man like Efraim took for himself no fish wife, one who scowled and sniped. *But*, she pointed out to Courtney, there were other ways of being mulish. Stiff-necked silence could be worse. "She will have to learn the hard way that, left alone, men do not come to their senses, stew in their own juice, or however one wishes to express it. I speak from experience."

"And I listen with an experienced ear," Courtney had assured her, plumping the feather pillow beneath her cousin's head and moving Donolar's pewter pot of roses where she could get a better view.

Courtney was remembering the words as she stared into the space above the rim of her coffee cup at breakfast when Roberta came into the kitchen. "Is something troubling you, Courtney?"

"You are up early," Courtney smiled in welcome, pouring Roberta a cup of coffee and refilling her own from Mandy's planished pot.

"No earlier than you," Roberta smiled back, seating herself and spooning sugar into her coffee.

"I sleep poorly. This is a miserable time for me."

"Yes, isn't it! I wish our insomnia were for the same

reason. I'm sorry, there I go again after promising myself I would do better. Forget I said that—and no, I do *not* want to talk. I want to walk! I finished the bookkeeping before dawn and if you feel up to it, let's watch the sun rise."

Outside, the world was hardly breathing in that mystical moment when a still-hiding sun paints the world from afar. Wordlessly, the two girls walked without direction, eyes following two kittenish clouds dozing comfortably between the peaks ahead before joining the congested traffic of the heavens. The little creek, unwatered for some time, murmured contentedly of a chance to rest in its mossy bed. The smell of pine was overpowering. And then it faded quickly. Too quickly. But, engrossed in their own thoughts, neither girl noticed that the trail of thick piney shadows had turned to the green smoke of deciduous leaves, too thin to hold back the rays of the rising sun. The stream grew silent. Only a dragonfly hovered, almost warningly. Then it, too, turned back to the forest. Courtney and Roberta walked on.

Suddenly the two of them stopped. It was as if, both walking in the same dream, they had awakened at the same time. *Swish-swish-CLOP!*

What was the totally foreign noise? Where had it come from?

Roberta lifted a silencing finger and Courtney, startled, placed a cautioning hand on Roberta's arm. There was no way she could run if the sound spelled danger, as it very well might. Because, too late, came the realization that their aimless drifting had brought them into full view of the cottonwood grove!

Swish-swish-CLOP! Again the noise which Courtney could have described only as a new and shining sound. Just why she would have been unable to say, unless it was a faint memory of Clint's having told her that once the trail was known as "The Path of Springtime Moons." But that was before the horrible sightings and—

Her thinking stopped. There, just ahead of them, in full view was a very young girl squatting beside a great rock, plunging a garment into the shallows, lifting and squeezing it, then beating it with a small round stone held in the hollow of her sun-bronzed hand.

The girl, who could not have seen more than 14 spring-times, was so much a part of the setting that Courtney found herself transported into another era—a time when this part of the world was new. Perhaps she was seeing through Donolar's eyes the women laughing, chattering, and singing together at their work...the shadows parting like doors to welcome home the hunter-husbands carrying the spear-slung carcass of their kill...giggling girls weaving wild honeysuckle and sweet clover garlands in their hair while watching for the sidelong glances of the young warriors...the an-cient tribal dancing some moon-brushed night...the primitive ceremony that created man-and-woman magic and found it good...and then the nut-brown babies clad only in ropes of coral beads around their fat middles wading into the shallows as young mothers beat clothes ...*swish-swish-CLOP!*

The repeating sound brought Courtney from her fan-tasy. They had no business here. Even though this was a part of the vast Kennedy holdings, something whispered that they were intruding. Why did Roberta linger? They must go—*now*. But it was the mystery girl who fled, black hair touching her heels. Then silence.

It was mystifying, Courtney and Roberta agreed as they walked back slowly. The men must know. Perhaps it was a missing part of the puzzle. On the other hand, how could it be? More importantly, what possible expla-nation could there be for the conflicting thoughts and emotions instilled by the sight of a young Indian girl, other than wondering why she had wandered from the reservation and was trespassing?

No solution had presented itself when they reached the Mansion. And there the mood changed so quickly from mystery to comedy to horror that the strange view might well have been a mid-morning dream.

"Suey, suey! You's filthy swine—trampin' down dem tater plants!" Mandy's voice, usually so mellow, told the world surrounding her garden that had women been fighting the Civil War, the outcome undoubtedly would have been different.

"Hold a civil tongue in yore head, woman! I'm comin' fer my hawgs. Touch one of 'em 'n I'll have ye arrested all legal 'n proper. That there's my prize brood sow—" Deacon Boggs was shouting back.

Mandy had grabbed a rake. "Suey, I tell y'all! I ain't keerin' iffen dem critters is wild boars, dey's gonna end up in pig-foot souce. Won't be nothin' lef' o' dem but de squeal 'n ah'll give it back to youself—it'd beat de one whut you's usin' in de choir!"

"Oh, mercy! There comes Mrs. Rueben," Courtney told Roberta. "She has the broom—and I honestly have no idea which side she will take!"

She took Mandy's. "Git or pretty quick vill I beat you—you Saul, out a-chasin mit der donkies ven you coudda be rulin' der land nearly. Git!"

The deacon got. And, oddly enough, the hogs grunted and followed.

Later, telling the story to Clint, it was funny. But then Courtney was too taken aback by something Roberta said. "Sometimes," she said slowly, "I think I'm a Saul—chasing donkeys—when I should be a ruler, taking charge of my life anyway—"

"Whoa!" The single-word command announced the

unscheduled arrival of Doc George's creaking road wagon. The one-seated vehicle with its two rustproof metal wheels and hickory shafts had been factory-guaranteed to last two years. With regular greasing of the axles and protection from the weather by a Gately-Ettling top attached by the smithy, the buggy had outlasted its life expectancy by ten years. The Brewster-green of the leather seat was no more faded than the owner's suit— or that of the man who sat beside him. Brother Jim!

Courtney sensed news even before sighting Dr. Freeman's horse in the little eddy of dust that trailed them. The commotion in the garden had muffled the sound of their arrival. Now there was complete silence.

Dr. Freeman, cricket-like, dismounted, tethered his horse to the gatepost, and approached the knot of silent women before the two larger men could climb from the buggy. He tipped his hat. He wiped his half-spectacles. Waiting, Courtney suspected, for his companions to speak. That neither did added to the threat of danger.

"Do come in," Courtney said, finally finding a voice.

Instead, the men shifted weight from one foot to the other.

"Out with it, George Washington!" Cousin Bella called from the upstairs balcony. "Whatever the truth is, we're stuck with it."

"The truth is, ma'am—ladies," Dr. Freeman said with studied calm, "there's been a catastrophe. Graves within the mission grounds have been—uh, disturbed. Remains scattered . . . and, Doc George, you have a say."

The twinkle had gone from Doc George's eyes. "There is what Indians on the reservation call a 'Great Sickness.' Half of them are wiped out and it is hard telling whether the continuous moan is from grief or is a death wail." His ruddy cheeks paled. "They refuse to let me doctor—"

"Or allow me to enter the gates," Brother Jim broke in. "Too miserable to listen to preaching—and are blaming the whites for it all."

"But—but the graves?" Courtney whispered. The men shook their heads.

CHAPTER 17
"Peace, Peace!"

☙

The news spread like wildfire. Truths. Half-truths.
And exaggerated rumors. Thanksgiving was near at
hand, a time for gathering together, usually at the Mansion, to count the Lord's blessings. Among them, *peace*.

Now, although the people were crying, "Peace, peace!"
it was as Ezekiel the prophet had said: There was none.
Not even in Courtney's heart. She neither ate nor slept
and found it increasingly difficult to maintain a forced
calm around the children. The heat held, causing the
three of them to break out in a rash—something Doc
George called "prickly heat." He prescribed an unsavory
ointment that reeked of sulphur and colored the skin a
sickly yellow. The twins, itchy and miserable, screamed
when Courtney tried to apply it. Jonda called Jordan a
stinkbug and held her nose. In retaliation, he rubbed the
stubborn mass into her hair.

"Stop it, both of you!" Courtney said angrily and spent
an hour trying to remove the ointment from the little
girl's curls. Jonda cried and called her brother names
that Courtney could only guess came from the kitchen. In
the meantime, Jordan snickered behind a chair. She was
ready to give both of them a healthy shake, which might
not help them but would do *her* a world of good, when
Roberta came to the rescue.

"I guess you know now that mothers are no saints,"
Courtney said.

Roberta laughed. "Neither are children, but what I

wouldn't give—forget it. If I take Kenney for a walk, you will have some time alone with those two."

Time *without* them would be better, Courtney thought ruefully—then was ashamed. It was true that she had little time for them and even it lacked quality. She was harried, her mind torn into fragments which flew all directions in search of peace they all once knew.

"I would appreciate it, Ro—I really would." She kissed the warm sweetness of little Kenney's elbow as he hugged her neck. As they waved good-bye, it occurred fleetingly to Courtney that Roberta was spending a great deal of time walking. Once she finished the bookkeeping Clint brought on his infrequent trips home, she set off on a hike and sometimes remained away for hours. The two women, to Courtney's disappointment, were scarcely together alone at all.

"Tell us a story," Jordan, now repentant and the personification of innocence, entreated.

"Story," Jonda, all forgiven, echoed.

Courtney suggested several of their favorite Bible stories, none of which fit the request. "We want to hear a story about the new baby, huh, Jonda?" Jonda's curls, now freed of sulphur, bobbed up and down like a shower of sunbeams.

Courtney's mind went blank. She had explained more than most parents would dare. What remained—at their level of understanding?

"How do we know it's coming? Did God tell you, like He told Mary?"

"Something like that—only He told Mary her child would be a boy, Jordan. Your father is better with the story—he should be here." Her words surprised her. Had frustration festered into resentment? Unexpressed but lying deep in her heart all along?

Forgive me, Lord, she pled silently. *It is no fault of his. Clint is doing his duty as he sees it—and, I am sure, according to Your will.*

"He said the baby came from a seed. How do we know if it will be a flower or a weed?" Jordan, of course!

Now, Lord, who could have anticipated that one?

Courtney wiped her brow with the ruffle of her over-skirt—not sure if the perspiration came from the continued warmth (had the heat ever lingered into November before?) or the pressing questions.

"It's—a different kind of seed," she murmured helplessly.

"Who plants it?" Jonda was doing right well with questions, too.

"God, silly!" Jordan said, scornful of her lack of knowledge.

"Does not!" Jonda's great blue eyes flashed with indignation. "Daddies do—only one time Daddy used to be our uncle, so how—"

As if in answer to prayer, the door burst open. Donolar had found a new kind of butterfly—one which may have come from the moon. The children ran after him as if he were the Pied Piper. Then, at the door, Jordan stopped. "Get Daddy to tell you about the baby," he suggested.

Exhausted, Courtney sat down by the window, straining her ears for a sound of voices. She should have inquired which direction Roberta would be walking. None offered safety exactly, with tempers flaring, every man suspicious of his brother, and one mystery after another enlarging the initial one—with nothing resolved. Roberta would have better sense than to take the Path of the Springtime Moons. Or would she?

Courtney consulted the dime-size enamel watch pinned to her muslin blouse. Unless Roberta brought Kenney back within the hour, she would go . . . no, she wouldn't. Clint had told her to stay away from the cottonwood grove and she would obey his wish. She sighed, knowing that her body was too heavy to allow much walking anyway. And her hips hurt more than during her previous pregnancies. She would just rest, think, and try to put together some sort of picture from fragments.

The population had more than doubled this year alone. Most of the newcomers were terminally ill of gold fever and, ignoring homesteaders' rights, "squatted" wherever they could hide out while they honeycombed the rich farmlands in search of fortune—clinging leechlike to empty dreams. The emigrants came empty-handed. They seldom stayed put long enough to raise a garden, and it would take more than an occasional deer and a few rabbits to feed the hungry hordes. That put a terrible strain on the supply of food. Two years ago the wheat crop had succumbed to rust and mildew from too much rain. Last year, fire destroyed it. And this year? The unusually dry summer and shortage of men willing to work spelled doom for the farmers. They had planned to sow a second crop in November, hoping for a winter crop. But so far, no rain. The outlook for farmers was as dismal for those who were ordained—or was it condemned?—to agriculture as for those who clung to the conviction that their fortune lay underground.

The mines! Just where *did* the Kennedy Mines stand? Clint made it no secret that they were yielding far too little to turn a profit and, if Courtney's suspicions were correct, Efraim's loan had been pitifully inadequate. How could they continue operating in the red . . . while trying to pay the farmers and miners a dollar a day whether it was for mining or building on the church and school? Tony Bronson said he could carry no more credit . . . cost him 35 cents a day to feed a family having no garden, livestock, and chickens. Courtney fanned herself with her handkerchief and wondered if the two sawmills were still operating. Mills—who was the man who wanted to raise enough wheat to build a flour mill, bake his own bread, and supply the valley? What an encouraging thought. Maybe he could do it, too, if only the men could strike a new vein. Or, she wondered for the first time ever, was it foolish to keep trying? The thought was so startling, she stopped fanning. Only to resume. Clint, being Clint, would pursue to the bitter end, if bitter it was. It was a sacred obligation. A moral charge. A bounden duty—even if it meant crawling on all fours up a glass hill. Nothing could stop him. Except her! And both of them knew she would never do that. Courtney smiled, remembering that once Cousin Bella had called her nephew "pig-headed." Granted, but that was one of the things Courtney loved about her husband. For her, it would be a sin to be a millstone—a heinous crime—

Crime! There was that to consider, too. From all reports, the city must be truly what Brother Jim described as the Sodom city. And, could his assessment of the valley be right? Was it, with the population explosion, beginning to resemble Gomorrah—in order to keep peace in a live-and-let-live manner? Oh, the marshals and their deputies would do their best to restore law and order, but there was nothing they could do to stamp out ill feelings between the two areas. Something had to be done to foster neighborliness again...maybe a get-together at the Mansion in spite of the drawbacks. Wasn't Thanksgiving the way early America brought together the white man and his red brothers?

Indians! Another scene flashed before Courtney's eyes, blinding her momentarily to all else. Could there ever again be peace until the Indians were given more than a small corner of what had all belonged to them once—given more than rights to hunt, but to search for and find love as well? Back in Cousin John McLoughlin's time, hearts of the missions had been pure. Then diversion. Incest. And savages became more savage. They worked less, cared less, and the few turned Christians worshiped less. Mixed marriages...half-breed children...and a failure on both sides to live up to their agreements. Missionaries turned to politics, their schools building up land holdings and working less and less with the Indian children. How long had it been since anybody cared? The government sent soldiers to guard the fort, most of them dividing their time between the saloons and the brothels. A few churches sent more missionaries. White women! This was no country for them—white women who knelt twice a day to pray, refused to "violate" the Sabbath by so much as traveling to the fort, and saw cleanliness as next to godliness. *Touch* those little animals? Impossible!

Disease had taken most of the Indians. Nobody knew for sure how many remained on the reservation. People outside the ruins of the old mission were as filled with fear and superstition as those within. There were strange whispers...and now the "awful sickness." And the unexplained appearance of what settlers were beginning to call "the living dead," corpses that could roam about...perhaps in search of their spirits....

Courtney shuddered—and then remembered the young maiden. Something about the girl who appeared and disappeared, a phantom figure in a sea of green, haunted Courtney. The illusion lingered. Roberta, too, had come under its spell. In some strange way, Roberta had identified with her. Was it the girl's peacefulness—or lack of it? Certainly, Roberta had no peace in her heart, and why had Efraim failed to put in an appearance? He had always been so attentive to his "little sister." There was no doubt about it, Courtney thought, getting up stiffly. There had to be a Thanksgiving feast! Of course, she must caution Mandy and Mrs. Rueben to be frugal. She would plan a menu, invite absolutely everybody, and things would be as they once were. Excitement built within her.

Smiling, Courtney opened her Bible at 1 Timothy 2:1-3: "I exhort therefore . . ." she read prayerfully, "that we may lead a quiet and peaceable life in all godliness and honesty. For this is good and acceptable in the sight of God our Saviour."

CHAPTER 18
How Many Heartbreaks?

🍂

Courtney's hopes were dashed to the ground a week later.

Without advance notice, all the men came home! Caught off guard, Courtney realized she had never looked worse. Clint liked her hair swinging loose as he had always known it, but the heat had caused it to hang dankly about her neck. So she had swung it up in a careless coil on top of her head. The dress she wore, a faded calico which she planned to burn like a paid-off mortgage at the end of her pregnancy, had split at the side and it gave her a certain satisfaction to let it gape!

But one look into Clint's weary face erased all thought of herself. "Oh, my darling—my precious darling!" She was in his arms, held as tenderly as if she were a china doll dressed in pure silk, kissed as hungrily as if she were a long-denied dessert.

Oh, to be alone . . . to talk . . . and talk . . . *counterpane talk*! But the others had gathered, with everybody talking at once and nobody making sense. There was so much to say and listen for, but Courtney was robbed of it all. Mandy, in a state of happy delirium, pulled her aside to ask if it would be all right to violate all rules and dig into the Thanksgiving breads and puddings. And then the children were there, all screaming, "Daddy—*Daddy!*" Courtney felt a sense of disappointment—childish, perhaps, or (as the valley women would say) due to her "condition," but it was as if being torn from her husband's arms were a foretoken, a whisper that all was not well.

How silly! Indulging in such thinking had stolen the opportunity she might have had of seeing Efraim and Roberta meet. Her brother was making his way to Courtney already, so the greeting must have been brief.

"Little sister—" Efraim said with emotion.

"How can you say that?" Courtney laughed, feeling the same surge of affection she always felt for her wonderful brother. "I look like a rain barrel!"

As his arms enfolded her, Courtney saw Roberta's face and thought that she had never seen her look so sad. Given a moment, Courtney would have whispered something—*anything*—to help. After all, Efraim always teased her about being a hopeless romantic, a matchmaker. Guilty on both counts. But the moment was gone.

Doc George had gone upstairs immediately and escorted Cousin Bella to the parlor. The others had swarmed in. Mandy wondered when to serve dinner. And Courtney must make herself presentable posthaste.

Clint took over as host, seating Courtney beside him at the table and the others at random. A certain grandeur was missing and Courtney wondered if the fine line between Cousin Bella's eyes was due to the lost formality. No, something else was bothering her. Did she share the sense of foreboding? Did they *all*? Donolar made no mention of his centerpiece. Unusual. The children were subdued. *Very* unusual. And, of course, Roberta was silent. It was going to be a strange meal, a revealing one. But Courtney's premonitions dissipated like squeezed-dry clouds when Clint took her hand and held it throughout the male-dominated conversation which followed.

"I guess the simmering pot has indeed reached the boiling point," Brother Jim said by way of openers for what sounded like breaking of unpleasant news to the ladies of the household. "We're going to have to mend the rifts before," he cleared his throat, "those liver-lipped outlaws start shootin' out the lights."

Doc George met his wife's eyes, then said with regret, "It seems that the more ideal we made the area, striving as we were for the model place to work, live, and bring up families, the worse element we attracted—bringing in riffraff, pestilence, and those with no respect for the law—or any knowledge of it for that matter."

"What did you find out—well, about the philosophical differences and plans for city government at the town meeting, Efraim?" Brother Jim blotted his mouth with the napkin from his knee, took another forkful of mashed potatoes, and added, "Efraim spent several weeks in town studying the problems—while Dr. Freeman looked for clues about the grave, rather grave*yard* mystery—"

So Efraim had been away? Courtney stole a look at Roberta. Her expression had not changed. She concentrated on her plate.

"About 30 men attended, mostly strangers except for Judge Wimple, the Southern gentleman, by his own admission." Efraim gave a crooked smile. "Then there was 'Cheyenne' Wills, wagon master who elected to remain here. It seems that the bank backed him and he is manufacturing wagonettes—sort of a cross between a draft wagon and a carriage, has two seats facing each other along the sides, with a driver's seat in front. Shoddy merchandise, like most that is pawned off on the unsuspecting public—"

"Where was this meeting?" Cousin Bella asked when he paused.

"Walloby's Board and Room auditorium, the only place large enough to accommodate that size crowd. And yes, Walloby's is the night spot—"

"Painted dancin' girls and the like on occasion," Brother Jim growled. "How sad, oh, how much we have need of our church, Lord!" He had lowered his voice into a prayer.

"I took the liberty of announcing our projects—church and school," Efraim told him. "They wanted to laugh it off, said the church was doomed to failure and would meet the same demise as the missions—and that schools were purely speculative without backing from the government—that big business would push us right off the map."

"That sounds like that gopher with a mouthful of gold teeth who calls himself a banker!" Brother Jim exploded again. "Isaac Jacobson, the tight-fisted money lover. We accept our Hebraic brothers for what they are, just unenlightened—"

Clint cleared his throat and Efraim continued his report.

"There was a charged atmosphere—ill feeling on all sides, and there are a lot of sides! Everybody represented, it seemed, except those needed most—miners, farmers, those dedicated to civilization and industry. Some want state sovereignty, others think we need the federal government. But the frightening ones are those who want no government at all, just complete autonomy—freedom to go on with the hellish lynching, hanging, no trial, no jury. Then there are the bigwigs who would like to see the exodus of the common man. In summary, Jacobson will lend us no more capital—no need to tell you what that spells out. And, as for news, I took it upon myself to circulate a petition, signed by our valley men, and submitted it to the State requesting aid on books and teachers for the school."

"Someday women will be allowed the voting franchise." Roberta's voice was low but determined. The fact that she spoke at all obviously jarred Efraim. "You have more franchise than you think—even without a suffrage law."

"If that were the case, some of this could be remedied."

Courtney squeezed Clint's hand more tightly. The air at the dinner table was suddenly as charged as it must have been at Walloby's banquet table underneath the bold shine of the gold-bronze chandeliers. It was as if the Glamoras had forgotten others were present. Both were on edge but behaving in a coldly civilized manner. They had problems that may have outstripped Roberta's inability to bear children, Courtney realized suddenly. Efraim had stiffened with a defensiveness she had never seen in him. And Roberta, she was certain, her quiver filled with verbal barbs, waited for provocation from her husband.

It came. She took careful aim and let an arrow fly.

"You don't say! Just how would you rearrange matters?"

"I *did* say. But not in those words. I would simply add some voices—women's. We could *all* vote on a representative here, send him—oh yes, it would have to be a man—to Washington, get the help we need for organizing. And, as for money—we—I have a solution—"

Their gaze locked. Neither flinched. Courtney fancied she could hear breaths exhaled in unison when Doc George asked if there was mention of the Indians.

Efraim's ashen face relaxed. A look of concern replaced the unexplained anger. "Unfortunately, yes. There is irrational talk of driving them inland—by whatever means."

"They have every right to be here, by decree of the government," Doc George said. "And by decree of the Lord," Brother Jim interrupted before the doctor could make further comment. "It is their right."

"It is their land," Donolar said, looking out the window as if he saw something invisible to the human eye.

There was uncomfortable silence, then Efraim went on to tell that while once the white man had refused

Indians strong drink, now he encouraged it. Why? It was common knowledge that Indians were unable to handle the stuff. And drunk—well, it was easy to say the "drunken savages" attacked a woman, so what was there to do but shoot him as one would a "mad dog"? Added to superstition and hostility was fear.

"They are hungry and afraid to venture from the mission ruins. Somebody unfurled a 'skull and crossbones' flag, perhaps as a prank, but the frightened people took it as a warning—and now this sickness. They are afraid to come out for treatment so have resorted to the ungodly practices of the medicine men. Naturally, they are dying."

"It is our Christian duty to rescue them!" Brother Jim said fervently. "But," he admitted, "you can't preach to hostile beings with backbones rubbing their bellies for want of food. Isn't there somebody in there who will act as interpreter—get a message in for us that we can help? Organized denominations are pulling up stakes."

The group was straining forward now, waiting for Efraim's answer. He had none with which to satisfy them. Spreading his patrician hands, Efraim said helplessly, "I am uncertain at this point that our own people, even those here in the valley, would agree to sharing— until our own future is a bit more certain. And what a waste of brainpower—as well as being a mission for which the Lord is sure to hold us accountable. There is a high degree of intelligence locked away behind those crumbling walls. But even Tony Bronson is denying them supplies—"

"You are right. The Lord *will* hold us accountable!" Roberta's voice rose to a shrill pitch Courtney scarcely recognized. "We can help—you *know* how!"

Efraim pointedly ignored her interruption and told a story which otherwise might have gone untold. Some of the Indians, who still called themselves chieftains, had gone away, obtained educations and chosen to return to help their people. Finding them hungry, one especially brave young man approached a storekeeper and demanded supplies. His boldness startled the proprietor who said, "How do I know you can pay?" The reply he received was, "White man, you may keep your paltry supplies and allow my people to starve. But remember this, sir! I have an uncle in Washington, D.C., whom I expect shortly to investigate matters. He is rich enough to buy you out and send you packing." The startled man put together a few supplies and mumbled, "What's his name?" "Uncle Sam!" The Indian lad had presented the grocer with a compass and marched out in dignity.

The story brought murmurs of approval. "And," Efraim concluded, "the sorrowful part is the rumble that the white men will assemble their own army, march on the mission and what remains of the fort in a massacre. That accounts for the flag that the Indians erected on the crumbling fence of the mission: WASHINGTON OR THE GRAVE!"

Courtney gasped in horror. "Is there a reason for the uprising—the hostility on both sides?"

"Devilishness—evil in the hearts of men!" Brother Jim stormed. "And, of course, the terrible graveyard incident—isn't Hank able to shed any light on this? And what about the sickness, Doc?"

"I am unable to get inside." Doc George's usually jovial face was serious, his ruddy glow dulled. Running a stubby-fingered hand through his cloud of white hair, he admitted failure at being able to appeal to the Indians— some of whose language he spoke. "And," he said with some embarrassment, "I guess I lack the nerve to cross the bobtails who have taken over the law. You see, I—I have been threatened. I am no coward, but when it comes to my family—"

Clint, who had been strangely silent, all but upset his plate. "They threatened the women and children?"

"I wasn't going to mention that—"

"You had no choice."

Perhaps Clint would have said more, but their attention was drawn to a rider pounding over the bridge leading from the forest to the grounds of Mansion-in-the-Wild.

Dr. Henry Freeman, the anthropologist!

Wordlessly, Mrs. Rueben met the guest at the door as the others shifted chairs a bit to make room at the table. Dr. Freeman handed the housekeeper his hat, fumbled with his pipe, then reached across to lay it in his hat's crown.

The twins were wide-eyed. "You may burn your hat up!" Jordan burst out in warning.

"May," Jonda repeated, "and the house—and all of us—"

"—like the Indians and the white men are going to burn each other," Jordan finished her sentence, then added a clencher, "like Satan does!"

Mandy, bless her, was first to recover. "Come with Aunt Mandy, now chil'ens—me 'n you's a-gonna have our cookies in de kitc'in." And, rolling her eyes heavenward in silent prayer, she whisked them away.

Usually Donolar followed. Tonight he stayed.

"Good evening, Dr. Freeman," Courtney greeted him with as much dignity as she could muster. "You are just in time for dinner." Which was true. So engrossed had the group been in talk that the food remained untouched except by the children and Brother Jim's two forkfuls.

Seated, Henry Freeman removed his pinch glasses, shook a freshly laundered handkerchief free of its folds, and polished the glasses. Without the spectacles, he looked helpless—somewhat like a nocturnal bird in search of a perching place in broad daylight. His report was equally blurred, lacking the full vision all had hoped for.

It was proper for the hostess to begin and close the meal. Courtney forced herself to pick up a fork as Clint started the dishes in their course around the table.

"You ladies are looking lovely this evening," Dr. Freeman said gallantly then swung into business. "Progress?"

Efraim explained, adding that the conversation had given Clint no opportunity to report on the mines or prospects for the wheat crop. "I guess you could say that bad blood is near to boiling over."

"Unless we select a representative to go to Washington—"

Courtney choked on a bread crumb. Clint was siding with Roberta? And the others were nodding! Courtney dared not look into her brother's face. But at that moment the handful at the dining table had cast their vote for Efraim Glamora, who one day would go to the nation's capital....

Dr. Freeman was talking. "—so the fragment of bone found in the cottonwood grove bears it out. The remains were those of Indians. But it is anybody's guess how they came to be exhumed in so grisly a fashion. Splinters of wood were weathered, but there's no way to know if the crude canoes were old or put together from old timbers. There were barefoot tracks and at least one trail left by a person wearing very large shoes."

"But the—the desecration done in the mission cemetery?" Courtney's throat was so dry she could scarcely give voice to the words.

"A mystery, my dear, a real mystery. We can only suspect the graves were violated at the hands of white men. Red men honor their ancestors—leave food for them by their earthly beds—and sadly, the graves held those laid away in Christian burial. This will lead to disenchantment—set back the clock on the Christian movement here—"

"What can we do?" It was unlike Brother Jim to be so subdued, to seek answers instead of giving them.

"I would like to attempt a crossing," Henry Freeman paused, catching the eye of each member in turn, "to Memaloose Island. With a proper guide, of course." He shook his head, loosening his glasses, and was in the process of readjusting them when Roberta spoke up.

"I think I can help."

"Roberta—stay out of this!" Efraim's voice shook with emotion. Fury or concern? It made no difference apparently.

"I will look into the matter." And with that, she asked to be excused, pleading a headache.

Efraim bit his lower lip for control. The others talked in twos and threes to cover the awkwardness of the moment, as the men stood politely for Roberta's departure.

"Perhaps we should get onto other matters," Cousin Bella said quietly. "The hour is late—and, George Washington, I should like to hear more about the disease among the Indians. Is it similar to the plague of long ago—the one that closed the mission down?"

"Very similar—something akin to the grippe, I think. And Lord help them for what they are doing. The Indians are great on sweathouses, you know. They heat their bodies with fires that would be too hot to smoke bacon, then plunge into the river."

An audible gasp circled the table.

"The result is death—of pneumonia. I guess it matters very little," the doctor continued sorrowfully. "They would die anyway—and to think that they were immune to colds until the arrival of the white man. They still hold us accountable. And now the townsfolk, ready to stampede at the flare of a match, blame *them* for this outbreak."

"We are responsible for their souls!" Brother Jim declared, his sparring spirit rekindled. "I've no use for wrestling with shadows—just bring it out in the open. How can I get in there?"

"It would be certain death to try until there is some kind of peace," Clint said. "The time has passed when the Indians trust us, and certainly shiny trinkets are no longer peacemakers. They need food, reassurance, friends—people who will do more than tolerate them, who will accept them as fellow human beings, love them. Only then will they listen to salvation through faith. I am afraid we have set a poor example."

Brother Jim looked unconvinced, but it was Dr. Freeman who spoke. "Strange thing," he said, scratching his temple with an index finger so as not to disturb a single hair, "twice now I have seen a Solomon's seal alongside the pile of rocks that once made up the mission wall."

"A what?" Courtney asked. She had never heard the term.

Donolar leaned eagerly toward her. "A lily of the valley. Oh, I should like it for my garden, and the butterflies would love its sweet aroma. Its name will interest the twins. It is so called because of the thick rootstock. Oh yes, we must go for it!"

"No, no, my boy! You must stay clear of the area. And this Solomon's seal is entirely different—an emblem in the shape of a six-pointed star—"

"Like the Star of David, the Jewish star?"

Doc George broke in before Henry Freeman could respond. "Somewhat, but again with a different meaning, Donolar. It is a sort of amulet, a guard against fever, although how the Indians came to know is a puzzle. It is in no way connected with their culture."

"Now I *know* we must break through—get inside—"

"Don't make me lose my temper, Brother Jim!" Doc George said firmly. "I want all public meetings canceled. Consider yourselves my prisoners until this epidemic passes. Do I make myself clear?"

"Clear as the Liberty Bell," mumbled the fighter, unaccustomed to losing.

Courtney choked back a sob. The order meant that there would be no Thanksgiving dinner ... no bringing the warring factions together ... no reconciliation ... forgiving ... praying together. No *hope*! Had she lost favor with the Lord?

She scarcely heard Clint's report on the mines. The bits her ears caught were dismal in spite of his effort to be of good cheer. Building was coming along. No hope for this year, maybe next. But their home library was a blessing. Thanks to his book-loving relative, Donolar knew most of the books by heart. Under Donolar's tutelage, the twins would have a head start, Clint said, trying to coax a smile. But how could Courtney go on smiling with a broken heart? Thanksgiving had represented so much. Now her world had crumbled like the mission walls.

But talk continued. "The wheat outlook?" Bleak, Clint said. And yes, silver was thinning, but the *faithful* men were staying. How long before the vein gave out completely? That would be like asking Doc George how long a patient was going to live. "Some things are best left in God's hands," he said. "We all tend to forget that."

"It is easy to see that you could use some prosperity hereabouts," Dr. Freeman observed, "and yet I would be less than honest if I failed to caution that aluminum's coming into its own. Once more expensive than gold, it's cheaper than silver now. Its uses are many—jewelry, tableware—thanks to France, where royalty is switching over."

"France," Donolar whispered hoarsely. "*She* lives there."

Their mother, Courtney knew he meant. Dear Donolar. Would he never forget how love was denied when he needed it most? No, neither would Roberta.

After prayers, Courtney cried herself to sleep in Clint's arms. That way, fortunately, she avoided one more hurt.

For Roberta and Efraim quarreled bitterly until the wee hours in spite of her efforts—schemes, really—to bring them together. Clint held her close. Someday his adored madonna must learn as he had that God is indeed in charge.

CHAPTER 19
A Private Thanksgiving

Thanksgiving was a time to praise the Lord for His goodness and mercy, and the number of guests did not determine the measure of faith. This Courtney decided once her disappointment had lessened. Cousin Bella was delighted with the change in attitude and asked Doc George to help her down the stairs so she could take a hand in the planning of the family's private feast.

"No, I do *not* want that silly riding machine, George Washington," she said of the wheelchair he brought home for her. "You just get busy and bring down some of those wheat-devouring geese with that gat of yours. You haven't forgotten how to shoot, have you?"

The doctor pinched her cheek affectionately. "I'll make you eat those words!"

"That's the general idea," she said tartly, expertly dodging another pinch. Arabella Lovelace loved the attention, Courtney knew, and always enjoyed the game she played—so girlishly "hard to win" and a little embarrassed at public display of emotion, while secretly willing it. "Be off with you—and no returning without a goose—a fat one!"

Her husband filled the order, bringing down six geese, made plump and sweet by the irate farmers' wheat. Dinner and conversation centered around his good fortune.

Mandy outdid herself with the cornmeal dressing. Best ever, everybody said. Lots of sage, she said. Then, she was sure that the Indians were right—camas did make a dish more "peart" than onions. Mrs. Rueben refused a hand with dressing the birds, and for once the two agreed on allowing Doc George to truss the six geese. After all, he'd had a heap of practice. The problem arose when they realized that no oven, no matter how accommodating, could open its mouth wide enough to hold half a dozen geese! Donolar, on his way up from the root cellar with a basket of apples, went to work without a word and improvised an outdoor pit. The twins danced around the flames in glee, followed by a jubilant shadow, Kenney, singing along with them although he had no idea that their merriment sprang from Cousin Bella's remark that this was a true old-fashioned Thanksgiving, after all.

Out came the breads and cakes that had been hidden and aging for weeks. Added were the fresh grape pies, sweetmeats, quince preserves, and pickles to accompany a table-size bouquet of vegetables. And of course there had to be corn. Corn pudding, Mandy's pride.

Excitement grew when an army of clouds clashed overhead and there was a volley of thunder. "What a blessing a rain would be!" Doc George said as he tied the last surgical knot.

Courtney, who had at his request served as "nurse" and held the plucked "patients," smiled. "Oh, indeed! Do you suppose the Indians are doing a rain dance?"

"Could be—just could be," he said soberly. "Such a shame, you know, all these pesky geese robbing the farmers blind and the starving people afraid to venture out hunting—and disarmed anyway."

"Oh, how I wish we could share," Courtney said wistfully as Doc George wiped his hands and removed his canvas apron. "Thanksgiving is for sharing. Look! Cara—"

Cara Laughten's face was pale. "Doc George, I need help. It's John—he's been hurt tryin' to bust a wild mustang. His back's all twisted—and I cain't lift 'im—"

The two of them were gone before Courtney could so much as greet her agitated neighbor. Doc George was back in short order for the wheelchair his wife had refused. Brother Jim would have said it was by divine arrangement. And maybe it was, as was the long series of strange happenings that followed.

"Back's not broken, thank the good Lord," Doc George said on returning, "but he'll be laid up a spell. Not that they can afford it. Some holiday."

"Yes, is it not?" Courtney smiled, feeling absolutely brilliant. "As long as you have to push that thing, is there any reason for it to go without a passenger?"

"Just what have you got in mind, young lady?"

"Well, let me think," Courtney said, faking concentration. "Oh, I have it—why not a stuffed goose? I was wondering how to dispose of six!"

Cousin Bella picked up a pencil and began to write. "I have been concerned over the surplus, too. How about Donolar's serving as runner and taking another of the critters to that new family occupying the old Lindsey cabin—and obviously as poor as Job's turkey?"

The day was taking on an unexpected sheen. Courtney, watching two spirited starlings—their colors muted by the grayness of the day, darting playfully to and fro— decided that the rainbow feathers symbolized her mood. What a joy it would be for the newcomers. The shack they occupied was unfit for habitation. Among the first to be built years before, its unhewn log sides were chinked together with chipped and cracking mud. And burlap hung over the lopsided cutouts which served as windows. There were no floors, just bare, cold ground.

Mandy growled something about parting with another of her cornbread-stuffed geese, then said she s'posed they all liked tater pie....

Courtney and Cousin Bella exchanged a smile. The private Thanksgiving was not so private, after all. And they were loving it. Roberta, rosy from her walk, came in the front door just as Doc George entered from the back. Their eyes met and Courtney fancied that he gave her a strange look, as if he were seeking an answer. None came.

The doctor turned away from whatever it was that troubled him. "I am more concerned than before about Laughten," he said with a professional frown. "Getting him into that wheelchair was no easy matter. The skeletal frame seems in order, but there's something unnatural about the movement of his legs—totally lacking in one, in fact."

"It will strengthen, George Washington. Have some coffee." His wife had listened to his worries over the valley folk for so many years that replies were automatic reflexes.

Doc George stuck his finger into the cake frosting Mandy was whisking, had his hand slapped playfully by her plump, black palm, and licked the frosted finger before replying. "Strengthen, yes, but there could be other problems—not deformity—but there are cases written up where such falls have an impact that goes deeper than the physical. The shock, added to John's worries over finances and the need to maintain his masculinity, could do just the opposite—render him impotent—"

"Well, they've a good-sized family. Cara would see such a state as no disaster. It would have no effect on how she feels about John. Problems only bring couples in love closer together. She would never cast him aside, make him feel useless—"

"Why not?" It was Roberta who spoke and her voice was sharpened by pain. "A wife has to feel needed, wanted. No marriage can thrive when one feels useless, locked out—it's—*unnatural!*"

"Not unless whatever brought them together—this thing called *love*—has died already," Cousin Bella fired back.

The doctor scratched his head. Caught in cross fire like this was more dangerous than risking another lick at Mandy's frosting. "No matter what happens to the Laughtens, it will be no disaster—unless one of them wants it to be, enjoys it," he said in what he undoubtedly meant as soothing syrup. Instead, it had the effect of rubbing salt into an open wound. Roberta was furious, anyone could see.

He reached for another forbidden lick of the frosting Mandy was now swirling onto a six-layer cake and dug far deeper than he intended. The slamming of the back door had startled him into a leapfrog jump.

Nobody spoke as the echo died away and then they stood still listening to and enjoying the clanging of horseshoes on the side lawn. It had been so long since ears had heard that kind of music. The symphony of hammers and saws had replaced it. But a change in timing was a healthy thing. Courtney's heart quickened when she heard Clint laugh deeply. The other men joined him and there was a pleasant crisscrossing of conversation. Doc George's face relaxed into a smile. Roberta's problem, unless she wished to share it, was her own.

Dinner preparations proceeded while the sun, moving downward, parted the clouds which had twisted themselves into gilt-edged giants, obviously clad in raincoats. The western sky was crimson, but its red sails said "sailor's delight." There would be no rain.

Dinner this evening at six o'clock would please Cousin Bella—and end a near-perfect day. Courtney was looking out the kitchen window, hoping to catch a glimpse of the obviously disturbed Roberta, when she was startled out of her senses by the sudden appearance of a strange lad—tall, she guessed, but bent over as if to dwarf his appearance. Indian? Yes, he had to be, even though the pale face (undoubtedly so by fear) was more ivory than bronze. A mane of blue-black hair swung over his bony face to rest on thin shoulders that had yet to fill out with manhood. What on earth was he doing here? She must alert—

But before she could make a sound or even move, he had snatched a roasted goose from the remaining four Mrs. Rueben had set on the outside counter to cool for better carving. He was—why, he was *stealing*, Courtney thought one moment. And the next she realized that his meatless rib cage told the story. He was dying of starvation.

Sickened, she edged to the door for air, aware only that the Lovelaces were moving into the sun room. Soon Cousin Bella would be dressing.

And there on the stoop stood Roberta, high spots of color in her cheeks, her eyes brilliant with triumphant tears. Turning to Courtney in surprise, she whispered pleadingly. "Don't give me away—*please*—"

It all came together then . . . the walks since the appearance of the mystery maiden . . . Roberta's silences . . . her offer to seek an Indian guide.

Tell? No, she would not tell. She would do nothing. The floor was rushing up to meet her. From far, far away, Roberta was screaming, "Clint . . . Doc George . . . *Efraim* . . . HELP!"

How beautiful. A roomful of colored lights flashing red . . . yellow . . . orange. And sounds that exploded like the colors—into stars. Beautiful, but undramatic. It all happened so fast there was no time for the boiling water (which nobody ever seemed to use, anyway). No time even for Doc George to remove his button-on cuffs before a surprise guest joined her mother on Mandy's cooktable.

Within minutes Courtney found herself upstairs, snuggled comfortably on her hospitable feather bed, looking down into a wee, pixie face. A tuft of black hair stood on top of the perfect head like an exclamation mark as if the wide-open dark eyes were dismayed at the world around her. Her mother was equally dismayed. Glamora coloring at last.

"A beautiful baby girl, a winner," Doc George said over and over as if trying to convince himself that birth which took place so fast could be so final. And then he was shooing all except Clint from the bedroom.

The twins balked. "Not until we name her, Daddy," Jordan declared. His words tumbled over themselves, "Jonda, Kenney, and me—we declare our little sister's name *Blessing*. God sent her on Thanksgiving and—"

"Blessing," Clint whispered, ushering them gently but firmly to the door, "Blessing Desmond it is. God must have whispered what I failed to hear."

"Blessing," Courtney murmured sleepily, her voice matching the reverence in her husband's. "All my blessings . . . Jordan . . . Jonda . . . Ken-ney . . . *you* . . ."

Then, blissfully, she was aware of Brother Jim's soothing voice coming from below reading the thirty-seventh psalm confidently:

> Fret not thyself because of evildoers, neither be thou envious against the workers of iniquity. For they shall be cut down like the grass, and wither as the green herb. Trust in the Lord, and do good; so shalt thou dwell in the land, and verily thou shalt be fed. Delight thyself also in the Lord; and he shall give thee the desires of thine heart. . . . Cease from anger, and forsake wrath. . . . For evildoers shall be cut off: but those that wait upon the Lord, they shall inherit the earth. . . . Wait on the Lord. . . . Mark the perfect man . . . for the end of that man is peace. . . .

The *Amens* rose in a heavenly chorus which dissolved into song: "We gather together to ask the Lord's blessing...He chas-tens and has-tens...His will to make known...The wick-ed op-press-ing...now cease from dis-tress-ing...Sing prais-es to His name...He forgets...not...His...own."

The two hands clasped across God's latest creation slowly relaxed. And the three of them slept...victorious in their harvest of love.

CHAPTER 20
Woman's Common Bond

Blessing was a good baby from the beginning, sleeping the night through without a whimper and greeting each new dawn like a cooing pigeon. The name was perfect—and she lived up to it. Consequently, Courtney was able to get on with her life with little change except for an enlargement of the heart to make room for her little "dark angel." Kenney adored her and, thanks to Clint's careful explanation of how parents' love could stretch to meet the needs of all their children, felt no jealousy. The twins achieved a new maturity. Weren't they in charge? And Donolar assumed the role of a tutor. There was so much his nieces and nephews must learn.

"Teach them well, dear Donolar," Courtney told him. "It may be some time before the school is ready. And Donolar," she continued, making her voice as normal as possible, "these will be your last students—our family is finished."

"I could teach more. I could show a dozen all the wonders."

"Plans have changed, darling. There can be no more. Mother Nature can be harsh sometimes—like withholding rain. This year's crop has dried up from thirst—"

Even as she spoke, Courtney saw horses, their riders carrying shovels, dusting up the road. They would dig a ditch as a fireguard around the fields, burn them, and plow the stubble under. Then they would pray for rain in order to seed another crop.

Had such a thing ever happened before? Not here, Clint had told her, but it was common in the Midwest. History would record the disaster as the "Year of the Great Drouth," but the settlers had no way to know. No way of knowing, either, that it would never happen again here.

"Are they sorrowful—the men? It must be a sad thing to be unable to produce grain."

A wave of sadness washed over Courtney. And then it passed. "It is always sad when nature fails, Donolar. But there will be other seasons, other good things to come. And sometimes God's surprises are richer than what we thought to be failures."

A stirring at the door alerted Courtney to Roberta's presence. How long had she been standing there? She had gone for her walk and returned sooner than usual. Eyes on the men who were shoveling dirt in the wheat field nearest the grove, Roberta greeted Donolar and waited until he was gone to speak to Courtney.

"Is it true, Courtney? Is—is Blessing the last?"

"There had to be some surgery to save the baby—it all happened so fast there was no time to talk, just act. It is all right—Clint understands, and—"

Roberta's eyes enlarged with such surprise that Courtney fancied she could see herself reflected in their depths. "You wanted 12—and you are willing to give up like this?"

Courtney laughed. "I am not giving up, my dear—just accepting."

"Like the men with their wheat?" Roberta's voice was bitter. "Well, I want more from life! I lack your patience."

She was pacing back and forth among the flower beds in the backyard where the zinnias and marigolds had twisted into pitiful skeletons and died. But their seeds would spring up with the first rain. They would bloom for Donolar's butterflies. Life would go on. Only—at this point—Roberta would not understand.

"I have not always been this patient," Courtney said instead. "I thought the world had ended when I miscarried—and I went into isolation when our second baby was born dead. I deserve no halo, Ro. Give God a chance."

Courtney regretted the words when she saw the anger they ignited. *Did I have to say that, Lord? Forgive me!*

Quickly, she changed the subject. "I wish you had postponed your walk. Oh, how I could use one! I have been inside too long. Shall we walk to Cara's? I want her to continue with the decorating. Not," she added thoughtfully, "that we can afford it for now—but with John in his condition, she needs money even worse."

Roberta turned on her heel and, without replying, started toward the Laughten cabin. They crossed the bridge in silence and then Roberta stopped. "Do you think things will be right with them—I mean, if he, uh, regains use of his legs? Will it be like before?"

"It depends," Courtney said slowly, "on how far apart they let themselves grow—if one or the other becomes warped—"

Roberta's hands went to her eyes, and she gave a little cry of despair. "We're talking about me, aren't we?"

This was Efraim's wife and her dearest friend. There should be no secrets. "Yes, my darling, I guess we are."

And gently she folded Roberta in her arms. Let the cleansing tears fall. Love. Love and the desire to give the object of that love the greatest gift a woman can offer. It was woman's common bond.

CHAPTER 21
"Rose Wind"

The day had been scorching. If only it would rain, the farmers were wailing. They wanted to be about their planting. If only it would rain, housewives moaned. Their children surely would be less cantankerous. If only it would rain, Doc George said with enough worry in his voice to make his the most valid of all wishes. He was losing the battle against the mystery disease. A killing frost usually followed rain, and it would take a cold snap to kill off the germs. It was dangerous to have the men working together. If one fell prey, all would. And it could all but wipe the slate clean.

Clint considered shutting down building, digging—everything—then changed his mind. After all, the real danger lay in the foul associations in the city where filth and evil communications were a way of life. The doctor agreed. "And I am afraid that conditions are equally unsanitary among the Indians—what few there are who have survived." He asked then if Henry Freeman had made an attempt to navigate the rough waters to the "Island of the Dead."

Roberta answered. And even she must have realized that she had spoken much too quickly. "He has a guide—so—"

Efraim had looked at her with a jerk of his head. Although nothing more had been said since the Thanksgiving episode, Courtney had known it had to come and braced her heart for it. But she still felt unprepared—

especially in her brother's presence. And here it was, striking with the speed of lightning from a cloudless sky.

"Do you know something you are not telling?" Efraim demanded. "This is critical to us all—do you?"

"It *is* critical to us all!"

"Does that mean *yes*?"

Roberta's hesitation was answer enough. But Efraim wanted more.

"I—I don't know—and don't get angry again!" Her tone was defensive.

"How can you not know what you know? And what do you mean angry *again*? We have never discussed this!"

He spun on his heel. His straight back and the way he stalked from the room spelled anger from Roberta's vantage point. But Courtney, who stood on the other side, saw his face—dejected, defeated.

Clint and Courtney had exchanged helpless looks. It was Doc George who tried to mend matters. "Wounded pride." He meant well, bless him. But to Courtney's ears, his voice sounded hollow.

Roberta's voice was equally hollow. "I'm sorry—I guess I destroyed my image of the dutiful wife—speak when spoken to."

"I harbor no such image, Roberta," her husband said. "Marriage is a matter of give-and-take, a sharing. Without that, we have nothing."

Roberta's smile was more of a leer—to hide a broken heart. "*Nothing* sums it up. I apologize for the scene— and (with a lift of her chin) Dr. Freeman does have a guide. I can tell you no more."

The sun dropped suddenly. The air cooled and long-fingered shadows reached across the valley. One maverick cloud floated westwardly and lingered to take on the sun's departing color—poised all the while for flight.

"Tomorrow will be fair and hot again," Roberta said tonelessly.

Dinner, once so relaxed, was tense. Roberta and Efraim avoided addressing one another. In fact, Roberta did not speak at all.

Efraim joined in the conversation regarding the mines. Clint had news—news which should have lifted spirits somewhat, however tentatively. But the mood of somberness hung over the table.

"My hunch was right," Clint said. "There *is* some silver on upstream—not much, but any will help. And it may indicate more."

"How much more, do you speculate?" Efraim was watching him closely.

"Hardly enough to feed our crew," Clint admitted, "but—well—maybe I am premature in saying this, but we found a bit of yellowish gravel again. The other time that happened meant—gold."

Clint's voice was so low-pitched that it took awhile for the words to sink in. Courtney was first to gasp. Her gasp echoed around the table.

Brother Jim was first to speak. "The Lord be praised! But you will need a bigger loan than old Jacobson will dole out. How much?"

"A thousand dollars for, say, 30 days—we could swing it on that, couldn't we, Clint?" The voice belonged to Efraim.

"A thousand dollars—all you need is a thousand dollars?" Courtney realized that her voice reflected the astonishment she saw in Roberta's face. Were they that low on cash?

"Chicken feed!" Brother Jim scoffed. And then he sighed. "For a banker, that is. Say now, would you believe that Shylock of a banker actually passed the time of day with me day before yesterday?"

"What were you doing in town!" Doc George's words were less a question than a chiding.

"I'm immune to germs," he evaded. "Satan knows he's out of his weight class with the likes of me! But, hear this! Isaac Jacobson was asking when the church would be finished, said he planned on taking part somewhat—and him a Jew! Now, I'm not swallowing that for one minute—especially with such idle threats as slipped out."

"Threats? What did Isaac Jacobson threaten?" Clint's voice was tight with concern. "More complicated relationships we have no need for."

Brother Jim was unable to hold back his news. "Began by quoting Old Testament Scriptures—they *do* know the law, you know. He's bound and determined that all groves should be cut down, burned, destroyed."

"Because of mosquitoes?" Doc George combed his hair with both hands. "Some groves maybe—willows—"

"*All*—says that's where the heathens worshiped idols way back when. And he does have a point, but what's that got to do with—"

Courtney knew then. It was the Indians he referred to. Her heart began to pound painfully. The cottonwood grove. The mystery maiden. The guide. It came as no surprise when Roberta rose, upsetting her water glass, and ran from the room.

It was the first time a diner had ever left the dining table of Mansion-in-the-Wild unexcused.

* * *

Cara accepted the work gratefully this time. No questions. No reservations. She and John must feed the children. It was that simple.

"This old quilt is very beautiful," she said now, "like ever'thing else in this part of the house. I ain't never been in here before." She surveyed the east wing in awe.

"We never use it, Cara—and I agree that the quilt is lovely, well worth preserving. I wonder if we can match this color. Where do you suppose such a shade of yellow-gold came from?"

"Looks like it coulda come straight from a gold mine, don't it just? But I'm guessin'," the girl said dreamily, "it likely's a scrap from a fancy ball gown." Cara held the quilt to her face, probably feeling silk for the first time.

The large, wistful eyes touched Courtney's heart. Someday, the Lord willing, when life became normal again, she would do something nice for Cara. How dear she was—so deprived, but never complaining. Or was she deprived at all? Cara gave and accepted love.

"What you want I should do with it, Miz—I mean, Courtney?"

Oh yes, the quilt. Cara was right. The worn patches needed replacing if the bed quilt served as a spread. The lovely yellow-gold's history probably went to bygone days when early settlers lived elegantly, before the arrival of the true pioneer, the poor, who carved out the Northwest with iron tears.

"Some lady probably won the heart of an admirer long, long ago wearing this very gown, Cara. I can almost feel the excitement and gaiety. There are trunks to sort through and it is possible that we will find something there. Roberta wants me to walk with her if—if I can arrange it. Else we would start today."

"Oh, let *me*! I will be so careful—and Courtney, iffen you're meanin' 'bout carin' fer th' baby—two's easy takin' care of as one. At this stage, all they ask fer's sleep, a little singin'—an' you gotta bottle? Feedin' makes 'em feel loved."

Courtney laughed, produced a bottle, and handed it to Cara, marveling at her homespun wisdom. "Cara," she said slowly, "tell me, if you had it all to do over, would you—?"

"Marry my John? And have his babies? Oh my, yes! I would'n wanta miss a dot or tittle! Even now, John's bein' laid up 'n all jest lets us be together more—and could be God's way uv lettin' me show my mate how much I 'preciate all his hard work fer me 'n the little 'uns.''

Cara bent over the cradle to touch Blessing's tiny mouth pursed in peaceful slumber as if awaiting a kiss. "She's *so* purty—feels like that silky quilt," she said, stroking the raven hair. "Takin' after you—you bein' so purty 'n all."

"Thank you, Cara. For the compliment. For being my friend, helping out here. And for what you said about— your marriage."

*   *   *

"You knew I was there!"

Roberta's words, spoken as the two young women entered the shady stretch of forest from which trails forked in all directions, were gentle enough. But they carried a hint of accusation.

"Yes, I knew. But the questions I asked Cara were not entirely for your benefit. Roberta, forgive me, but I sense a bit of paranoia. It bothers me, because we love you— all of us."

"All?"

"Yes, all—and that includes Efraim. Your behavior is—well, unfair. Please, darling, stop punishing yourself and him. I would be unable to bear it if anything came between the two of you."

"What would you have me do?" Roberta asked stiffly.

Courtney sighed. "Nothing, I guess—strike that! I want you to be open with him, tell him how you feel— and stop hoarding secrets."

Roberta stopped. "There are things you do not know."

Courtney picked up a pinecone and began idly peeling off the fluted bracts. "What is important is that Efraim knows."

Roberta sucked in a breath. "He knows what we quarrel about. Your brother admires my mind and uses it to his advantage, then refuses to listen to my suggestions. I am unable to accept growing old, becoming a drudge, held hostage by mines and farms when there is an easy solution—today like yesterday and tomorrow to come—"

"Are you bored, Ro? Somehow I thought you married Efraim for love. Does it matter that he has taken an interest here?"

"Of course I married for love! But did *he*? And bored? Not bored—disgusted, discouraged, heartsick, and so *weary*. Please don't press me further."

Dear Roberta. "I will not press you," Courtney said. "I will pray for you instead."

They walked in silence, concentrating on the pointed toes of their high-topped shoes rearranging the dry pine needles carpeting the path.

"You know where we're going." Roberta's words were a statement.

Courtney nodded mutely. "Only I am stopping here. Call me the *dominee* or whatever legal phrase you might coin. But Clint asked me to stay away from the grove, and I shall respect his wishes. Besides, it is dangerous. You know that."

"Yes, but *she* doesn't."

"Who?"

"The girl we saw—Rose Wind."

Rose Wind. It was a lovely name. Courtney sat down on a large rock on which the moss had managed to stay green. Slowly and deliberately, she scraped at a spot of pitch which had collected on her heel. A fingernail snapped and she hardly felt it.

"The boy who took the goose is Swift Arrow—supposed to be her brother but isn't. It is all very complicated. I will explain—with Rose Wind's help. With a bit of persuasion, I think she will come here with me. The goose was a token of friendship in the girl's simple view of life. Warn me with a whistle if anyone comes."

Courtney was to confused to speak. But there remained one surprise more. "Swift Arrow and Dr. Freeman have gone," Roberta whispered over her shoulder.

CHAPTER 22
Sweet Story of Love

❦

An infant wind flicked the cottonwood trees and set the leaves to dancing. The streamside alders parted and through their green archway two shadows emerged. Cautiously. Then swiftly.

"This is Rose Wind, Courtney. She knows things."

Courtney found herself without a voice as she gazed at the hauntingly beautiful face before her—so perfectly sculptured in fine marble. The youthful body was thin, almost sinewy, her hair dark and sweeping, and her parted lips would have appeared sensuous except for her total lack of guile. Flawless skin caused the great, clear eyes to look even darker than her hair. But they were so troubled. An innocent child of nature and its mysteries.

The mysterious girl's imperious air and the totem-pole straightness of her body said *Indian*. Her scant clothing echoed the word. But the skin, so pitifully visible beneath the animal-hide sarong draped over one shoulder and hanging loosely to cover her body, said something quite different and the cheekbones were not quite prominent enough. She stood for inspection with patient grace. Embarrassed by her simple dignity, Courtney stood up, wondering how to address the beautiful stranger. A smile spoke all languages, did it not?

The girl did not smile back. "I speak your tongue," she said in a voice as sweet as a flute.

It was a dream. It had to be a dream. "You have nothing to fear," Courtney found herself saying, marveling that she found a voice.

127

"I have much to fear," the girl replied. "I am in grave danger if you reveal my secret. Then there would be no peace left to beg and share from the Great Sky."

Courtney nodded, not understanding at all. "You are not Indian, then what—?"

Rose Wind stood even taller, a faint smile of pride carving her face into a certain joyousness. "I am Hebrew, stolen away when I was very small. A rabbi taught me the language and the law. But I know the ways of the tribes hidden away, as well. I can be of help—unless you turn me away. Then I shall die. And perhaps you shall die, too. As lovely lady tells you, I know things."

The musical voice went on and on in the saddest story Courtney had ever heard. After she was stolen, there was war between the tribes along The Border of the Sunset. Prisoners on both sides were taken and the strange balance created a fragile peace. Each year, however, fire must be exchanged between them and each tribe must return two straight-shooting braves. Although the young men were slaves, they were treated as equals and on occasion became blood brothers by slashing their little fingers and crossing each other's foreheads with a drop of blood. But there could be no marriages between tribes which often brought broken hearts as fair maidens leaped to their death in the Great River Beyond. Rose Wind herself was the jewel because she knew things . . . she was educated . . . and she could look into the Great Distance. And then she met one of her own, Frank of the Hebrew nation. Now she would not marry Young Chief. But this she had kept within her heart, lest the young Student Prince (her name for the Hebraic lover) be put to death by Old Chief. It was hard to keep Rose Wind's tenses straight.

"Student Prince, so beautiful of mind, was not of mortal making. His God sent him to find me. We met in secret with the help of Swift Arrow, called my brother to establish a kinship qualifying me for marriage to Young Chief. And Swift Arrow continues to serve me."

The sun shifted and strange shadows twisted themselves among the trees. Calls of the night birds commenced. And it was as if time were of the essence. Rose Wind must hurry her story along.

"We were married, Student Prince and I, Rose Wind. But he could not take me to his people. We must wait, allow him to learn more from the Great School. Our marriage was done by ways I knew, sacred vows beneath arches of blossoms with his God as our witness. Someday, we knew, we would be married by the Jewish Master. But I must be older and my beloved must be wiser in the eyes of his people."

"But were his people not your people also?" Courtney asked, feeling a stirring of great compassion for the girl.

Rose Wind spread her hands and studied the fingers one by one. "They did not know. They thought me to be Indian and pagan—"

"But your birth—your education—all say otherwise."

"This they would never have believed unless proven by Great White Father. The Master who taught me now stands in life's shadows."

"I am trying to understand," Courtney said slowly. "Great White Father? Is that not the Indian's title? And you were taught by a rabbi. Yet, you refer to your lover—"

"Husband!"

"Forgive me," Courtney said softly. "Why do you make mention of your husband's God as if He were a stranger to you?"

Rose Wind shook her head in perplexity. "I know things, but this is one which has not been revealed. I was brought up Indian. I lived by their laws—except in love."

"Rose Wind," Roberta said the name softly, "do you wish to share the rest of your story with your new friend?"

Dark eyes surveyed Courtney, revealing nothing. "Are you my new friend? Can you keep my secret, protect me and—"

Courtney lifted her hand to stop the flow of musical words. "I am indeed your friend, dear child—"

"I am 16! Perhaps you think that is too young for love?"

Sixteen. The age she herself had been when Mother sent her to the Columbia Territory where she met the love of her life.

"Love knows no age, Rose Wind—one is never too young or too old to love. God Himself is love. Please believe that, because what I am going to say may be upsetting otherwise. You see, I want very much to protect you. But I am unable to promise to keep your secret if—if it means deceiving my husband—or my people—"

A strange feeling passed through her being, almost overpowering. She felt drawn into a spell, losing control. Even her language sounded like that of the Indian maiden, she thought.

"Oh, I will tell you other secrets—secrets which will help you to defeat the enemy. It is only my one secret which must be guarded. It is the gift left to me by Student Prince, my departed husband."

"Departed?" Unaccountably, Courtney was clutched by grief.

"My tribe took his life—bore my beloved to Other World, leaving me alone with only one gift. No clothes have I and no food. I have only one gift which I must protect with my life, lest all of love should perish as grass in the fields. I can never return."

Courtney longed to invite the girl to share her secret and to offer whatever it took to shield her from the tribe which at this very moment must be pursuing her. The only contact would be Swift Arrow. He could take food and clothing as the days grew colder. But dare she?

And then the terrible reality of it all struck her. Rose Wind was hiding in a dangerous place. There was even talk of torching the grove. But where could she go? What could she do? She was possibly the key. But this was not a matter she and Roberta could decide alone.

A sudden crackling sound in the dry brush brought the girl to her feet. Up from the rock and through the ferny dell toward the cottonwoods she went, bare feet appearing to tread the air. A rabbit hopped into full view, sat on his haunches, and looked curiously at the two astounded young women left behind. It was almost as if the things of nature were in harmony with the girl of the forest, understood, and would protect her until others learned what animals and Indians knew. . . .

"What do you think?" Roberta asked uncertainly as they hurried back. "Poor little girl, caught between two cultures—and now trying to enter a third."

Courtney felt as if she were emerging from a dream. Back there she had been so aware of life with the shining awareness she knew as a child—holding the hand of nature, near to the heart of God. But now? She looked upward, watching a wispy cloud scarfing the sky beyond the Mansion. The real world. She was glad she had not sworn silence. "I have to think, Roberta." *And talk to Clint*, her heart added.

Cara met them at the door. "I found the scrap, Courtney, so I'll be fixin' the quilt! And here's a real old fiddle that was in the chest. And this here's a old, old envelope—I hafta go git John's supper—"

But Courtney hardly heard. Her mind was on the sweet heartbreak of love.

CHAPTER 23
When Storms Strike

How would the story of Rose Wind or the history of the valley have differed had there been no storm? There were those who said it signified God's anger. Others said it was His answer to prayer. Courtney wondered if it could be both—or was it either? Brother Jim, shaking his head when questions were heaped upon him, gathered the family to read from Isaiah:

> Let the wicked forsake his way, and the unrighteous man his thoughts.... For my thoughts are not your thoughts, neither are your ways my ways, saith the Lord. For as the heavens are higher than the earth, so are my ways higher than your ways, and my thoughts than your thoughts. For as the rain cometh down ... and returneth not thither, but watereth the earth, and maketh it bring forth and bud, that it may give seed to the sower, and bread to the eater: so shall my word be ... it shall not return to me void....

Courtney listened carefully, meditating on the words, which, after all, were the alpha and omega of wisdom in any language. She marveled at God's manifestation of power and love through nature. She had come to appreciate and understand so much since Rose Wind had come into her life. Surely, the bravery and courage of the brokenhearted little maiden was a part of His plan.

Never had there been a more trying period in the valley. A period of more uncertainty, fear, need, and desperation. Yet in spite of the threats on life itself, so real that nobody knew for sure who the enemy was, there was progress. The men worked fervently on the buildings, Doc George and Brother Jim—the only two now who ventured into the world outside the Mansion—reported. Both church and school were almost finished. And yes, there would be State funding. But money for supporting families, seeding the crops, and manning the mines was another matter. Why was a loan so hard to come by?

Rose Wind knew things. She knew who the enemy was. Courtney was convinced of that. But to bring her here? She and Roberta disagreed about the matter. Courtney felt that it was risky at best (yes Roberta, she realized what one's Christian duty was, but she knew her duty to her husband as well... and there was Cousin Bella). Roberta was bewildered. After all, Courtney—not Arabella Lovelace—was mistress of the Mansion. True, but...

The matter was unresolved as December came in, cooled by misty fogs which rose from the river, but without the promise of rain. The epidemic worsened. Two new undertakers opened temporary quarters near the fort. Quarters? Makeshift shanties, Doc George said in disgust, ready to move on to the next disaster if ever he could bring this one under control. "Vultures, rapacious creatures, offspring of the unclean beasts of the Ark!" Brother Jim snorted. "I hope the Lord loves them enough for the rest of us!"

Clint had been home for a whole week—under circumstances which were far from ideal. The four children came down with measles all at once. The twins, not as sick as the other two, were demanding and ill-tempered. It took Clint's firm hand to keep them in bed in a darkened room, essential so the disease would do no damage to their vision, Doc George said. Kenney ran dangerously high fevers. Somebody must be with him every minute, careful that he did not get too hot then chill, which could cause pneumonia. Blessing, bless her baby heart, should never have been exposed to measles. Was the tiny heart strong enough to withstand the disease? She was fiery red and fretful and once, while Clint catnapped, Courtney slipped away to check on little Kenney. The result was disaster. Jordan and Jonda, curious and well-meaning, slipped from their prison, saw the flaming face of their baby sister, and fanned her furiously. The rash disappeared to their delight—and their mother's dismay!

"Oh Clint—Clint darling, they've done it, those two! Doc George said if the rash were to be driven in—"

Clint consoled her and took over. Sweat her and the rash would return.

And so it went. A week together which was a nightmare. If only Cara could come, perhaps she could take over just briefly. Donolar checked on the Laughtens and returned with the frightening news that the dreaded malady had struck closer home. Every member was down with the strange disease that was threatening to wipe out the whole population.

Courtney felt a surge of resentment. Roberta, who professed to love children so much, was of no help. Instead her time was spent away from the Mansion. Courtney could only suppose she was with Rose Wind.

Be fair, Courtney, she scolded herself. For Roberta had made it clear that it tore at her heart to be around children. And now that Clint was home . . . Courtney sighed. Only a mother could know that it took more than two bone-tired parents, whose nerve endings were exposed and raw, to understand how much a pair of extra hands would mean.

Cousin Bella was no longer able to move about alone. Mrs. Rueben stayed with her much of the time while Mandy made chicken soup in her scrubbed-out washpot in the backyard, even sending up hosannas that "heb'en dun helt back de rain, aftah all—so's hit woud'n watah down de stew!"

It was hardly the time to tell Clint about the mystery in the cottonwoods. Courtney remembered later that there had been no opportunity, either, to inquire about Dr. Freeman and Swift Arrow's findings on Memaloose Island. Those matters seemed far away. Her real world revolved around the sick children.

The night before Clint left, Courtney forced herself to hold her eyes open, although they were dry in their sockets and every brain cell begged for the mercy of sleep. Was it 24 hours since she had slept? Or was it 48? Still, she fought against surrender. It would render her unconscious, dissolving all her muscles, bones, and organs and stuffing the husk of her body with nothingness. No! She *must* stay awake . . . see Clint . . . be held for a blessed moment . . . and *talk*! Despite her efforts, she dozed off.

A movement awakened her. In a semi-conscious state, she felt Clint ease himself onto the bed, careful not to disturb her. She reached for him in the darkness, then suddenly was in his arms.

Efraim could have chosen no worse time to come home. Courtney lay still in Clint's arms until she heard the creak of the top step of the stairs. Tensing, she listened for the turn of the doorknob leading to the suite he was compelled to share with his wife. Now she could relax. Except that the battle of words began immediately.

"It could be a lot worse," Roberta was saying as if they had taken up where an unfinished quarrel left off. "We can manage the money without Jacobson's help. The man is out to get you—I feel it. And the papers you have drawn up are all wrong. He wants you down on your knees begging—"

Efraim's laugh had no smile in it. Courtney had never known her gentle brother to be so sardonic. "*Beg!* I could crawl on my hands and knees until the birds nested in my beard, and he wouldn't budge. It's as if he *owns* the bank . . . and what do you mean, it could be worse? You know the loan is due and you know from the ledgers that Kennedy Mines are in the red—and what a rock the farmers are against—"

"But—"

"Let me talk!" Courtney heard his footsteps—pacing, pacing. Now he was on the carpet, now the bare floor— and once she was sure he stopped to kick a chair. " 'Free as air, take the land, get rich'—yeah, but nobody mentions equipment, help, seed, cost of shipping—and eating—and taxes are coming—days of *volunteering* money to run the provisional government are gone."

"I've bent over backwards to help!"

"I don't want your help. It's *my* problem." The banging must have been Efraim's fist pounding on the nightstand. "I'm still the man of the family—or have you forgotten?"

"Stop talking to me as if I were a woman when you don't believe it any longer!" The voices were getting louder, angrier. "I thought marriage was a partnership. *Your* problem, Efraim? I would have supposed it was *our* problem!"

"I—am—not—taking—your—money!" Each word was spaced out as if Efraim were explaining a lesson to an inattentive child for the millionth time.

"Then quit! Give up! You and I see a *supporting* wife differently!"

The words caught Efraim by surprise. And before he could recover, Roberta was reversing the roles, making him into the child—not inattentive perhaps, but stubborn, willful, and driven by a stiff-necked pride that went before a fall. "Efraim, for heaven's sake, *listen*! You are going to let us all suffer, maybe be done in completely, by the stupid obsession that somehow *I* would be a threat to your manhood if you accepted what is half yours anyway! Yes, the money is a part of an inheritance from my mother, but my father arranged the annual paychecks as a wedding gift—not for *me*, for *us*—"

"I won't listen—"

"Oh yes, you will! Has it occurred to that stubborn head of yours that maybe this latest setback is the last straw—that it could be a sign that somebody wants you to quit? That you may be flirting with danger and refusing to be bailed out?"

"That sounds like preacher talk—or *Indian*—"

The air was charged. And then a cable snapped. "I give up," Roberta said quietly. Why was Efraim unable to hear the tears in her voice? Or was he enjoying punishing Roberta to punish himself?

"Oh Clint, my darling—my darling—I am glad I have no money."

"It is more than the money, sweetheart," Clint mumbled from the gateway of slumber. "Nobody—shares—what—we—have—"

Courtney tiptoed to close the door. If there was more, she could no longer bear to listen. When she crept back into bed, Clint had succumbed to the grip of exhaustion. She took his hand and laid it gently against her breast knowing that she, too, was on the brink of sleep's mysterious netherworld . . . and perhaps she would meet him there . . .

In that euphoric state, she didn't hear Efraim slamming the door, the sound of his horse's hoofs on the sunbaked road, or Roberta's muffled sobs.

* * *

Courtney was afraid Roberta would leave. When to Courtney's relief she remained, prayer after prayer went up as to what she should say that would help mend the widening chasm. Roberta adored Efraim but found what she considered his stubborn attitude and unswerving loyalty to failure something she was unable to live with. But could she—*should* she?—live without him? Efraim *had* sounded a bit like the king who could do no wrong. Maybe that is what happened in marriage when obstinacy kept the couple from praying together. When they tried one another's patience until nerves were as taut as the steel cables that brought the men to safety from the dark bowels of the mines. *Knowing* God could help and ignoring Him was more grievous than the heathen who knew nothing of the Divine Helper who watched over His own.

It was He who intervened, after all. In His own way. . . .

The children improved rapidly, just as Clint had said they would. Courtney had found a love note pinned to her pillow the morning after Roberta and Efraim's quarrel which, in Courtney's opinion, was a showdown. Clint's note was so beautiful it brought tears to her eyes—while so personal it brought color to her cheeks and sent her heart jogging like a schoolgirl's. Then, in closing, he changed from devoted husband and lover to the concerned father. All fevers were down, he told her, and went on to remind her what they both had learned together—that children spring back as if they were molded around rubber balls. He would not awaken her . . . she must send Donolar if there was a setback. He ended by cautioning her to be careful. He would be home for Christmas.

Christmas! How sad that they must break with tradition—especially when Cousin Bella would have loved to show off the Mansion with its changes and repairs. Everything about it said "Welcome" and they would be unable to throw open the doors of hospitality. The mistletoe was bone-dry and the needles of the firs, pines, and balsams had faded. Well, they would make do with cones, ferns from along the riverbanks—and somehow Donolar always coaxed his Christmas rose to bloom. They must get at their baking—including enough for the Laughtens, who were still recovering.

All this was running through Courtney's head the day the horror which was to haunt them forever began. It started with a smell of smoke. The valley was a tinderbox and even the livestock recognized the danger. Tails over their backs, they ran in wild stampede toward the ponds—dancing, prancing, and sending piteous calls of anguish to their own kind.

From the beginning, Courtney knew. Fire. It had to be. And somehow she must have known, too, that its origin was in the cottonwood grove.

"Rose Wind, *Rose Wind!*" Roberta was screaming as, together, she and Courtney ran toward the grove without pausing to consider any plan of rescue.

It was hard to breathe. Smoke spiraled upward only to swirl downward, obscuring their vision and eddying about their skirts. The downdraft meant wind. Wind meant the spreading of fire. And she had left the baby unattended. There was no way to make Roberta, who had outdistanced her, hear above the roar of the flames and the whistling of the wind. Courtney gave one more desperate cry then turned back, praying aloud for the safety of them all and a miracle that someway would save Roberta . . . the Mansion . . . and the mines. A new fear gripped her heart. The mines! Fire could trap the men. Oh Clint . . . Clint! Tears streamed down her face as she rushed through the gate, not daring to look over her shoulder for fear of being drawn back to search for Rose Wind or try to persuade Roberta to come home.

Then came the mighty explosion. Tops of the cottonwoods, sucked dry of all moisture by the merciless sun, burst into flame with a mighty boom that well could have heralded the end of the world.

Courtney had no memory of screaming. But she must have. The entire family—even Cousin Bella with the aid of Mrs. Rueben—met her at the door. All was in confusion. But Mandy held Blessing—praise the Lord for that!—the twins, proving once again that they could stand tall when in charge, were comforting Kenney, and Donolar was pointing wide-eyed at the cinder-covered Roberta stumbling from the woods. Her clothes were shredded. Her face was wild with hysteria. And she was alone. Courtney rushed to meet her.

All was still in a state of wild confusion when the men arrived as if blown in by the wind. They had seen the smoke, recognized the danger, and already a crew was digging fireguards around the area. It was in their favor, someone said, that the grove was a sort of island, somewhat isolated from the other timber, and that the ground was soft because of the spring in its midst. And over and over the question: *How did the fire start?*

"Jacobson—Isaac Jacobson! Could he possibly have been serious about the grove being ungodly?" Brother Jim tasted the words and his expression said they were even more bitter than quinine.

"The Injuns—" one of the other men began.

"It is no time to speculate!" Clint said grimly. "We—*Roberta!* Where—what—?" His eyes sought Efraim's.

Efraim's face paled and in one giant stride he was by his wife's side. "Are you hurt? I want Doc George to take a look—and then we will talk."

Roberta seemed not to hear. Her ears were undoubtedly deafened, as well, to the prolonged roll of thunder, the only overture to the storm which struck like a swooping hawk. The wind continued to kick up dust and fill the gutters with ashes, but its voice was lost in the drumbeat of rain. Trees bent like bows through which limbs, stripped of foliage and sharpened into arrows, shot fiercely. The apple tree by the window writhed and groaned like a feverish body. And then came the hail. White sheets of it, blotting out the world beyond the Mansion.

Nobody heard the knock. Suddenly she was simply there, the "Snow Maiden," the twins called her. Rose Wind, midnight hair lank and dripping and flesh purple with cold, opened her mouth to speak—and then collapsed in a little heap at their feet.

CHAPTER 24
Student Prince's Gift

🍎

Shyly, but without hesitation, the little Hebrew girl answered the men's questions. Wrapped in heavy blankets, her feet in a basin of hot water, she sipped Mandy's chicken soup gratefully—refusing a spoon but lifting the bowl to her mouth instead. All this Rose Wind would accept with appreciation. But with fear in her great, dark eyes, she refused to allow Doc George to examine her.

He did not press her. And to Courtney's relief, neither did the other men. When she hesitated or appeared afraid, they let the matter drop as gentlemen should. Here was a need and they would meet it as was the way of the valley folk. But here, too, was a valuable resource person—someone on whose answers they could rely. Perhaps she could help them unriddle some mysteries, even point a finger at the enemy or enemies—at least some of them, as there appeared to be many.

"Do you wish to hear something of life within the mission?"

Yes, that would be helpful.

There were many dogs, she said. It was a mark of man's worth to own the animals even when they ate the food so needed by women and children who were starving. The men worked—but by their own standards. No longer could they hunt freely. And they did not welcome the white man's tools. They were far too miserable to listen to preaching or be interested in garden hoes missionaries offered, hungry and dying as they were. And yet they clung to the old ways, even celebrating with their ancient dances, their use of the medicine man, and their belief that nature sent them many gods—friendly gods, not angry like the One the missionaries introduced.

Yes, people came occasionally and "rescued" the children. But they did not wish to be rescued. They did not wish to rake gardens and attend the white man's schools. They either pined away or escaped and returned to their people and their ancient ways.

And yes (here Rose Wind hesitated), a few escaped—but this was unwise—dangerous. Yes, her own life was in danger. Even though her ancestry was far different, in their eyes she belonged to one of the tribes—a tribe which had chosen a husband for her.

At that point, Rose Wind skillfully shifted the direction of the conversation. "The women have a sad plight, a great source of grief to my rabbi. The red housewives and their slaves never finish their work. At 15, they are eager and ready for marriage. At 30, they are aging—and before 50, they are very old and very wise. The men make canoes—and war—"

Again, the girl stopped. "No more questions tonight," Doc George ordered. "This child must have sleep—Courtney, Roberta, a hand?"

Upstairs, Roberta poured water from a pitcher into the basin and brought fresh towels. Courtney brought a full, pink flannel nightgown. Rose Wind stood in awe of it all, glancing from one piece of furniture to another. Then, as she started to wash her hands, the soap slipped. As she bent to recover it, the wet garment she wore dropped and she stood nude and bloated with Student Prince's gift—a child!

CHAPTER 25
After the Storm

❦

The rains kept up—a blessing, farmers declared. They planted their wheat fields during a brief intermission. The timing was right, just ahead of winter's white rule when hibernating creatures sought dark refuges, birds hushed their song, and the wee, brown seeds lay sleeping until spring unlocked the earth. Then they would spear the ground in response to March's hoarse call and, like a miracle, be transformed to an ocean of waving brown gold.

Of course, before this wondrous transformation, there was a winter to survive. A winter filled with hardship, almost untameable emotions, mystery, intrigue, and then new life—as symbolized by the dying of the grains of wheat....

The rains were a blessing in other ways, too. It allowed men to remain home for what amounted to reacquaintance with their families. It could have spelled victory for Doc George over the deadly plague. But that, sadly, was not the case. Surely the freeze would snuff out the life of the germs. But that did not happen either. Later, however, he was to say a prayer of thanksgiving that the often impassible roads, while creating hardship for his dying patients, at least allowed him some time to "renew the courtship" with his "best girl." Arabella Lovelace was overjoyed . . . the first real joy she had known for awhile . . . and her last.

During the month-long storm, much took place in the town—rapidly muscling into a city. "Organic laws" were adopted, although nobody was exactly sure what the phrase meant—other than the formation of an executive committee of three "founders" (nobody being sure how they were chosen—certainly not from among families of the original homesteaders), a supreme judge, a clerk and recorder, a high sheriff (to "oversee" the one now serving), three constables, a major, and three captains (selected from the militia at the fort).

Owners of the "dens of iniquity" (so the story went) were so happy over the shoo-in of men they thought to be pushovers that all spent half the night in the saloon, the other half in jail. The story tickled the funny bone of Brother Jim, which was much in need of tickling. Next would come a governor, sure as shootin', he predicted. Great things happened when the Lord was at work. And history was to prove him right—at least, a governorship came to pass. Other matters were a powder keg of controversy, waiting for a match to light the fuse and set it off. That, too, was to happen.

Out in the valley, other matters were so pressing that nobody paid much attention to politics. The farther that farmers and miners could stay from the city's evils, the better. "A cesspool—a reg'lar cesspool," they mumbled in regard to the city, its charter, and its government. Besides, something resembling a town was springing up around the valley people. But even that would have to wait until the air was cleared. What with all the sickness, the growing threat of the Indians (real or imagined), domestic needs—and the "downright scary stuff" like disappearing cemeteries with graves opening to give up their dead, then that fire . . . well, it *could* be rained down, they guessed . . . there was no room left in their troubled minds for Sin City.

Inside the Mansion, a drama all its own was unfolding.

Seemingly, Rose Wind had not looked beyond the moment of coming here. "I am your hostage," she said, meeting all eyes in a clear, straightforward manner, then bowing submissively. "I know things and am protection against the enemy."

"More of a threat, I would say," Efraim growled uneasily. "Your family will come searching for you—" He spread his hands hopelessly.

"My family is dead," the girl reminded him gently. "I am not Indian."

"Be that as it may, that is how the tribe laying claim sees you. They will attempt a rescue. Who knows you are here?"

"Only Swift Arrow, and he will never tell. He will die first because he knows that they will kill me—not rescue me, as you say."

Efraim shook his head. "I find all this very baffling— that they should keep you, groom you to marry the young chief—then want to kill you." Suddenly, he turned on her. "This comes at a bad time. Tension between the tribes. Tension between Indians and the government. Tension between Indians and whites. Just *why* are you here?"

"For protection—and to offer help." Rose Wind's flute-like voice remained low and musical without a hint of impatience at what she had repeated over and over. This time she added a line: "You see, I have betrayed them—"

The conversation was leading nowhere. Actually, Courtney did not wish it to at this time. The finger of suspicion would point to Roberta without giving her time to prepare the defense.

"Look, there are questions, Efraim—and solutions we must look for," she interrupted. "But please let me suggest that you postpone them until you know the background. I have recorded it all in my journal which, in this case, I am willing to share. I have only one request. Since some of it is very personal—I—I want Clint to read it first. Then—"

"I hereby accept the job of censor!" Clint smiled, chucking her beneath the chin. "I can hardly wait," he whispered, his grin a little wicked. Courtney turned away to hide her blush.

The awkward moment had passed.

It was remarkable how smoothly the adjustment was made, once Mrs. Rueben finished with her fumigating and Mandy overcame her fear that this "po' baby" did not bring an ancient curse. After all, she shared "that ole-time religion what was good 'nuf fo' de Hebrew chil'drun."

The two women made up a room for Rose Wind and told her a bit about the family routine. Yes, of course, she ate at the table. 'Twasn't theirs anyway, 'twas the table of the Lord.

Roberta offered clothes, but Courtney shook her head. Roberta nodded. Of course, some maternity things—

A look of dread passed over Roberta's face as she helped Courtney lay out some loose cotton garments. "You—you didn't record about the *baby!*" The whisper was desperate.

Courtney shook her head. "But I must—"

"No!" Roberta jerked a pink over-blouse from a hook. "They'll know soon enough—" The girl reached for the blouse with a gasp of pleasure.

Rose Wind stared at her reflection in disbelief. How like a child she looked, so innocent, so sweet and unspoiled by the world. And yet she had known heartbreak, had no claim on a future, and her life was in danger. All this she faced stoically. The answer came even as Courtney watched her in fascination. Rose Wind spoke a few phrases (Hebrew?) and then translated simply: "The Lord is with me."

Cousin Bella invited Rose Wind to her quarters. The two of them talked while Roberta paced the floor, wringing her hands for fear the girl would say the wrong thing. Courtney overheard Clint and Efraim discussing the situation—a real dilemma, they said, and Efraim was glad *somebody* in the family was open about the matter. Brother Jim loved the girl on sight and found that she possessed a great knowledge of the Old Testament and the Law. He arranged quiet times for them to talk together, seated cross-legged on the bearskin rug before the fireplace in the library. Someday he must try, with the Lord's help, to undo the frightening misconceptions well-meaning missionaries had instilled and introduce her to a loving Savior. But, wisely, he waited. The child must be handled like the tender flower she was. Doc George, too, waited, although Courtney was sure—and told Roberta so—that he knew her secret. Rose Wind answered all questions with a willingness that touched Courtney's heart—and eventually the hearts of them all. The girl was genuine. On this they agreed.

Donolar and the children adored her and would have monopolized her time completely had Clint allowed it. "I want to be absolutely sure in my mind," he told Courtney, "that they know the difference between her legends—lovely as they are—and the Bible stories."

Courtney agreed completely. One of the wonderful things about children was their *belief.* Unexposed to the outside world in their formative theology, everything adults told them was truth—or it was that "awful word," a *lie.* That the beautiful "Snow Maiden" could lie was unthinkable, something which they would be unable to understand.

"Isn't it wonderful how they have come to accept her? It has been a wonderful experience for them. They enjoyed every minute."

"Why past tense, beautiful? It is good for us all—as are you—"

Clint was holding her close, kissing the top of her head, and she loved it. How good, how *wonderful*, to have him with her. And yet her mind was wandering. Why *had* she spoken of Rose Wind's presence as though it had drawn to a close? An unexplainable sense of uneasiness came uninvited and settled around her heart. Maybe it had been there all along, hovering over them all, just waiting for a host....

Rose Wind's manners were faultless. She ate heartily, accepted whatever Mandy set before her without question. Her second helpings were high praise as was the visible pleasure in her eyes. "Ain't nec'sary uh body be talkin' all de time—us cooks know by de glow! De po' baby dun looks lak she's been t'church, praise de Lawd!"

One evening at dinner, Rose Wind spoke without being spoken to for the first time. "I know things. Have you no wish to hear?"

There was a brief silence, then Clint explained: "We do not wish to press you, Rose Wind. For the time being, you are our guest—not our hostage."

Rose Wind closed her eyes. Then, opening them, swept aside her dark curtain of hair. "The men, they will return tomorrow—bringing news from the Island of the Dead. It will not be good, but not so bad that seeds will die in their graves or cattle drop their young untimely—"

Dr. Freeman and Swift Arrow arrived the day following, the day before Christmas Eve. Their account was horrifying. Waters were at flood stage, stranding them on the desolate island. Only Swift Arrow's ingenuity kept them alive. He speared fish and found an edible moss.

All gathered around the two, bringing dry clothing, offering food and hot coffee, asking questions. Yes, the graves there had been opened. But the remains were back...if, indeed, the bones were the same as those which appeared and disappeared so mysteriously.

"They are the same," Rose Wind said.

CHAPTER 26
A Christmas Carol

❦

Christmas Eve and the downpour continued. In some houses, perhaps, there would be mumbling and grumbling. Conversations would be reduced to monosyllabic mumblings and mutterings—even among the valley folk. In the city, there would be unholy carousing. But, in spite of foul weather and unsolved problems, there was a certain peace in the Mansion-in-the-Wild. Life was simple, happy, and as uncomplicated as one could hope for.

"The winter crop will be bountiful," Rose Wind said, "perhaps the best you have yet harvested. Come spring, new seed will go into the ground and (dropping her head modestly) fertility will prevail."

Courtney believed her. She also recognized a certain plaintive pleading in the childish voice—as if she were asking again that her gift be kept secret, while at the same time asking that it be revealed. Courtney, snuggled with her back to Clint, his arms securely around her middle between the flannel sheets, told him that night of Rose Wind's pregnancy—such a special night to disclose the coming of a child. She heard his sharp intake of breath. But he gathered her closer.

"How strange—a little Jewish girl. We will make room in the inn," he said.

A chilling wind whistled down from the reaches of the mountains during the night. Lidding mud puddles, cattle pools, and Mandy's rain barrels. It moaned and fretted through the firs and, around dawn, made good its threats and laid a heavy blanket of snow over the entire valley. The children were ecstatic as Donolar pulled their sleds from the attic of his small cabin. Doc George's spirits soared to the upper ozone layer. What greater gift than this germ-exterminating cold snap? Clint and Efraim said it was the boon farmers needed, locking in the bedded-down seed. Mrs. Rueben, her nose red and raw, complained bitterly that the wind could bite through wool, freezing flesh and bone. Mandy, in an oversize apron with a design as busy as a Christmas wreath, bustled about—purposely ignoring the housekeeper's discomfort. "Purtiest sight evah I laid mah eyes on—white as washed-away sins fo' de redeemed," she said pointedly.

Accustomed to Mother Nature's sense of humor, the the men, fortunately, had had foresight to wrap the pump. There were prune cakes, green-tomato mince pies, and pumpkin bread left from Thanksgiving. No problem a'tall puttin' gingerbread men in to bake onct de ham was a-cookin'—be ready 'fore de tree was up, Mandy promised the children. Courtney, pushing all dark thoughts to the far corners of her mind, carefully avoided mention of the strain between Roberta and Efraim as she helped her wrap the few small gifts ordered from the mail-order catalog. Rose Wind, wide-eyed with wonder, divided her time between helping in the kitchen and assisting the children with making paper chains for the tree. She knew how to do wonderful things with vines, leafless and without color in their dormancy, but taking on new life when woven into strange and interesting shapes and threaded with bright yarn.

Doc George brought Cousin Bella downstairs and she sat dozing intermittently as her bright eyes took in the scene contentedly. The family was together. What more could she ask?

In the evening, around a crackling fire, Brother Jim read Luke's account of the Holy Birth, then told the

Christmas Story in his own words. Rose Wind, like the children, listened raptly.

"I think the Baby Jesus must have been very beautiful—like Blessing. But it is a sad story. My people took away His life—and we must bear the burden of punishment, wandering from place to place without a welcome. Yes, it is sad."

Cousin Bella rallied. "You are welcome here, my child."

"Amen!" Brother Jim boomed. And then he lowered his voice as if revealing a secret to Rose Wind. "And you do not need to carry a burden of guilt or be punished, little one. It is all too much to try to understand at one time—just take it slowly, a chapter at a time, as we must take our earthly walk. Already you understand better than lots of folks I know. You can accept and give love—and that's what the story of Jesus is, a love story."

Rose Wind's dark eyes pled for more. "Make me understand—how can I know things and yet not understand this? My people do not believe about the Baby. The missionaries said God was angry with us. And the Indian tribe which brought me up taught me their ways—that there are many gods, and it seems they are always angry."

There was no sound in the great library except for the shifting of a log in the fireplace. "We will pray about this, all of us," the big preacher promised. "Just accept in your heart that there are no angry gods, little Rose Wind. God Himself is not angry at your people, although it must have hurt Him very much to have His gift of love refused. But He is ready to forgive—"

"And love me?"

"He loves you already!"

The girl's small hands went up to cover her eyes as if to blot out an ugly scene. "Oh, I wish my people knew—and the Indian tribe—" she moaned softly.

Brother Jim reached out to touch the trembling hands and hold them in his enormous ham-like ones. "Someday they will, my child. That's what we are all working on. Just open your heart now and invite the Christ Child in—your heart is the only earthly home He has."

The prayer he prayed was beautiful. Tonight Courtney had seen a new side to the man so dear to the hearts of them all. A more gentle side. A loving, compassionate side so in keeping with the spirit of Christmas. How well she understood Rose Wind's confusion. Hadn't she been through it? The memory lingered of a side to Brother Jim that frightened her. He was right. Understanding took time. It was something, she knew now, that he too was working on.

There was a restless stir among the children. Doc George scrambled to his feet. "All right, kiddies!" he called out merrily. "How about opening these packages? Arabella, we need a Santa Claus—"

"Your suit is laid out on the bed, George Washington!"

There was a shout of joy and then a state of happy confusion. Courtney knew she would hardly be missed if she tiptoed up the stairs. Moments later she was back. "This is for Santa. You do the honors," she whispered to Clint. He obliged without questions.

Taken by complete surprise, Doc George tore into the package and found the two most important nonliving items of his life—items he had all but given up hope of seeing again. The mysterious brown envelope. And his precious violin.

"Well, I never!" he said, a broad grin creasing his Santa face. "I will need a lawyer on this," he said as if addressing himself, then made sure the envelope was sealed before laying it aside.

Courtney and Clint exchanged glances, question marks in their eyes. A lawyer? So this was a legal document. But a *lawyer*—when there were two of them in the family? It made no sense.

The "ohs" and "ahs" rising from the group turned back to Doc George. Carefully, with a sort of reverence, he removed the well-preserved violin from its worn case. With exaggerated ceremony, he positioned the instrument beneath his white beard, lifted the bow, and pantomimed its movement across the strings.

"Play! *Play!*" The chant grew louder.

The merry twinkle of his blue eyes faded. In its absence, the round face was so profoundly serious that it was almost beyond recognition. A faraway look in his eye, Dr. George Washington Lovelace bowed with a flourish to Arabella Kennedy Lovelace, the love of his youth and the joy of his old age.

Momentarily, the sparkle came back to Cousin Bella's faded eyes as he played Johann Strauss' waltz, "The Beautiful Blue Danube," and then "Tales from the Vienna Woods." Cousin Bella wiped a tear from her eye with her lace handkerchief, her expression begging for more. Turning to Mandy, the master struck up a lively version of "Dixie" to which she clapped loudly. Next, he serenaded Mrs. Rueben with "Der Doppelganger," and for Rose Wind, the sad-sweet minor key of some ancient Jewish piece Courtney did not recognize.

"Aw, sweet bird of youth," he said nostalgically. "There was a time Arabella will recall when I wished to be a conductor—"

Doc George played beautifully—so beautifully that for some unexplainable reason it made Courtney's heart ache. Clint reached to hold her hand, his grip saying that he felt the same emotion. The musician struck up a Christmas carol then. All joined together in singing. Then tenderly Doc George put the instrument away—for the last time. . . .

CHAPTER 27
God's Mill

Snow turned to rain. Rivers rose as the snow melted, sending sudden floods of murky water over the lowlands where the cattle loved to graze. Carcasses of the dead animals put a stench to the air which even the steady downpour could not remove. In most cases, cows had perished because of being stranded and unable to escape, so their owners were unable to reach them and dispose of the remains. Doc George shook his cloud of white hair in despair. Wells would be polluted. Disease would spread. And he, too, was stranded. The minute the waters receded it was imperative that he get into town for medical supplies.

Meantime, he made a point of becoming better acquainted with Rose Wind. While the others concerned themselves with her mind and heart, he was concerned with her body. Courtney, having suspected all along that the gently wise doctor knew the girl's secret, was relieved. She was concerned with the trials of her little friend. Although Rose Wind appeared at peace with the world, Courtney agreed with both Doc George who said there was something "patently wrong" physically and Brother Jim's comment that something was "out of kilter" in her soul. The child was carrying some secret she was afraid to reveal. But what could it be that they had not touched upon? "God's mill grinds slow but sure" was among the repertoire of Brother Jim's ancient proverbs. And that it was grinding now there could be no mistake.

"Well, well!" Doc George sang out the first morning there was a lull in the rain, a painted cloud portending better weather. "I do believe I could find a dry spot for the sole of my foot if I took the trail across the backcountry."

And he was off, the brown envelope tucked securely beneath his arm as his old buggy wheels sliced the water with a creak and moan. By the time he returned home the sun was peering out playfully from between thinning clouds. Tomorrow would be fair. Most likely, the men could return to work. That news was like the dove's return with an olive leaf to the Ark.

God's mill wheel took some interesting turns at dinner. Doc George had gathered a lot of information. Did the family wish to hear?

"Barcus is willing," Donolar said without inflection. Courtney and Clint exchanged a quick, secret smile. *Willing!* How many at this table would *survive* without the sharing—including Doc George, whose very vest was about to pop its buttons with his eagerness.

"The two towns—theirs and ours, at least, what's *going* to be one, centered around the mines, their business places, the school, and church—are separated only by a creek. But miles apart in philosophy. That den of Satan was nigh onto being washed away by the flood. Such a pity the rains stopped! While we (Doc squared his shoulders and twirled the gold chain holding his 17-jewel engraved watch in the pocket of his vest)—well, we may never become the state's queen-city, but folks can settle and prosper here in a saintly fashion. Such a glaring contrast. But getting down to cases, let me say that I took care of my business—found a lawyer who's smart enough once you get past that bowl-of-bland-mush personality. Make that reheated mush—without salt!"

Again Courtney wondered why he had bypassed Efraim and Roberta. There was to be no explanation apparently, as the animated doctor was moving on to other matters. Maybe she was the only curious party. Certainly, Efraim showed no concern. Of course, he had made it clear to his sister years ago that he had no driving ambition in the field of law—that he would swap every book in Harvard for buckskins. But did his wife know? They quarreled so much about other things.

Right now, Efraim was speaking. "Think we'll merge?"

Doc George looked puzzled for a moment. "Oh—the someday-towns? Yes, yes—I do. It's inevitable if we are to survive without one's demise. The question is: Which one's ghost would prowl the remains? They envy us—and still fear us." Doc George shook his head, combing heavy hair with his fingers in perplexity. "We Christians are a strange breed, but how to convince them that, while we walk in the Spirit, we live in temples of flesh is another matter."

"It boils down to voting," Efraim said, avoiding Roberta's eyes. "I have proposed an election. If our man wins—or our *woman*—"

When he hesitated, Roberta said quietly, "A vote is all we ask."

"I understand you have outlined the plan, Efraim. Keep after both sides. We'll need a representative in D.C. to reconcile differences here on the frontier." Doc George ignored the Glamora exchange.

"Plan on trouble from Ike. The man's obnoxious by choice!"

"Ah yes, Jacobson. That reminds me—I saw him and am convinced our meeting was no accident. Naught he does ever is! He followed me to the livery stable, looking too fit and satisfied for my comfort. Asked too many questions, too—kept mumbling about duty demanding that he order the militia into what's left of the mission. That we could do without."

Throughout the conversation, Rose Wind had picked daintily at her food, wearing a single expression of wide-eyed expectancy as if waiting patiently, with concealed anxiety, for something to happen. It was about to—and Rose Wind sensed it.

"And so it goes. And so it goes," Clint said wearily. "When will the feuding end?"

Doc's moment had come. He leaned forward, recovered the corner of the napkin he wore tucked in his collar from the gravy bowl in the nick of time, and prepared the diners by rapt expression for an explosion of news.

"Would you believe the old coot claims to be ready to join forces with *our* side of the creek? Says there's no cooperation in a town with a dumb sheriff, a crazed mailman, and a—*she-house*—pardon me, ladies, *his* words—claiming to be employed by an antique dealer. Funny if it were not so downright filthy—funny, in that those painted women-of-the-night are downright antiques themselves!"

"Well, he's analyzed the situation with some degree of accuracy," Brother Jim declared. "But something tells me there's more."

Doc George nodded. "He claims the Indians have stolen his niece."

"What?" "Say that again!" Clint and Efraim, alarmed, spoke simultaneously. "They have taken no prisoners for years." Clint picked up the conversation cautiously. "The cemetery . . . the children's sightings at the church . . . the fire—but all circumstantial. We have no proof."

Rose Wind's face paled. Efraim took note. "Did you see anyone that day, Rose Wind?" His voice was not unkind. "The day of the fire?"

"I saw." Rose Wind's musical voice trembled like an instrument holding a note.

"Would you recognize him—or her?" he probed softly.

"I would—but I must not. Oh, please—"

Roberta reached out to put protective arms around the girl. "Efraim—*please!*"

Efraim nodded and Doc George turned to the subject of doctors. New "quacks" had flowed in, he explained, to replace the ebb of the tide washed out to sea when gold fever struck. No ability. No supplies. And certainly no knowledge of the Hippocratic Oath of medical science. The frauds simply wandered around like minstrels with a pair of unsterilized scissors and a saw stashed in a saddlebag. Sawed off limbs like so much cord wood. Any ill-fated woman who allowed herself to be attended by one of the ignorant charlatans was bound on putting her trust in some pixie called chance. Why, 'twould be wiser if the poor soul delivered *herself*. . . .

Roberta had dropped her head and Efraim was drumming impatient fingers alongside his plate. Uncharacteristic of him, but these days everything was. "Interesting, Doc, but what has this to do with—"

The doctor was unperturbed. "Good question, Efraim," he smiled. Courtney hoped hard her brother failed to notice that the smile was almost patronizing. She never knew because Doc George was speaking again. And what he had to say, shattering as it was to those who had no prior knowledge, was destined to be the cause whose effect brought tragedy to the Mansion-in-the-Wild.

"Rose Wind, love, do you wish to tell him—or shall I?"

Courtney caught her breath. *No, no! He must not reveal . . . break the sacred promise . . . expose the girl's secret.* And then, although her heart kept up its frightening rhythm, threatening to break her rib cage in its bid for escape, the truth dawned on her as clearly as if spoken by God Himself. *The secret did not belong to Rose Wind alone.* Perhaps even the girl had realized that, extracting no promise from the man she had learned to trust. Oh, how good that Clint knew, too!

The moment had come. Rose Wind raised her chin bravely and, although her voice was low, her dark eyes shone with pride and joy. "I am with child," she said, "and it is for this reason that I must live, for it will be a male child. He will crown Jesus King in his heart as have I."

CHAPTER 28
Irreversible Decision

❦

"You are making a mistake, little sister," Efraim said flatly.

"I am surprised at you, Efraim—and a little disappointed. What has happened to you, you who offered every stray cat refuge? Surely your heart tells you that Rose Wind has no sanctuary but here. If it were anybody except my adored brother, I would suspect a bit of prejudice."

"You know better than that!" Efraim bit off the words as if biting into a bullet. "Where is Roberta anyway—with *her*?"

"The name is Rose Wind, Efraim," Courtney said quietly. "And she is teaching Donolar and the children the art of basket weaving, thinking ahead to Easter. The baby should be here by then."

Efraim stopped rummaging through papers heaped on his desk to face her. There was fire in his blue eyes—not deep-lake blue like her broad-shouldered husband's, but so like the twins' and little Kenney's that he could be their father. "Bellevue blue," Mother had called them. But the beautiful eyes lacked the tenderness heretofore reserved for Courtney. Had his relationship with Roberta done *this* to him?

"Meanwhile, you are to be her—Rose Wind's—guardian angel, and then what? Or have you bothered to think ahead—providing we all make it until then?"

Courtney was startled. For the last half-hour, she had been following Efraim around as he ransacked drawers

161

in search of something unnamed. They had been too busily engaged in Courtney's insistence that Rose Wind was to remain here. In fact, it was the topic of their conversation with each meeting since she, as mistress of the Mansion, had announced that the girl was staying on. Efraim had been the only one registering dismay approaching anger.

"I am not sure I like you when you are like this," she said now. "You seem to like the girl—"

"Which has nothing to do with it! Courtney, you may be endangering the lives of us all—"

"*I* may be!" Suddenly, Courtney stood very straight. "You sound as if we women go from door to door looking for trouble while you men are thoroughgoing pacifists— only I know better!"

His face paled. "Calm down, little sister! Let's stick with the problem. We may be dealing with a mass murderer—bent on hiding out, while watching our every move. Do we dare take a chance?"

"Yes, I guess we do. We have no proof that Rose Wind is a part of the unrest. And (her chin went higher in an effort to meet his eyes directly) even if she were, I would never turn her out to the mercy of the world as you describe it out there—a brawler's paradise, and her expecting a child and—oh darling, please, let's not quarrel. I followed my Christian conscience—"

"To whom?"

Courtney's anger faded to sadness, but her purpose never wavered. "My decision stands—irreversible. It will not be put to a vote."

Efraim looked at her sharply, then his countenance softened. "A real Glamora among us and I am just finding out. Where *is* Roberta? I am going into town and need the mine's ledger."

"So it's the ledger you want, not Roberta? It is in the library."

CHAPTER 29
Strange Findings

It was a bleak, sunless February morning but there was no rain. Courtney arose, as cheerless as the day, too on edge to eat even though her stomach felt as if it had been running on empty for days. Too long she had weighed and reweighed the situation at the Mansion, at the mines, in the shapelessness of the little town that cried for birth around them . . . crops . . . what lay ahead for Rose Wind . . . and the tension between Efraim and Roberta.

All night they had quarreled, voices rising and falling like the wind. No matter how hard she tried muffling out the sounds (as she had done to close out the intimate sounds of flirtations in which Mother indulged, while Father slaved for her), the words came unbidden.

Ironically, Efraim and Roberta bickered about everything except the real thorn, Roberta's insecurities and sense of worthlessness. The subject of children was a dead issue—dead but not buried.

"What you're saying is that you are above having a husband who works at mining or farming instead of making momentous decisions in a courtroom. Then maybe you choose to have a life of your own!"

Could this be Efraim—dear, sweet Efraim? And could the irate voice which responded be that of the shy, retiring girl to whom only his love gave meaning and caused her inner beauty to bloom?

"No married woman has a life of her own! And what do you mean I'm *above* your way of life? All I ever wanted was a husband, a home, and—well, that's all I wanted, that and being a partner instead of being shut out because of my education—"

"Stop it, Ro! You are wrong, wrong, *wrong*! We *are* using your education. I have no objection to your having a life outside the house. What do you think I planned—to use you as a substitute in case one of the mules had the bloat?"

"I would, you know—only you wouldn't appreciate it because that would be *helping*. And *that* you are unable to take!"

"That, I take it, is an indirect reference to your money. For the last time, I am not taking one red cent! I will make it here on my own or we'll starve together—that is, if you plan to stay—"

Their voices trailed off and Courtney cried herself to sleep near dawn. *Reach out to him, Ro,* her voice pled. *Take her in your arms, Efraim...hold one another... never let go...never relax until a difference is settled ...God tells us that and you both know Him...*

* * *

The children's happy patter helped Courtney pick up the pieces of the day and put them into a semblance of order. What a blessing they were, *all* of them. Even the rounding-out, curly topped Blessing seemed to understand how needed her coos and squeals were. They filled a special place in her heart, but they filled in, also, the chambers left empty when Clint was away and the void she had known since Cousin Bella gave every appearance of failing more each day. So much so that Courtney was no longer able to talk over with her the problems her wisdom could have helped resolve.

This she was thinking when the sound of hoofbeats on the bridge announced visitors. Who? The doctor had forbidden visiting. She was so hungry to talk to other women and to the people she loved so much at church. But they would not be coming.

Curiously, she pulled back the upstairs drapes just in time to see Dr. Freeman dismount. Then she saw that another man was with him. Both were tethering their horses at the hitching post. And, for some unexplainable reason, Courtney felt a ring of apprehension form around her heart. Who in the world was the stranger?

Henry Freeman politely doffed his hat. "Mrs. Desmond, may I present Adolph Heinz? He is the saloon keeper and knows many people."

Saloon keeper—*here*? Courtney managed a word of greeting and noted his appearance as the three of them entered the sun room.

Adolph was German, she decided, judging by the short stockiness of the man. His head, resembling a pumpkin with a thatch of bleached straw where the stem ought to be, sat on his shoulders as if placed there by someone who forgot the neck. "Ach, Frau Desmon', you are vrien' of Herr Doktor, so I hep—you see," the man said in a molasses-thick voice that set *r*'s to rolling and *s*'s to hissing.

"Thank you, Mr. Heinz," Courtney said, taking his worn felt hat with a pheasant's feather waving from the band and handing it to a saucer-eyed Mandy. "Mandy, will you please send Mrs. Rueben in?"

Introductions over, the housekeeper and bartender talked what Courtney often heard referred to as a "blue streak." She suspected that they veered from the topic of concern frequently, but no matter. The poor dear seldom saw anyone who spoke her tongue. And, after all, they did get the information they sought—at least, as much as the willing talker knew. Courtney had but one concern. Should she have admitted anyone from the outside in view of the spreading epidemic? Well, it was done, so she put the matter to rest and listened.

In spite of the language barrier, the four of them communicated fairly well. It all boiled down to what Adolph Heinz had overheard spoken by men who were in a drunken stupor. "Wan' der truth? Der truth you git from der drunks ven I put dem up in der room mit der drape wid no door."

And the truth was that it had been warring Indians who resurrected the remains of their own people from the mission cemetery. One tribe—no, he did not know one from the other—moved their dead to a secret cave. The other prepared a "waiting place" in a grove, making ready to transport them by raft to Memaloose Island, building new canoes and preparing food for them for their journey. But (and here Adolph grew very excited) white men—*yes*, he was sure!—stole away some bodies—or tried to—before the Indians discovered them! One man this big (he made a circle with his arms) tried slipping through the Indian guards and, oh, it would make Frau Desmon' sick should he tell how they disposed of der remains. That incident was just one reason there might be a raid.

The desecration in the cemetery? Not done by Indians (the pumpkin-head appeared about to roll off so violently did he wag it from side to side), 'twas white men again. Many men but only one leader.

Although Dr. Freeman pressed for an admission that the bartender knew the leader's identity, he repeatedly denied knowledge. He only understood that it was a mighty important man—more feared than respected. He knew nothing regarding the fire either. Indians maybe?

Or maybe the same unidentified man. Rose Wind had said *he.*

Dr. Freeman and Courtney talked further when Mrs. Rueben took Adolph into the kitchen for "real German kraut straight from der churn."

"What he says coincides with Swift Arrow's accounts—

except that I think the boy knows more and is afraid to tell. He agreed that the bones were Indian and helped match the soil, but he is fearful of a Great White Stranger." Courtney was beginning to be, too.

CHAPTER 30
"Take Care of Rose Wind"

Clint came home three days later. Courtney almost burst into tears in her joy and relief at seeing him. Her mind had been in such turmoil that she was weary from lack of sleep. Maybe her brother was right in saying that she was flirting with danger. Maybe—oh, so many things to which she had no answer. To her, it seemed that they had reached a dead end—and yet there was no room for turning back. Or was she deliberately punishing herself? Stoking the fires of pessimism instead of turning matters over to God and resting awhile?

Clint immediately sensed her mood and suggested a night stroll. The air was crisp with cold, but there was no wind and the sky poured dipperfuls of stars above them—so close, surely they could have gathered a bouquet. Clint talked cheerfully about the mines (saying nothing really), proudly about the children, hopefully about the crops until he sensed that his approach was not working.

He stopped, drew her to him, and pointed to the stars overhead which seemed caught in the treetops. "He who hung the stars in the firmament understands, but your husband does not. What is it, darling?"

"Oh Clint, I love you, *I love you!*"

And then she poured the whole story out.

"Sweetheart, we are investigating this from every angle—"

"Not the right one, Clint. The answer is out there—just hanging, waiting to close in on us. I feel it."

Clint's arms tightened around her. "Courtney, listen to me, my precious. You have had too much responsibility put on you and it can smother you like an avalanche if you continue taking on the world's problems. You *are* doing that."

"I guess I am—*our* world's. But Clint, they *are* mine—"

"They are ours. You are not alone. Repeat after me: 'I am doing a good job.' "

Courtney drew back. "But, oh darling, I'm *not*. Everything has gone wrong." she whispered. "If Cousin Bella were in charge, none of this would have happened."

Clint pulled her back into his embrace, parted the hair on her forehead with his chin and kissed her tenderly. "Do you think—*honestly* believe—that my aunt could have prevented the trouble with the Indians, changed the complexion of that city, kept peace between Efraim and Roberta, and prevented the mines and the weather from running amuck? And do you think she would have shut Rose Wind out—or even—" Clint slowed down at that point, choosing words carefully, "led to the capture of whatever cowardly, conniving person or persons possibly lurk out there?"

"I am confused, Clint. I—I am unable to answer you. But I doubt if she would have admitted Adolph Heinz today. Oh, he is harmless, but it would be a last straw if—if he brought the germ—"

Clint laughed. "The chance is a million to one against it. *Now*, repeat after me!"

To her surprise, Courtney felt a little giggle coming on, but she repeated solemnly.

* * *

Courtney tried to relax. When the black imps of fear begged devilishly for an audience, she gave them none. Until the news came that Adolph Heinz was very ill—

mysteriously so. Looked like arsenic poisoning, so the story went.

Or it *could* be the disease Doc George had fought a losing battle with for so long. If so—no, no, she would not think like that. And then came a thought which was even more disturbing. If the poisoning story was true, who was responsible—and why? Had anyone seen him at the Mansion?

"I am doing a good job," she tried repeating. But what had that to do with this? And, she admitted, saying did not mean believing.

On Saturday the bartender died. And on Sunday Doc George came home complaining of weariness. A little rest and he would be as good as new. But, just to be on the safe side, he would steer clear of the family. "Please respect an old man's wishes," he said with a dismal attempt at a smile.

Why, then, did he summon Efraim? *Oh come, Courtney. Is that really any of your affair? Turn your mind to other matters.* And so she thought of how fortunate that Efraim was there—Efraim and Clint. She and Clint would play with the children and—

But as they started up the stairs, they met Efraim coming down from the spare bedroom where Doc George was "resting." Courtney longed to question him, but he put a warning finger to his lips. And he was so pale. Something else registered in some small niche of her mind. Something a little irregular but familiar . . . oh, yes . . . he carried the brown envelope.

In the frolic that followed, Clint tumbling on the floor with both twins astride his middle and little Kenney, his round cheeks scarlet from trying to pump "Daddy's wegs" (for whatever reason), life's concerns floated into nothingness. Courtney sat in her favorite cricket rocker, her chin buried in Blessing's curls, and hummed a lullaby. *Save us a little corner like this in heaven, Lord,* her heart whispered.

"Where is the music coming from?" Clint asked as, with the children fast asleep, they turned to their own bedroom, exhausted.

It was a strange sound—strange and familiar. "Rose Wind!" Courtney said in surprise. "It is the ancient song Roberta and I heard when first we discovered her hiding place—but why—?"

She and Clint must have located its origin at the same time because both were hurrying to Doc George's room. Rose Wind must not risk exposure to illness. The doctor had cautioned them all.

At the door, they paused, neither of them able to speak. The girl was leaning over her beloved friend, holding his hand and humming a soft shepherd's song that must have been as old as the hills of Judea. "Nobody ministered to the Messiah in His distress. I see His hands bruised by spikes, the tender flesh torn—for you and for me. But there was no vengeance, just forgiveness for what my people did."

The doctor's eyes were closed, but he reached and touched the small hand that smoothed his brow. "*His* people, my child."

"And yet they do not know love conquered. Can you hear the angel harps? Heaven rings with them."

"God bless you, my child—" the tired voice faded.

Clint stepped in quietly then and pulled Rose Wind gently to her feet. "He must rest now." A tremble in his voice suggested unshed tears.

"Take care of Rose Wind," the doctor said softly. "She—she is right—she knows things. Now, if I could have my violin—and Arabella—alone."

Doc George's bow never touched the strings of his beloved violin to mingle with the angel harps. But he did see his Arabella before slipping away...

Shock paralyzed the household. Cousin Bella was in no condition to attend the small service the family held in the parlor where Brother Jim tearfully read George Washington's favorite Scriptures. They laid him to rest on a little hill which rose above the new church, knowing that life could never be the same.

CHAPTER 31
In Spite of Sorrow

❧

The black crepe wreath blowing in the March wind was only a symbol of sorrow behind the Mansion's closed doors. The real pain twisted the hearts of the great house's inhabitants. Mandy's mellow singing was hushed and, united in sorrow with Mrs. Rueben, she lacked the spirit to point out the housekeeper's talents for blunders.

Brother Jim's voice no longer boomed. Try as he would to bring solace to them all, he seemed more in need of comfort himself. He had lost his best friend. Without warning. Without time to pray.

Courtney, more concerned about the others than herself, wondered who would be on hand to deliver Rose Wind's baby. The beloved doctor had only ill to say about the men calling themselves doctors in town, and she trusted his opinion. Doc George had been no faultfinder. She must talk with Roberta, help her prepare in case of emergency. Thank goodness for the peace, however temporary, between the Glamoras.

Clint was wonderful, spending every minute he could spare with his aunt. For it was Cousin Bella who had suffered the greatest loss and, in her fragile condition, nobody had expected her to survive her husband. Doc George himself, who recognized the uncertainty of life more than anyone else, had prided himself on honoring, consoling, and pampering his childhood sweetheart. "One should treat a mate as if every day were the first day of a lifelong honeymoon—while recognizing that it could be the last." And by that creed he lived—and died.

Remembering, Courtney squeezed back tears. Life must go on in spite of sorrow. "Just hold us up, Lord," she whispered over and over, needing to hear her own prayer. "Take charge of my heart, my home, my life. Make me Your instrument in time of pain."

And in her prayer for others, Courtney found her grief turning to a gentle sadness which allowed her to carry on in the grand tradition of Mansion-in-the-Wild. It is what the doctor would have wanted.

"I am so proud of you," Clint told her, "a *brick*, as Doc George would have said." His voice broke in half.

"The Lord is holding me up, darling—make no mistake about it—His strength and your words I pledged to repeat: 'I am doing a good job.' "

She snapped open the lid of her pin-on watch. It was time to remind Mandy to start the stew. Dear Mandy, so torn by grief she could no longer function efficiently. "How is Cousin Bella, Clint? I have been unable to get a word from her."

Clint inhaled sharply, concern creasing his forehead. "She is a million light-years from here. I thought under such sad circumstances she would cling to me, but she is lost—more dead than alive, in need of security but hiding inside herself. She talks—rather moans—something to do with Efraim and Roberta. Do you think she should see a doctor? Strike that—it was a stupid thing to say."

"Nothing you do is ever stupid, my darling, but—like you—I am frightened about my dear Cousin Bella. She is the only mother I ever had." Shuddering with a sudden chill, Courtney locked herself in his arms.

It was only later that she remembered something Clint said. Why would Cousin Bella be concerened about Efraim and Ro? If only there were some way to get through to her, it would be a relief perhaps to know they were no longer sniping at one another—almost as if to say that, however small, one remnant of good had come from the great loss.

Other good things happened, too, as the days of readjustment crept by. Miraculously, the sickness stopped. It was beyond explanation. Perhaps it had run its course and a sort of immunity set in. Or (and Courtney found satisfaction in this theory) perhaps it was Doc George's legacy. One of his attempts to cure may have worked.

Also Efraim received word that his proposal to vote on sending a representative to the capital was well-received. Surprisingly, there was no objection to the voting or the formation of a committee to see that the vote was kept "honest, no stuffin' of the ballot box." Each of the two embryonic cities would choose a candidate.

Efraim's pleasure was touching. It had been far too long since Courtney had seen that look of adventure she so loved about her brother. And then he looked a little embarrassed, as if it were in poor taste in view of their cousin's bereavement. She was relieved to see a spark of interest in Roberta's face. Her voice was almost teasing when she spoke.

"And will women be voting?"

"Of course," he said matter-of-factly. "Although I must tell you that a first draft of the state constitution failed in Congress, after passing in Walla Walla. The reason for rejection? It included a provision for women's suffrage. Nevertheless, we will not back away."

"Thank you, Efraim." Roberta's voice was humble.

Courtney's heart throbbed with new hope. A natural-born matchmaker, her brother had called her. If only one or the other would reach out . . . but no, it was going to take more than this. If only Cousin Bella—

But Arabella Lovelace was beyond helping, Courtney

knew, when she took the children to see her cousin briefly. She paid only token attention, then turned to gaze out the window as if watching for her George Washington to come home.

CHAPTER 32
The Lovelace Legacy

Courtney and Roberta talked more now, although so far they had skirted the subject of Roberta's relationship with Efraim. Conversation centered mostly around Rose Wind and Cousin Bella.

Winter may have tiptoed out or it may have swung open the door of spring without knocking. Courtney simply awoke one morning near Easter knowing that spring had arrived. The mountains were burgeoning with color. Sweetbriar and trailing arbutus, strung with new buds, crept from beneath the dead, sodden leaves and tied it all together with loops and bows. Children, freed from quarantine by a shiny-bald, puckish-faced doctor who claimed to be "state-appointed," would be stripping long johns to wade the still-swollen creeks, their squeals of delight bouncing against the hills as bare feet tested the icy water. "Dey's dun gon' plum crazy, lookit dem monkey shines dey's cuttin'," Mandy said. And Courtney sent up a little prayer of thanksgiving when an indulgent smile creased the ebony face. It was scary to hear the beloved cook, so needed in the household, moaning over and over, "We-all dun hafta bow to de Lawd's will...He dun give and He dun took away...Hit's de Lawd's will...an' we dun hafta—" she reckoned as if in a trance.

Courtney reckoned, as well. It had to be said sometimes—but must it be repeated now? It was not the Lord's will that life stop for them all, and Doc George

177

would have been the first to say so. Nature knew better. Life renewed itself, the old giving way to the new. And new life in human form would bear testimony soon— very soon.

Rose Wind, suddenly lethargic, withdrew. Strength seemed to have emptied from her fragile body. No more daily walks. But she needed this "preparation time," Rose Wind said—time to commune with God instead of nature.

On the morning that Courtney discovered spring, she asked Roberta to join her for a walk. It was Roberta who suggested that they follow the Path of Springtime Moons. They had been nowhere near the rubble since fire had destroyed the cottonwood grove. The children begged to tag along. Tag along? Donolar came with them, as did the Laughten nine, and they all raced ahead, dragging little Kenney, to swing on low-hanging limbs and wild grapevines in what Mrs. Rueben called a "jollification."

Roberta laughed (and that, too, gave Courtney's heart a lift). "I feel like a lady Pied Piper—and love it!" Roberta said.

"I am glad you are noticing the children again," Courtney said, immediately wishing she had made no issue of it. Quickly, she shifted the emphasis. "You need to be prepared to help when Rose Wind's time comes. We may be unable to get a doctor, you know."

Roberta nodded soberly. "Doc George made them all sound like clumsy midwives wearing britches—or worse, more like butchers. But, Courtney, I know nothing—" Roberta's voice dropped to a whisper, "Courtney, *look!*"

They had come upon the ruins of the grove before Courtney was aware. And there in its center were two men, one of whom she recognized instantly as—of all people!—Isaac Jacobson. He was as impeccably dressed as always, looking almost dainty in contrast to the stranger beside him. One startled glance revealed to her a gangling man with dark hair that curled jauntily beneath a stocking cap. The red cap all but covered his eyes and a wide Roman nose spread across his face. Add several days' growth of stubble on his chin and the amazing picture resembled that of a horse. As did his gait. The two men were quickstepping the length of the scorched land, pointing nervously back and forth, both taking notes.

Isaac Jacobson spotted them, his small eyes widening with shock that said he wished the earth would open up and swallow him. Even in her own state of shock, Courtney found herself thinking that should that happen, the earth would regurgitate.

"Ah, Mrs. Desmond and—uh—?"

"Mrs. Glamora," Roberta supplied quickly, her eyes—like Courtney's—taking note that the banker seemed shaken by the name. He recovered quickly.

"Ladies, may I present Jud Askov, mapmaker by trade and—"

"What are you doing here?" Courtney demanded calmly in spite of a hammering heart. "You have no permission, as far as I know."

"Permission?" He feigned surprise. "Why, I supposed you knew there was to be a merger and this land (did he actually lick his lips?)—well, its ownership may be in question later anyway in view of business affairs that beautiful ladies would not be expected to understand."

Roberta's eyes flashed. "I am a lawyer, Mr. Jacobson—a good one. As such, I suggest that you vacate the premises. The land is *not* up for grabs—nor will it ever be!"

The small eyes narrowed. But the beginning of a leer was cut short by Courtney's single-word order, "*Go!*"

They went. Jacobson looked over his shoulder to yell,

"You haven't heard the last of this! This is not the end—"

"That's right!" Roberta yelled back in a manner that made Courtney proud.

* * *

"How much do Clint and Efraim owe that awful man?" Courtney asked Roberta after the children were put down for naps. There had been no chance to talk coming home. It took both women watching the little ones. The Laughtens, accustomed to looking after themselves and inventing their own games, were determined to teach the others how to "skeet" rocks across the river. No? They knew another game, they said with a shrug. They could cross the creek on stepping-stones and "first 'un what falls in, gits dunked!" Adult talk was out of the question. If the children all got home safely, it would be a miracle.

"Jacobson?" Roberta was saying now as they had a needed cup of tea. "Nothing, but a sizable amount to the bank—not enough, but too much, if you follow me."

Courtney nodded and Roberta talked on. "It's the interest that chafes. The mines barely yield enough to meet that and the principal just hangs over their heads. Cousin Bella said it best: Laying claim to a loan was 'rented money' and Cara calls it 'share-croppin'. If the loan goes unpaid—well, that vulture is right. He can foreclose."

Roberta stirred her untasted tea. "I have a feeling you know the options. *I* could pay the loan off if your brother would bend—"

"It is a matter of pride for a man to be the breadwinner, I guess."

Roberta's eyes flashed fire in the final flare of the setting sun. "So he would rather have a vampire like Jacobson do it!"

* * *

Donolar and the children were filled with chitchat about the day at dinner, but neither Clint nor Efraim appeared to be listening. Courtney and Roberta had agreed to bide their time in relating today's upsetting incident. So they waited as the men talked about the promising look of the wheat fields, the hope that a small new vein at the mines had given the workers, and the progress on the buildings. God willing, there could be an upswing.

"If only we can hold the bank at bay," Clint said slowly. And then, taking Courtney's hand beneath the table, "Forgive us, ladies, this must be terribly boring."

"Oh no, not at all—*not at all*," Courtney said hastily. "As a matter of fact," she said, looking into Roberta's eyes for support, "we—"

But she got no further. The squeeze of Clint's hand communicated so many things. This time she felt it was silence. She was right.

Efraim was holding up an envelope. Worn. Brown. It had to be the one Doc George had wanted. And then she remembered helping her brother locate the envelope and seeing it tucked beneath his arm. But what—?

"The contents of this," Efraim said, fingering the worn flap as if to build up interest in his audience, "will make a world of difference. I—I—" Efraim fumbled for words in a manner totally foreign to his nature, "I am sure," he gulped, "you will be as overwhelmed as I. He— uh—Doc George left this to me—that is, to Roberta and me—but it is the lifeboat we never expected—never suspected he owned."

Roberta was leaning forward, eyes shining as they had not shone for longer than Courtney could recall. "*What?* What is for us, Efraim—*what?*"

"The controlling shares of the bank!"

His voice echoed and re-echoed against the walls and a gasp circled the table.

There was laughter. There were tears. And everybody seemed to be hugging everybody else at once. Oh, if only Cousin Bella could know . . . but, Courtney realized, she had to know. She and Doc George were too close for it to be otherwise . . . and hadn't Clint said that her few words centered around Efraim and Roberta? Oh, what a legacy!

Jonda, casting great violet eyes around the group, decided whatever this meant, it must be very important. "We'd better wake God up and tell Him," she said.

CHAPTER 33
And His Name
Shall Be Called...

❦

A certain fulfillment was reached. Once again Mandy filled the house with songs of praise. Brother Jim's vigor returned and he began drafting sermons for when he returned to the pulpit. Donolar, not quite sure of what it all meant, realized that the new church must bloom with roses and concentrated on removing winter mulch and fertilizing and pruning. And lessons, of course. School just might be opening in the fall and his pupils should know more literature than any of the others, recite more Scriptures, and excel in their knowledge of butterflies and their life cycle. Arithmetic he would leave to their teachers.

Now the men could be paid and—oh, everything was wonderful aside from the still-unanswered questions. Everything except two critical points. Two—unless one counted the serpent of prejudice which had ceased to rattle but was coiled and ready to strike.

One of the problems, of course, was Cousin Bella's manner. "It is as if she has chosen to live out her years canonizing the past, insulating herself against reality," Courtney told Clint.

"Reality can be painful. Something I had trouble dealing with during my blindness—so I understand."

"So do I, darling. I went through it when I lost the babies. Even now, I look back and wonder how I could have saved them—"

"There was nothing you could have done, sweetheart.

In your heart you know that." Clint's voice was husky. "Tell your mind that!"

"I know—but sometimes it seems that the mind has a mind of its own. Once one crosses the border of fantasyland, it is hard to come back—to face reality. Slowly I came—or am coming—back."

Dear Clint. Dear, wonderful Clint. "And better than ever! 'In my weakness I am made strong.' "

At the moment Courtney was satisfied. Later, reviewing their conversation, she realized that they had failed to take age into account. Cousin Bella felt that she had lived her life out, seen most of her dreams come true. Going back over it chapter by chapter was an effective balm for the survivor's heart. The Mansion was the cover of her life story which had unfolded within its walls. As long as she had it, she had her mate. He visited her once, she said (as probably he did in her dreams) but was too busy to stay. One day he would take her with him. After one of the delusions, she asked to see Cara and, pointing to Doc George's old violin, asked if John would like to make music to while away his hours in the wheelchair "until George Washington returns."

"Oh yes, ma'am, he'd be mighty grateful. 'Course he cain't go frettin' them opry notes, but he loves fiddlin' 'Turkey in th' Straw' and has learnt 'In th' Sweet By 'n By' since bein' baptized."

After that, Arabella Lovelace put her voice to rest, seeming neither happy nor unhappy. She divided her time between watching the road and stroking every piece of furniture or tracing the outline of Cara's needlepoint as if sending each detail to her brain for storage.

Courtney's other concern was Rose Wind, who—if the girl had counted the "moons" correctly—was overdue. Her dreamy-eyed listlessness rivaled Cousin Bella's.

Courtney's concern was well-founded.

On a misty May afternoon, just before a late Easter, Mandy asked Donolar to drive her to the Company Store for supplies. Mrs. Rueben, who would never be convinced that the cook could shop, insisted on going along. Another good sign of normalcy. But, although they begged long and convincingly, Courtney had reservations about allowing the twins to go, too. It was Roberta who pointed out that they would be starting school in the fall and needed to get the feel of being somewhat on their own. Well, they were in good hands and Kenney must become accustomed to being without them.

Admittedly, it was nice to be alone with Roberta—alone in a sense, anyway—so they could have a long chat. They sat over tea, elbows almost touching, and talked on and on. Roberta would have been unable to suppress her pleasure at Doc George's gift to them even had she tried. It resolved the mystery, she smiled, as to why their benefactor sought someone other than themselves for legal advice. But why would he have never revealed ownership of the shares?

Courtney was sure Cousin Bella knew, she said. To which Roberta nodded, saying that the doctor was a charter member of the bank's shareholders.

"Well," Courtney smiled, "the shares settle the financial problems between you and Efraim, Ro. I am so thankful for that—much more than the money itself, although it will resolve problems for the other families."

Roberta looked at her squarely. "My money would have done that, too. Oh well, why beat a dead horse? I guess we women simply find rejection of any flavor hard to handle."

Were they still talking about money? "Ro—if I am not prying, how are things now, between you and my brother?"

Roberta leaned back and smiled. "Intruding—*you*? Impossible. Sometimes I think I married Efraim to get you for a sister!" She colored slightly and lowered her voice. "Not the whole truth and nothing but. To answer, we no longer wave a red flag in each other's face. But we—uh—well!" Roberta, once again the shy maiden, the blushing bride, the newlywed in a marriage that was unconsummated—yet.

Courtney squeezed her hand in understanding. "Give yourself time."

Both heard the sound at the same time. A moan so faint it might have been one of Mouser's kittens begging at the kitchen door. When it was repeated, they knew it was human. Rose Wind!

Out the door of the sun room. Up the stairs, two at a time. Down the hall. Given to privacy, what if her door was locked? Courtney turned the knob just as Roberta drove her weight against it, causing both of them to tumble inside.

And there she was, bunched in a little heap on a small braided rug in the center of the room. Her legs were crossed, Indian fashion, and she was rocking back and forth in pain.

Carefully, they got her into bed and into the position Courtney had learned from her house calls with Doc George. "Relax, my darling," she whispered. "Roberta, wet a towel. Her face is soaked with perspiration. Relax, Rose Wind . . . breathe in . . . Roberta, *hurry!*"

Courtney's mind was spinning like a mill wheel. Nobody was here to help. It was up to her and Roberta. And, by her own admission, Roberta would be of no help in the delivery. *So Lord, how—*

The answer came before she could finish the prayer. "I will manage the delivery, Ro. You talk to her . . . keep her breathing deeply."

Grabbing sheets and tearing them into squares, she laid them aside, poured water from the pitcher into the basin and soaked towels. Now, for the disinfectants. Oh yes, in the children's rooms.

The rest she went through in a dream, reacting rather than thinking. Yet, strangely, although her own mind seemed to be in a white fog, the conversation between Roberta and Rose Wind was clear.

"I have talked much with God," Rose Wind gasped between contractions, "and He has told me I am for-given—if I accepted love without the kind of marriage —the world recognizes—"

"Oh yes, darling, *yes*. Marriage is sacred no matter how it is performed. Your faith has made you whole, that's what God's Word tells us—"

Rose Wind breathed in as Courtney ordered. And with breath indrawn, she whispered, "There—on the table— bring the Book That Talks. I do not want to hear—about law—just love—"

Roberta, voice trembling, read passages Rose Wind had marked in her Bible: "Repent and believe the gos-pel...be not afraid, only believe...if thou canst be-lieve, all things are possible...whosoever believes that Jesus is the Christ is born of God..." and then, without pausing, Roberta read her own favorite, John 3:16: "For God so loved the world, that he gave his only begotten Son, that whosoever believeth on him should not perish, but have eternal life."

"I believe," Rose Wind whispered faintly. "I *know*—I know God and He knows me—I am with Him—"

Her agonized scream came without warning, filling the room with pain. Courtney bit her own lip, the taste of her own blood filling her mouth. At that moment, Rose Wind's pain became her own for she was reliving the moment of truth which seared her heart with an agony far greater than the torch of pain wrenching the girl's body. Rose Wind's baby was wedged in the birth canal, buttocks where the head should be. Again, as when Kennedy was born, Courtney was the mother and Doc George stood in her tracks...and she was struggling to give birth...to hold her son's head above the swirling black waters of death...her own life counting for noth-ing at all....

Until the doctor's voice stilled the waves. Now again, she heard his voice—or was it her own?—pleading, commanding: "Fight...breathe...bite down on this ...I must turn the baby!"

More screams followed by sudden calm. "Weary—so weary—go home—meet Student Prince." Rose Wind's childish voice faded to otherworld utterings, mumbled, jumbled, barely audible. And there was a gurgle in her throat. "I—go—leaving gift—"

"No, no," Roberta pleaded. "Live, Rose Wind—for your child, for God. You must take His Son's message— *Courtney!* She's not breathing!"

"Keep her talking!" Courtney ordered, struggling desperately with only memory as her guide. *Lord Jesus, help me, HELP me!*

"Roberta—take gift. Man needs male child—carry name. Swift Arrow know—but not tell Evil One...hide from uncle...always I plan gift for *you*."

Suddenly Courtney could go no further. Waves of exhaustion washed over her. Her legs were lead, her body granite. Of course! It was she who was dying. She welcomed the warm surrender...no more struggle. And then she rallied. The baby! It, not she, was choking. God's newest creation would never know His breath of life without her. Fighting off lassitude, she worked fiercely, driven by a Power beyond herself. All the while hearing whispery, meaningless words: "—carry on—teach him—love of Jesus—my ways preserve, too—teach Indians—"

It happened so quickly. Suddenly a child was born! Courtney grabbed him and by instinct pumped life into the small body. In some far corner of her mind she was thinking: *It is a dream. How could this infant stranger be identical to Blessing? Did God plan this?*

Rose Wind never saw her gift. "His name shall be

called—Yada," she murmured, "Hebrew for 'to know'—
he must know—God—and—His Son—"

A small sigh of contentment. A faint, angelic smile.
And she was readied to meet Him—and her Prince.

CHAPTER 34
Good Friday
❧

It was only natural that a person should feel depressed on Good Friday, Courtney told herself, as she dug into her layette in search of tiny clothes for Baby Yada. The shadow of the cross hung over the hearts of Christians. And the heavy clouds that hung like ill-fitting shrouds over the mountains contributed to feelings of sadness, helplessness, and failure.

Down the hall, she could hear sounds that belied her generalization. Roberta, in spite of her sadness at losing Rose Wind, was ecstatic over the baby. *Hers*, she said. *All hers*.

"Not all, Roberta. Not yet. The child must have a father. Wait, darling—it is a great decision, something you and Efraim must decide. It is a complicated matter," Courtney had suggested.

"What complications?" Roberta's eyes were bright Christmas stars—not at all the practical eyes of the lawyer trained to examine all the facts.

Courtney laid down a wee shirt, tenderness filling her heart. Were Kenney or Blessing ever this small, little hands grasping air—and her heart? She and Clint had been denied those moments with her sister's twins. But because they had come in much the same manner as Rose Wind's gift, Courtney knew the pitfalls of trying to gain full custody. And this could involve much more. They might be dealing with both the Jewish community and the Indian tribes, who were at war among themselves and hostile with the whites. How thankful she was that Cara's son was on his way to tell Clint and Efraim. The men had not undergone the emotional experience and could be more objective.

But would any decision bring consolation to her own heart? Deep down, the sense of futility clung like a second skin. In some unexplainable way, she must be responsible for the swarm of tragedies . . . Cousin Bella's withdrawal from life . . . Doc George's death (could the bartender have brought the deadly germ?) . . . and now losing Rose Wind, undoubtedly through her own clumsiness. She clutched a navel band with such force that her nails dug painfully into her palms.

Burrowing her head into the chest of sweet-smelling clothes, she wept bitterly.

Voices. Steps on the stairs. And everybody talking at once. Obviously, the family had returned simultaneously with Clint and Efraim. Well, of course—Alexander would have spread the news. Too late, she wished she had cautioned the boy against that.

All was confusion. Jordan and Jonda were everywhere at once. Their shrieks of delight awoke Kenney, who—rubbing sleep-heavy eyes with chubby fists—joined in without knowing the source of the celebration. And, in the wise way children have, the three of them pulled a protesting Blessing from her cradle. "See?" they whooped, "a twin for you—now you're just like us, half of somebody else!"

Courtney, still heavy of limb, viewed the commotion with detachment, hoping that the noise did not disturb Cousin Bella. Startled, she realized that she had failed to tell her. Or, was waiting wiser until the inevitable storm had passed? Would the family let their minds or their hearts rule? Surely there would be those who pointed out the sensible thing to do, showing Roberta all the risks involved in keeping this child. The pendulum of Courtney's mind swung from one side to the other. After all, she and Roberta felt a special kinship with little Yada. All either of them would feel was a certain rejection at the willingness on the part of people they loved and trusted to put him into the hands of anonymous people some-where . . . without identity . . . without love. Her heart ached with pity and a fierce kind of protectiveness. The great clock downstairs struck the hour, reminding her that time refuses to wait on such decisions. The storm that was brewing was overdue.

But there *was* no storm!

Roberta had washed the baby's ivory body, coaxed the dark hair into a finger roll on top of the perfectly shaped head, and wrapped him in a fluffy blue blanket. She stood in the doorway of the room she and Efraim shared as strangers, a proprietary gaze fixed on the baby's puckish face. Yet, when the moment came—when Efraim was really there—the eyes she turned to him were wistful and pleading, all defiance gone.

Mandy and Mrs. Rueben waited anxiously to take turns in the "viewing," but respectfully they waited. Brother Jim would have broken through the ranks except for the restraining hand Efraim placed on his arm. Courtney's breathing was shallow. Something in Clint's pocket scraped her face as he put his arms around her from behind. She was conscious of the wound but not the pain. The hurt would come if Efraim were callous, indifferent.

Without a word, he lifted the corner of the blanket to peer in bewilderment at the transparently thin eye-lids closed in sleep, the tiny mouth puckered like an un-opened rose. "You—you mean—you and my little sister de-livered—this beautiful child—boy—girl?" he stumbled.

"Boy! Yada—a boy to carry on the Glamora name—*oh Efraim!*"

Efraim touched a wee hand. The dimpled fingers clung to his.

"Well, don't just stand there—*do* something! Surely some doctor's call of duty takes him beyond doling out pills! Get him for—our son."

CHAPTER 35
Burial of the Past

❦

Quietly, unceremoniously, sadly, Rose Wind was buried beneath the starry night sky. "We should dispatch the child to her Maker as speedily as possible," Brother Jim suggested uneasily. All agreed that for security reasons they must make no use of Farnsworth's Funeral Parlor which had opened its doors "in time of need" (in time of *greed*, Brother Jim corrected with probable accuracy).

Almost in a whisper, he quoted from memory some of Rose Wind's favorite biblical passages and then told the Lord informally what the little maiden had come to mean to everyone in the Mansion. "But we know, Lord, that You are the Master Architect and, as promised by Your Son, have many mansions in Your house. Please reserve one for the little pilgrim who met You on her journey."

The family stood, hands briefly linked, and murmured the Lord's Prayer. Courtney's throat ached to sing "Rock of Ages," but she knew they dared not. And so, without speaking, the women stood as the men laid Rose Wind to rest beside Doc George. Theirs were the only two graves in the new cemetery, differing only in that the new grave had no distinguishing mound. Instead it was smoothed to ground level and covered with dead pine needles as if the earth had never been disturbed. And there could never be a headstone. At least, not now.

It was all so impersonal. As if nobody cared. Inside, Courtney knew, they all ached. She knew, too, that all would guard the precious legacy Rose Wind left in their charge. Single file and buried in their private thoughts, they moved through the dark of the forest. And all were burying the past in their own prayerful way.

Courtney shivered when a wolf howled and instinctively moved forward to touch Clint's hand. It was then that she saw or felt a sweeping of the branches along the creek. A person? An animal? At first she thought it was advancing, and then she caught a single glimpse of motion so swift that it seemed to slice the darkness, letting in a fleeting second of light—and recognition came. Swift Arrow! And, living up to his name, the boy was gone.

* * *

Efraim was enchanted with Yada from the beginning. The enchantment was mutual. It was clear that the baby would have been happiest in his vest pocket. Roberta bloomed, her color rivaling the blush of Mandy's early-June peaches. Under full sail, all flags flying, her every gesture said love was renewed. The shadow of the cross was gone. Resurrection had performed its miracle again.

"But how can they be sure," Courtney asked Clint, "that all is in order—that the baby is theirs?" She swallowed so hard it hurt. "It would kill them to lose him when all is going so well."

"I know. Efraim is seeking legal advice. And bear in mind that he, himself, gained experience in getting full custody of the twins for us."

"True," she said reflectively. "I guess it is hard for me to bury the past."

Hard and sometimes impractical, Courtney was to decide. For, although all went well when he consulted the attorney who had handled Doc George's will, the matter must go before the judge. When Efraim reported that matters would be over shortly, a sort of twilight gathered over Courtney's heart. Had he forgotten the judge was Isaac Jacobson?

CHAPTER 36
Sunrise

❦

Roberta's whole world changed. Up came the sun in never-before radiance, dispelling the gloom, and bringing a vibrant glory to her recently lusterless eyes, curving her lips into an endless smile which she divided equally between her husband and their child. Once more she was beautiful—because of love. Courtney fancied she could hear the song in her sister-in-law's heart.

How, then, could she be required to face the awful truth to which happiness had blinded her? Courtney compelled herself to play the little game with her— drawing a thin curtain of pretense between what was and what could be. After all, where was her faith?

That same sun rose over the entire valley, illuminating each household. Loans were settled. Money was assured for next year's crops since Efraim would be in charge of the bank's purse. Hay was cut and tossed into golden mows. Housewives were putting up more fruit than seven years of famine could threaten. And, praise be, school *would* open this fall. And already the neighborhood had gathered to "shake" the roof and erect the cupola of the new church. Everybody liked Miss Lizzie, a plain "ole-fashion" girl, little older'n some teachers who warn't yet married, still 'n all, she'd brung a heap o'books.

Maybe she'd be meetin' some nice man here—men bein' so plentiful on the frontier. Where would she stay? Likely at the Mansion, they reckoned, enough room there to quarter the cavalry.

So they aired and mended their Sunday clothes. They let down hems and took older children's shoes to the cobbler for half-soling for the next child in line in preparation for some "real schoolin'." And, my goodness yes, they must be putting together a welcome quilt for the new teacher. That would call for a quilting bee for sure!

It was at the quilting bee that the loosely organized committee of husbands found them and asked for signatures on a petition. A petition? Well, a petition was—uh—sort of like a prayer. It was an *asking* of not God—though some praying was in order—but asking men (that was, folks—men *and* women) for a right. No, not begging.

"Humph! A lawyer coulda twisted facts better'n that!" Widder Morris observed, biting off a thread.

Boots Thomason, who supposedly had taken a "shine" to the widow, looked relieved. "That we got—right here, ma'am."

It took Efraim some time to pare his language down to suit the ladies. And longer to convince them that *they* could sign the petition for the two growing communities to merge into a bona fide community, as crime-free as they could make it. When they understood, there was a scramble to get hold of the ink bottle and the pen staff. Imagine, women in politicking! About time, of course.

Efraim apparently did a better job than he took credit for. Not only did the measure pass, to his surprise he was elected as representative from the valley side. And, to his own surprise more than theirs, he found himself the winner when ballots were cast. Mr. Efraim Glamora would be going to Washington—at a date to be established later. But that was to come later without the preamble of a dream. His dream, at the moment, was to complete the process of making Yada his son.

CHAPTER 37
High Noon

There comes a time in the solar day when the sun reaches its apogee, seems to stand motionless as if in debate, and then starts downward. Throughout July and August the valley seemed at high noon.

Bypassing national bureaucracy, the will of the settlers gathered new iron from thin air. Unaware that they might be planning and plotting a city on land which they were not entitled to claim legally, the men on the valley side worked out a plan as brilliant as the midsummer sun. Clint and Efraim burned midnight oil studying the ledgers, their sad story told in red figures. Farmers had turned to mining when crops failed. Should miners, in like manner, turn to farming since the mines that had failed slowly at first were now at a near-standstill?

"Someday," Efraim said tiredly as Courtney took them coffee on one of those wee-hour nights, "we'll be compelled to decide between the scythe, hook and cradle and the picks and shovels, considering all the land you own."

Clint nodded before answering, pausing to stroke Courtney's hand as she spooned sugar into his cup. "Green gold, no quartz, no clay. But that is a farmer's dream—"

And you are no farmer, darling, Courtney's heart cried out. For some, raising wheat was almost a religious experience more than an occupation. Watching the weather . . . kneeling in the newly turned earth . . . sifting the rich soil through their fingers. But not Clint.

"Washington's soil is rich, productive. You would do well, for this is basically an agricultural area and my prediction is that it always will be—or are you interested?" Efraim said tentatively.

Clint's long fingers pushed back his sun-bronzed hair. "Interested—but not for Courtney and me. I realize we will need to expand into something more, but—call it sentimental or some such—I think we agree that we want to keep Aunt Bella's dream alive."

"To that I say 'Amen!' It is slaughter to think of transforming 5000 acres of virgin timber into a wheat farm, no matter how productive. So I take it you plan on scaling down on the mines?"

Courtney walked behind Clint and wrapped supporting arms about his neck. Anything he wanted was *her* gold mine. Even an ark on dry land!

"Right, but I am giving thought to harvesting some of the timber. Actually, the fir, hemlock, pine, and cedar are crowding out the oak and maple—sapping each other as well. With the sawmills in town and the harbor so close, there is every opportunity for shipping."

"Ever think of a newspaper?"

Clint leaned forward. "Did you? All that wood pulp—"

Efraim grinned. "You read me like a book. People are news-hungry and with two helpmates like ours, how could we lose even my election? My little sister here's a born writer." His face became animated. "And Roberta could proofread at home—couldn't drag her away from that baby. Oh, what a baby he is! And—not intending to jump the gun, but—well, in case I *do* go to D.C., Ro knows as much about running an office as I. It would be in good hands."

Courtney felt her heart pick up speed. She was as excited as the men. And there was more to come.

She heated up the coffee on the wood stove that Mandy stoked and left burning on work nights. Mrs. Rueben, whose tongue was as sharp and sure as a well-honed bowie knife, came into the kitchen to dig into the larder for the cook's hidden cookie jar. The woman had mellowed considerably since Yada's arrival. The baby was the darling of the household. On that she and Mandy agreed. And the withering looks of disapproval reserved for one another were fewer and farther between. Courtney accepted the cookies and, on impulse, leaned over and kissed the weathered cheek.

The sharp eyes, so capable of firing shots of indignation, softened. She straightened as if inviting the world to take a second glance. A German emigrant could be somebody, after all....

"So it's all settled, and that's downright gentlemanly of you, my friend." Efraim's voice trembled a bit as the two shook hands.

"Cookies to celebrate! Go wake Roberta, Courtney."

Roberta looked radiant, in her glory, even in her nightgown with her hair tumbling and coiling like that of the Greek goddess, Medusa. Holding the wee bundle that was Yada cradled to her breast, she moved to Efraim's side. It was a tender scene—meant for the two of them alone. But neither Courtney nor Clint could tear their eyes away as Efraim rose to put his arms around his little family and closed his eyes.

Clint cleared his throat and they all shared a laugh. Then the men, talking at once, explained how they planned to convert shares owned by the workers in the mines into shares in the City Company yet to be formed. Yes, it was necessary in order to file application for a charter before construction could begin, providing, of course, that there were more *yes's* than *no's*. How long it would take the application to reach the top of the stack heaped up on some cigar-puffing legislator's desk was anybody's guess. Clint would spread the word among the farmers tomorrow. Efraim would take the completed petition into town. It was best to push this thing, he said, as valley folk needed all the support they could garner and soon prospectors would be moving on while farmers holed up for the winter. Clint wondered one last time if their side stood a chance, but Efraim's hopes were unfaltering. "Of course," he said with the kind of conviction that turns dreams to reality. "The Lord is on this side of the river!"

Roberta had become so excited during the planning session that, when Efraim told of the parts he hoped she and Courtney would take in publishing *The Territorial Gazette*, Courtney feared Roberta would let go of the baby as she swung the bundle back and forth with such abandon. Fat chance! Her hands were laced around him so tightly that the grip told the world she was first a mother, then a businesswoman.

Suddenly, the swinging stopped. "Tomorrow? You will go *tomorrow*?"

"I will," Efraim said solemnly. "And to stall off the question you have asked one million and one times, the papers should be ready by then."

They were.

Efraim came home walking ten feet off the ground. "That judge is so upset about the length of our petition and talk of my being the representative the valley will choose, he never knew what he was signing! He owns most of the town, grabbing it from those in debt to the bank, I am guessing. So, of course, I am the enemy now that I have control. He made no secret of wanting to foreclose on our people, too—the weasel (Brother Jim's title, but fitting). Most of his dealings are illegal it is easy to see. Ah, for a peek into that oversize Union fireproof safe, with a lifetime guarantee, he says—which might not be so long, after all, judging from the enemies the man delights in making. 'To Know Him Was To Hate Him' would be a fitting epitaph—"

"Efraim!" Roberta scolded gently.

"Strike that, Lord," Efraim said in a prayer-soft voice. "But I did bring home a book on tombstone selecting. Brother Jim thinks we should have one ready to erect at the first worship service. Cousin Bella will want it simple—I—hope she realizes—"

"Doc George would want her to see," Clint said, "but—" and he shook his head. Arabella Lovelace was incapable of making a decision.

There was silence. Then Roberta could no longer contain herself. "Efraim, tell us more about Yada's papers. Do you really think we can trust them—*know* that he is ours?"

Efraim patted his vest pocket. "As safe as the crooked judge's vault, which is as strong as steel and cement can make it! Congratulations, Mrs. Glamora. We have ourselves a son!"

* * *

September came in golden. The wheat. The sun. The mood. Even Jonda and Jordan—so fair of skin after a summer in the sun—looked like bronze angels. And behaved as well! There was something sobering about school's opening soon. Too, they were "older" now, they informed their parents. Yada's arrival, like Kenney's and Blessing's, gave them a new status. Courtney, basking in the warmth of the weather and of love, put away worrisome thoughts and paid little heed when her brother announced that Washington was now admitted to the Union and an election on the constitution would follow on October first. Great headline material for his newspaper in this remote part of the world. An interview with the Republican gubernatorial candidate, Elisha Perry—sure to be elected—would be of interest. More interesting, Courtney thought, would be the kind of thing she jotted in her journal: everyday life, beauties of the land—and the Indian affairs. She frowned, remembering glimpses she caught of Swift Arrow, making her aware that high noon did not last....

CHAPTER 38
Terror in the Afternoon

🍎

Kennedy School, the first nonsectarian school, opened its doors in mid-October. The single-room structure could be added to from all sides, depending on increase in enrollment and state funding. At present, a proud three-member board decided, it was prudent to hold some of "Miz Arabella's bequest" in reserve for repairs and such. Donolar, with all the pomp of a King Arthur knight, took Jonda and Jordan in the buggy to meet the new teacher. From then on, all the three of them could talk about was "Miss Lizzie Jennings" who carried all the world's wisdom around in a satchel. Donolar took roses daily to the lady-genius. And Mandy, narrowing her eyes at the twins, said one of her apple barrels was "gittin' mighty low since dat school begun."

Since Jonda and Jordan could read, write, and cipher, Miss Lizzie assigned them the task of helping the Laughten children with their language arts. They could "figger," the Laughtens told her. And they were right. Come to think on it, Alexander Laughten told Donolar, if he wanted, they would help Donolar if he would help them learn "a mite uv that lit'trary stuff an' Injun his'try." A satisfactory compact.

The grateful parents, Cara and John were touchingly humbled. If ever they could do anything—"jest any little ole thang—"

It was their kind offer that led to circumstances under which a tragedy that rocked the valley occurred....

It was a blue-ribbon day, one which begged grown-ups to be children again. Courtney, in kissing Clint good-bye as he left to do some final cleanup work at the mines before the new and smaller digging, wished for the kind of picnic they used to share.

"Apples and jerky," she smiled, remembering their early days together when everything was magic.

"The time will come again, sweetheart," Clint promised. "And we will make up for lost time—eating off the same apple—"

"You take the first bite," Courtney teased, "then I won't be held responsible for what happens afterwards!"

It was a sweet, stolen moment both of them would remember more poignantly than they remembered their courtship picnics. At the time, however, the day seemed quite ordinary—wonderfully so. Clint remarked that the air had a bit of a nip and Courtney ransacked the closet for his buffalo flannel overshirt.

"By the way," he said as he shrugged into it, "Efraim wants Roberta to go into town with him, helping choose the site for the newspaper. Why not go along?"

It sounded wonderful. How long had it been since she and Roberta had been away? "But nobody could persuade Roberta to leave Yada. He is still of the spirit, not flesh and blood."

"Three *would* be a handful for Mandy and Mrs. Rueben," Clint agreed, "and I overheard them planning to make apple butter and cider—but wait, there's Cara! Leave Kenney here and let Cara keep the wee ones."

It took some insisting on Efraim's part, but Roberta finally agreed, then spent an hour going over details that were routine with Cara. How did she manage to keep her face straight and keep repeating "Yessum"? Naps? Oh, her John would "fiddle" fer 'em . . . not to worry . . . he put their brood to rest "thata way—nothin' as restful as a good hoedown."

Town was a place of strangers. A place in which happiness had died and drunken revelry had moved in to replace it. Courtney was sickened and diagonal looks at Efraim and Roberta told her that they shared her sentiments. But the story was still unfolding. She was willing to wait for the merger. Willing also to wait for her brother and sister-in-law while they attended to business.

And, waving away Efraim's objections, she sought out the women's shops. Browsing would be exciting. And, once inside, browsing turned to buying the pamperings so dear to a woman-in-love's heart: a bottle of cologne; a fringed shawl with tassels, like memories, attached; and a lovely one-of-its-kind dress of thread silk. The saleslady, who could have been 20 or 40 or any age between (it was hard to tell when her oversized mouth was painted barn-red and her face so powdered she looked as if she had been rescued recently from the flour bin), had an eye for business. "Bee-yootiful hair, young lady an' a complexion Cleopatra with all them milk baths couldn't match. Now, with a teeny-weeny bitta help, your beau—"

"Husband," Courtney corrected, lest the woman be working around to offering her a "night spot" in some tawdy "parlor house."

The well-padded woman attempted to bow from the middle. "Beggin' your pardon, ma'am—we never know. Well, with that hourglass shape, you'd appeal to Napoleon hisself in this empire gown."

"Wrap it, please!" Courtney said impulsively of the high-waisted, blue silk with its long, flowing skirt and daringly short puffed sleeves. Tonight, she decided, they would resume the "dinner-at-six" tradition.

Roberta might wish to shop a bit, too, as it would be a "proper" meal, which meant all would dress accordingly, as Cousin Bella once required. But when she met Roberta and Efraim, they were laden with packages:

peppermints for the children, calico for Cara's sewing machine to tailor school clothes for her children, a Bible for Brother Jim (his being pounded to pieces) . . . and Efraim, glancing at the slanting rays of the sun, declared that they must be getting home. After lunch.

"I would prefer making a purchase for Clint," Courtney declined. "I could do without a meal—"

"So could I," Efraim chuckled, "but Mama here is caving in! One would think she is nursing that baby of ours!" He squeezed Roberta's hand affectionately and his reward was a radiant smile. "A bowl of chili maybe—there's little these places can do to spoil that surely."

Tucking his hand beneath the girls' elbows, he steered them across the dusty street, cautioning all the while that they keep their ears open, ignoring the gibes, and their mouths dutifully shut. It would tax his strength, he grinned, to fight for the honor of his two "best girls."

Efraim chose the most substantial-looking building in the so-called "mining town" (whose livelihood most likely came from professional gamblers and women of questionable virtue). Conversation stopped when the trio entered, and grizzled, ragged, unwashed patrons gaped. Courtney and Roberta were the only ladies and Courtney admitted later that she felt as out of place as a shotgun in a church house.

To his credit, the proprietor wore a white apron and his fingernails were clean. Best chili in town, the prune-faced little Mexican assured them, licking his lips in endorsement. Man had to fight "tooth, toenail, and prayer" to hang on. But, señor, he was a-doin' it!

Stopping at the *Chili con Carne and Otros Hots* delayed them, but Courtney insisted on a quick purchase at the open-front men's goods concession. There, with a laugh, she bought a lumber jacket in bold red-and-blue checks for her future "logger." She felt festive for the first time in ages—until an incident, small though it was, caused her stomach to knot in a way that had nothing to do with the chili.

"Mrs. Desmond, I do believe?" A man stepped from behind the counter.

Isaac Jacobson! Courtney acknowledged the judge's greeting with a brief nod, paid, and hurried out, conscious that his shifty eyes followed her. Something was irregular—as if he made a point of being seen.

She made no mention of the encounter on the way back to the Mansion. Efraim and Roberta were talking nonstop about handpresses, newsprint, printer's ink, and the temporary building for the weekly publication which would become a daily in no time, they predicted, spouting their lines like well-trained actors on stage. Once they picked up subscriptions for ads . . . made the newspaper free for awhile . . . then . . .

On and on they talked as the buggy wheeled along the narrow, curving road at the foot of the mountain, sometimes losing itself in the massive ferns, cattails, and rushes alongside the river. From the outside seat she occupied, Courtney could, by straining her eyes, catch a glimpse of the mines—men, ranging in age from teens through seventies, rushing to close up and get on to other ways of making a fortune.

But, closer, something else caught her eye. The bent-over figure of a man or boy running alongside the buggy. She was about to alert Efraim when the figure straightened. Swift Arrow! And he was waving some kind of signal she was unable to translate. That it could be a warning never occurred to her, although she did feel that the message was intended for her alone. What could it mean?

There was no further time to give it thought. Efraim was addressing her. "Forgive us, little sister, for seeming to ignore you. There is just no stopping newspaper people or lawyers. And being both compounds it—two in one family—my, my!"

"My, my, indeed! My, my, how wonderful!" Courtney laughed. "I am so happy for you—in every way. Efraim," she said slowly, "is there any way you could use John Laughten? Any menial task would help. Cara says he is deteriorating, especially since Doc George's death."

They forded a shallow spot and crossed the creek—a shortcut from the bridge. Wise, since the slanting rays of the autumn sun were probing the forest like warning fingers. The afternoon was fading.

"I have given it thought. What John lacks in education, he makes up in what Doc George always called 'horse sense.' But—well, John is his worst enemy. It is sad, but he feels that every lamp in his life has gone out—Doc George . . . the mines. . . . He hates his lot, but makes so little effort—and never misses a chance to air his grievances."

Courtney nodded. "More dead than alive, poor Cara says. He sees the wheelchair as a prison rather than the blessing it is—"

"Let's not be judgmental!" Roberta broke in quickly. "Kill a man's pride and you kill the man—"

Amens came from both Efraim and Courtney, each remembering.

There seemed to descend a sudden quiet as they neared Mansion-in-the-Wild. The three of them felt it. Roberta's knuckles were white on the armrests and Efraim urged the horses forward. Fear made Courtney's heart beat so loudly she would have been unable to hear a cannon.

And then they saw Cara. Running. Screaming. Holding something square above her head. *Blessing's music box!*

Irrationally, Courtney leaped from the buggy and ran to meet the hysterical woman, feeling no pain when thistles tore at her flesh and her flying hair caught in low-hanging branches. A lady Absalom—and not caring. "Forgive me—forgive me—oh, I wish I wuz dead!" Cara screamed.

The two met and, frenzied, Courtney shook Cara. "What is it, *what*?"

"They took 'er—Injuns, painted 'n awful, with guns 'n war paint! I—I," she panted, "I took 'er out fer airin'— John inside—'n they grabbed me 'n helt—'n said they'd come fer their kind. I'm guessin' they come fer Yada.... Oh Lord, strike me dead—dead! Blessin's stole."

CHAPTER 39
...And into the Night

❧

Condemned by her accusing conscience, Courtney's feet were planted in the whispering, sun-dried grasses. If only she had remained at home. Or listened when her brother would have hurried...told about seeing an Indian lad slinking through the brush...if only—

But her mind was no more capable of functioning than her body. A sense of futility seized her throat, rendering her without voice. How many tragedies she could have prevented—*if only*—

Suddenly, then, a wild surge of emotion she was unable to understand freed her. The primitive maternal instinct which, although not removing her from the nightmare, rendered her able to move in it.

"Which direction did they go, Cara?" Courtney asked through clenched teeth.

But it was Cara's turn to freeze. Her face went blank with shock.

Courtney felt abandoned. Totally alone in the world. Somebody had stolen her baby—hers and Clint's. And there was nobody who could help her. For Roberta, without waiting to hear that Yada was safe, had ignored Efraim's tug at her skirt, jumped, stumbled, and then run wildly in the general direction of the Laughten cabin. The team had panicked and Efraim was trying desperately to hold them. Donolar would have gone for the twins. Clint was still at the mines.

With supernatural power and speed, Courtney ran to

the stable, saddled Peaches, and—unbeknownst to anyone—was riding like the wind astride the little mare
without thought of direction, conscious only of the soft
breeze that strummed the pines in somber notes of a
dirge.

But one thought was clear in her mind. Her baby, her
precious, innocent baby, was the pawn in some kind of
senseless scheme. The best plan was to find Swift Arrow.
He was her only hope of contact with the Indians. And,
knowing how she had befriended Rose Wind, he would
never betray her or Roberta. Nobody else would understand that. Even family members would be inclined to
say an Indian was an Indian. . . .

Twilight wrapped a purple scarf around the shoulders of the ancient firs, lending mystery, but obscuring
the Path of Springtime Moons. Soon stars would fleck
the sky, but it was the dark phase of the moon and
visibility would be close to zero. Peaches, dear faithful
Peaches, would know the way.

An owl hooted almost overhead. Courtney did not
flinch. It was as if she were a stranger living in a body the
other Courtney had abandoned. She knew no fear for
herself. Just fear for little Blessing who was being held by
unfamiliar hands. And white rage! Gone was the sense
of kindness toward life and love. Good did not reign as
she had thought as a child. She no longer thought as a
child. Reality was the stalker. It had snapped joy and
kindness like a fragile twig. The culprits must be caught,
punished. After they had given her baby back! But what
if . . . no, no, she would not look beyond the moment
when mother and child were reunited.

Reining in near the spot where she and Roberta had
first seen Rose Wind, horse and rider sat statue-still
beneath the obliging shadows of whispering pines. A
midget cloud caught one last ray of the fading sunset,
reflected in golden threads through the sword ferns,
then faded to inky darkness. Time snailed past.

At first, Courtney thought the soft, poignant notes were those of some distant shepherd's song. But when the melody repeated, it was closer. "I am here." The voice from the shadows was unmistakable.

"Swift Arrow?" Courtney whispered. "You must help me!"

"My heart and head are sore with thinking," the lad whispered back in their ghostly conversation. "I know things as did the loved one I called sister—but these I do not know—where is child. I saw men—but Swift Arrow not think men are of warring tribes or hostage tribes. But the forest whispers and spirits hear. It is a time of great feasting—feasting of hearts, not feasting of body, for there is no food. But fires must be carried between tribes for Spirit's blessing—"

"Blessing!" Courtney, forgetting, cried out—the word wrenched from her heart. And instantly she felt the boy's wiry finger across her mouth.

"Must be very quiet—and I show you Great Feast, if you swear silence. Black trouble if tribes know—death for me—and you, too—hostage, ransom for food—"

Courtney removed his fingers. "Ransom? You think—"

"I do not think tribes have child, but who knows what Great Spirits do in time of feasting. Fires burn deep—follow! It is hard to find."

Swift Arrow was right. Barefoot, he led Peaches along an unfamiliar trail. Courtney, still unafraid, prayed that the little mare did not give their whereabouts away with a sudden snort or whinny. And then, when they stopped, it was in a world of silence. This was a celebration? She had thought the Indian feasts were noise-filled and happy.

Longing to ask questions, Courtney bit her tongue. The promise had been silence on her part. She waited. She was to learn later that all fires were extinguished. In the midst of the measureless dark there was a fire stack waiting. Around it the Indians would be huddled, waiting for its lighting by the Great Spirit. And the waiting was worst of all. Perhaps it would not come, the fire, and then they would all die. For years now it had been burning low—and look what the white man had done. . . .

Courtney stiffened. The air suddenly filled up with the smell of charring. A solitary spark flew upward, followed by a shower, then petals of flame opened into a giant blossom which lighted the world. There was a great shout. Fire was born again. Hands of warring tribes, at peace for this solemn moment, linked. The two tribes holding hostages each released one in "good faith" and to "appease appetite of Great Spirit."

There was chanting and dancing to the muffled rhythm of wolf-skin drums and, as the red tongues of flame leaped skyward, all faces were illuminated. There were toddlers and babes-in-arm—naked and nut-brown—but there was no white child.

Swift Arrow's hand closed over Courtney's. His signal to flee, and she saw why. The dancers had formed into a long line and were snaking their direction. Quietly, and with heavy heart, she turned Peaches—hardly knowing whether to be relieved or disappointed. It was becoming increasingly difficult to feel anything at all.

A sudden sensation of aloneness overwhelmed her. Swift Arrow had disappeared. *Lord, lead Peaches*, her heart implored in the silence.

The trek was long and arduous. But now there were sounds: hoofbeats, voices—and arms! "Courtney, Courtney, my darling . . . my dearest . . ."

Clint was crushing her to him and she was clinging, clinging.

". . . sheriff . . . posse . . . red devils," men were muttering. Then, "But we'll have to wait."

Courtney rallied. *Wait? Wait for what?* "Morning," somebody said.

CHAPTER 40
Reality of a Dream

❦

Did she sleep? Courtney was sure she did not. Although too weak to resist when Clint unlaced her shoes and placed her on the bed, stroking her feverish brow until he thought she had dozed, her mind was alert as assorted persons—some recognizable, others, strangers—moved in and out of the saffron shadows of her vision.

How many knew that the Mansion was all but deserted, that Blessing and Yada were with Cara? Indians, Cara had said, but in her agonized state of mind, who could be sure? *Think, Courtney, think ... it is important that you review today's* (or was it yesterday's?) *circumstances and any other suspects that came before.* Why, oh why would anyone take her darling? What motive— unless Cara was right, that it was a case of mistaken identity? Even so, why, *why*, WHY?

She reentered the dingy cafe where she, Efraim, and Roberta had eaten. The waiter looked different, pot-bellied, a greasy apron pulled tight over a bloated belly. And how had she failed to see the bar before? The man had to be shocked at the sight of an unescorted lady entering a saloon, going boldly to the bar. But must he yank at his walrus moustache? And why was he motioning with a wink to the gaping, snickering men gathered around a sticky, wet bar that reeked of stale alcohol? "You wan' sumpin', *señorita*—yes?"

"Señora!" Courtney corrected with all the bravado she could muster. "Yes, I am looking for a baby—"

The snickers became guffaws. "A baby in here? Lady, you gotta be crazy. All we got's rotgut," the pig-eyed, near-shoulderless man bellowed, pouring the contents of his glass on the floor. "But I saw one ridin' on back of a pestle-tail mule—tryin' t'outrun Injuns. Now, iffen you want, you 'n me could chase 'em. Come t'think on it, there's other things we got t'offer she-patrons here—eh, men?"

Sickened, Courtney stumbled from the place, aware that the woman staring from the upstairs window across the street was watching. Her face was familiar—oh yes, the saleslady. What had she revealed to the woman? Courtney wondered. But wondering was cut short by the sound of footsteps behind her. She whirled to face her stalker. Dressed in black that set him apart like an undertaker, the man was hard to see in the darkness. She was unable to distinguish the facial features but could see the long talons serving for hands reaching, beckoning. . . . Death? Run, she must run—outrun the creature, outwit him—for surrender would mean that he had laid claim on both her and her baby.

The darkness parted briefly. Someone had lighted a lamp and, in the pool of light spilling on the ground, the face of the man she collided with was clearly visible. Something about him was familiar. Where had she seen the yellow-green, heavy-lidded eyes that could belong only to a reptile? Was the creature truly a man—or evil itself? The eyes narrowed even more, then widened into a blank stare that revealed a terminal sickness in the heart and brain, if such he possessed. No, she had never seen him before—but why did the feeling persist that he was no stranger at all? Oh, the voice! It was the voice she recognized.

"Mrs. Desmond!" Pale lips drew into a thin line that could never pass as a smile. The resemblance to a reptile was not confined to the squinting eyes. Any moment a forked tongue would reach out and take its prey. "You have looked in the grove, I suppose? Oh, that's right, the real problem's solved, ain't it now? Fire purifies—even those subhuman bein's callin' theirselves red men know that. Of course, my job's to help people work their way out of this purgatorial town—even ladies like you who come at your own risk. Easy for you to get yourself scalped. What if I wuz to tell you I know who kidnapped that kid—what camp they got her in? You look healthy as a colt, but colts is helpless away from the mare. Lean on me—"

A pain had lanced Courtney's heart. The world was a carousel spinning out of orbit. Nothing seemed to matter. And yet it must. She must stop this carousel, get off... *Leap, Courtney... Run!*

Panting, she escaped the grip on her arm and ran with her eyes closed, aware only of a foul, acrid taste in her dry mouth and the inability to breathe. Why not let this blanket of darkness wrap around her, blotting out the dark? Already it was changing, becoming a wash of casket-lined gray. It would be so easy—but what was that? The distinct cry of a baby. Not just any baby. *Hers!* Mothers know their own, just as the Good Shepherd knows His sheep. *Blessing!*

The silver-studded sky was painted with shadows. She had reached the woods. Only then did she dare stop. And listen. At first, all she could hear was the sound of her own breathing. And then footsteps. There was no fear, just a flood of relief. Swift Arrow had come.

"Come," he whispered. "Very old and very wise squaw has baby. No harm will come. You will believe only that which you see, for you do not as yet know things as did our Rose Wind. Come. Old Squaw help—"

"But you have cautioned me to stay away—saying the Indians would take your life, call you a traitor. Do we dare?"

"It is the only way. We are near—"

* * *

"Old Squaw, you befriended our Rose Wind, took her to your breast when her own would not. Now, you must befriend another who befriended her."

The old woman let drop the tanned hide covering her body, massaged her joints, and squatted on a low stool, blinking in the glow of a candle Swift Arrow had lighted. "Ah yes, many moons ago I, too, was befriended—never wanting to return to my people, having built memories here. Yesterday is gone. But what is it you seek, little one? You are pale and your eyes say sad things. Medicine man—"

"No, no!" Courtney protested weakly, feeling somehow that she must record each word in her memory—even the sour smell of the woman's old flesh, the sagging, leathery skin, offset by a bone structure which spoke of great beauty in another age. "It is my child I seek."

Old Squaw began to babble in a way that reminded Courtney of Donolar—things that made no difference to cover things that did. The candle flickered and went out. "You must go. Dying fire is signal of great sorrow. Go—it is not your child I have here."

Courtney lifted an arm in which the bones seemed to have melted, feeling for the withered hand in the dark. But it was as if she were alone in the tent-like structure. "Please," she whispered. "Please—oh, do not go. You *do* have a child, dark and beautiful."

"Black sorrow come if you do not go. It was her child."

"Rose Wind—I know, I know—but, oh please, you have the wrong child!"

* * *

A strangeness had come over the world. The air was fresh and for a moment the earth felt newly created, a place where one could breathe. The commotion outside seemed out of place. And then reality came back with a rush. Dawn was breaking and search parties were amassing. The sheriff would take one group...Clint another...and Efraim...Brother Jim...Dr. Freeman ...somebody called "Cheyenne" Wills, a wagon master...and all the valley folk—miners, farmers, sheep raisers, united in time of trouble...but—but *Isaac Jacobson*? He must not be here. Courtney must tell Clint what she knew—the dream that was a revelation.

And then she sank back onto the bed, little beads of perspiration forming on the flattened plane of her stomach. What did she have to tell him? Nothing that he would understand. He had been sweet and tolerant of Rose Wind's knowing things. Courtney could expect no more for herself. She only knew she must find Swift Arrow.

"Filthy vermin," somebody was saying. "Murderin' renegades"..."or could be them Injuns jumpin' outa th' graves—cain't be sure...." Firearms, they said. Outraged and all good shots—Courtney shuddered, then hardened her heart. Anybody who would steal an innocent child deserved what he got. *No, Lord, forgive me—I—I don't mean that....*

"No violence, men!" Brother Jim was ordering the militia. That could have its funny side—only nobody could laugh. "Let me at 'em. Me and my iron fists can cast out devils!"

Clint entered as Courtney was getting dressed. "Lie down, young lady!" Gently he tried to steer her to the bed. Wordlessly, she resisted, even when he whispered "darling" over and over as if the words were torn like ragged little scraps from a bolt of cloth. Courtney shook her head. Bits and pieces were coming together like a mosaic, even though the artist had yet to recognize his own design. She must find Swift Arrow.

"I have explained to the children," Clint whispered, "and now the men are calling me. Oh, I love you, *love you*—we *will* find our baby."

"No," she said, her voice flat and without inflection, "you will not."

* * *

Swift Arrow found her as she had known he would if she waited beside the creek in the ferny dell. Terrified, the youth panted out a story of pandemonium among the tribes. But, sadly, "No, baby is not there."

CHAPTER 41
Waiting—for Disaster

❦

Courtney had returned to resume her duties at the Mansion. Heartsick. Weary. And all prayed out. Back and forth she paced over the Brussels carpet with Mandy wringing her white-palmed hands and crying out, "Po' baby" and Mrs. Rueben, equally grieved, saying the lady of the house was wearing a path on the rug, *tsk, tsk.*

One day passed. Two. Three. Then Courtney lost count. Trying to carry on normally in front of the children was more than she could manage. And not knowing the fate of little Blessing was more than she could bear. Cara and Roberta were no help. Cara beat her chest in remorse, weeping with guilt and anguish one day, and told of John's deteriorating state of mind at being unable to help the next. Roberta, on the other hand, suffered paranoia. Yada was sure to be stolen. It was only a matter of when. She alternated lighting all lamps for protection against the kidnappers one day and huddling in darkness to hide her whereabouts the next. They were going to move, she said—go as far away from this place as travel allowed. Start over. Under an assumed name. Build a small cabin. And live in anonymous peace.

"Peace!" Courtney had had all she could bear. "You mean isolation! That is no solution. We have to help—if you can think of my baby instead of yourself!"

"You mean—you are going to join the men?"

"It was you who said we were equal! Yes, I am going!"

Roberta shrank back like an animal that has been struck without knowing why. "Where?" she whispered.

struck without knowing why. "Where?" she whispered. "To find my baby!"

* * *

The men had thundered away in all directions. A little fog had risen from the river and the riders looked like ghosts floating inside it. Maybe they were. . . . How many would return? Emotions were high. Too high for them to listen to a woman who admitted herself to behaving as if under some strange spell. Who could expect a mother whose baby was stolen away by the Indians to be rational? Nope, it was a man-sized job. They'd find the culprits, and why bother with a trial? Indians had no respect for it, didn't understand it, and didn't want to— the heathens!

Courtney forced herself to ignore some of the talk. They all meant well. In fact, some—never having had an opportunity to take part in frontier drama—were downright boastful. She could depend on Clint and Efraim to be just in any situation. And between Brother Jim—in spite of his intolerance of the evildoers and fist-shaking at the Evil One who beguiled them—and the sheriff's men, a means of punishment could be worked out that stayed within God's laws.

Even so, Courtney felt no reassurance. Something was bothering her. Something that she was unable to pin down. A presence of something or somebody alien, out of place among the searchers. And a whisper as wispy as the river's dissipating fog that they were looking in the wrong place for the wrong people. Something would have to turn them in another direction or her black-haired, cooing Blessing was lost to her and Clint forever—like Rose Wind. Or worse . . .

And something did happen. Not what she would have expected or even asked for had she been able to pray. Oh no! Something so terrible that it seemed God could never have had a hand in it.

A ransom note!

Courtney had on riding clothes—high-top boots beneath a long riding skirt over dark trousers. Donolar had Peaches saddled and waiting. Dear Donolar. The boy had scarcely spoken since the tragedy, but how would she have managed without his caring for the twins?

The November sun was growing more reluctant to climb the eastern mountains but had sent warning flares of pink across the pillows of clouds heaped along the passes. Swift Arrow's hair, light for his Indian heritage, appeared pink as his head rose unexpectedly from behind a clump of laurel. Glancing furtively over his shoulder, he waved a piece of paper at Courtney, causing the little mare to snort and raise her front feet upright. Courtney soothed her and took the paper.

Then with heart throbbing painfully, she read the crudely lettered note. Money. Money for her child's life. More money than the bankers would keep in their vaults. *If you want to see your child alive.*

The words rang out like a cannon. She was too stunned to speak. She had faced everything but the baby's death. *Oh, Clint. . . .*

But Clint was not here. "Where did this come from?" she gasped.

The frightened youth could only shake his head. And then she saw the gashes and bruises. The boy had been beaten unmercifully.

"Oh, Swift Arrow—I'm sorry—"

The boy stood erect, chin lifted proudly. "Swift Arrow brave—no hurt. Swift Arrow help, come!" Courtney mounted without hesitation and prepared to gallop behind him. But he hesitated, then said, "Indians not want money—want food. White man want money, and yes, he will kill. No time for talk—" and, like the river fog, he was gone.

Where were they heading? And for what purpose? There should be money in her saddlebags if she hoped to negotiate with this killer. There was a little at the Mansion. Not much. But enough maybe to stall this madman, make him listen to promises, until she could get more help. Hindsight. She would have to trust Swift Arrow— see him as an angel-in-the-flesh the Lord had sent. An angel with wings on his feet. For Peaches, ears back, could scarcely keep up with him in the heavy brush on an unfamiliar trail.

Unfamiliar? Yes, but with a striking resemblance to another which she had never seen either. Courtney shook her head to clear it. She was, she *had* to be, living out a dream. . . .

Courtney did not see the hut improvised from fir branches anchored between the protective roots of a button-willow until Swift Arrow stopped in the eerie green light of the heavily wooded area. "Grandmother Old, I have brought her to you. May we enter your hiding place?"

The drooping branches parted with the help of two dark hands, twisted with age. Green shadows fell across the crinkled crepe of the old woman's face, half hidden by a heavy veil of hair.

"Black sorrow follow child born in shame. High Chieftain not pleased. Bring anger of gods. Child must be destroyed."

Courtney stared at the green ghost, a cold creeping over her to tighten around her heart. "But the child is not Indian," Courtney whispered through lips now stiffened with cold. "She is mine—ours."

The woman squatted and, closing her eyes, began rocking back and forth as if reliving an agony too great for words. "My Rose Wind not Indian, too . . . but Grandmother Old keep her safe under wing of night . . . my child die taking baby with her and I thought to me: What

harm? And now my Rose Wind die, too... taking secret ... but leaving child because gods are angry ... send
great sickness to punish me. I must sacrifice and destroy
child—"

Courtney felt the very blood in her veins freeze. "No,
no!" She dropped to her knees, grasping the old squaw's
legs in pleading, but feeling them go rigid with fear.
Dropping her hands helplessly, she whispered, "Oh, have
mercy! You are kind. You have loved and cared for a
child—please, I beg you, give mine to me!"

Tears were streaming from her eyes, feeling hot to her
cold face. And to her surprise, the old Indian wiped
them away with a rough thumb.

"Child not here—yet. Wisdom is mine. Like my little
singing bird, I know things. I will know if child belong to
stranger when white man bring."

White man!

Courtney was about to cry out in horror when the
scene shifted so quickly it might have been a dream. The
walls of the hut went back to being willow branches,
hiding their secret. And Swift Arrow was gone. Peaches'
ears had gone up as if alerted to a new danger. And then
the air was filled with wild screams.

Donolar! Babbling as if in an unknown tongue instead
of using his usual signal, the soft whistle of a mountain
quail. She grabbed him and found the thin body wet
with perspiration through the shredded garments, rent
by the thorn thickets through which he had come.

"Get hold of yourself, darling—what is it, *what is it?*"

She caught the one word *fire*, saw a gnarled hand
reach through the branches in a sort of pact, motioning
her to duties beyond the moment. And, hardly aware of
what she was doing, Courtney helped her brother up
behind her. Moments later, they were swallowed up by a
cloud of smoke. Nobody needed tell her. Somehow she
knew. The Mansion was burning and disaster after disaster lay ahead.

CHAPTER 42
The Lost, the Found,
the Lost

❦

What time was it, anyway? The sun, a dim outline like the moon in total eclipse, squinted through an ugly glow that had nothing to do with the turning leaves. Black smoke, like that from a laboring train's smokestack, billowed from the west only to be tossed to the east. How long had the wind been blowing? It seemed to come from the four corners of the earth, polarizing near where the Mansion stood. Through it forked tongues of flame licked at the dry leaves and sent them swirling like red shooting stars all directions, threatening the entire valley, transforming it into an inferno. Courtney realized then that a ring of fire had formed to rage gleefully around Mansion-in-the-Wild.

"Clint!" Courtney tried to scream only to choke on a mouthful of smoke. Clint, her wonderful Clint, whom she had neglected—thinking only of her own torment—was nowhere to be seen among the hooded men who were vainly trying to enter the doors of the Mansion. *Clint will be among them ... and Efraim ... and, oh dear God, Cousin Bella ... and MY BABIES!*

Someone was hoisting a ladder to Cousin Bella's window. Oh no, they must not climb that. The window, even should they reach it, was barred. And reach it they never would for flames were licking at the ladder's top rung and hungrily devouring the sides. Again she tried to scream, but her voice echoed as if she were in an empty tomb. The heat was unbearable. Quickly, she ripped off her overskirt and covered her head—racing ahead, not sure of what she had in mind.

Immediately, a restraining hand jerked her back roughly. *Clint!* He was pointing to where a large group congregated beyond the fiery circle and gave her a shove. Mandy, her groanings too deep for description, folded Courtney to her heaving bosom.

"Miz Bella—Miz Bella—may de Lawd haf mercy on my soul ..."

"The children," Courtney, beside herself with shock, screamed above the awful roar. "Jordan, Jonda, Little Kenney? *Mandy!*"

The inhuman utterings continued, but somehow Mandy managed to hear and reply. "Dey's in de well— Donolar let 'em down 'fore de Injuns come screamin' and throwin' fiery torches—oh, Miz Bella—"

"Mandy, Mandy, *which* well?"

But Mandy, in her incomparable grief, was stricken dumb. Her dark eyes rolling backwards, she collapsed, just as a frenzied scream went up from the horrified spectators. John Laughten, a wet quilt wrapped around his body and face, was pushing through the flames in his wheelchair. Cara cried out in anguish, but in vain. A sudden burst of energy had coursed through the wasted body and, rolling the wheels faster than the other men could run, he entered the door—

Just as there was a terrible explosion. And the building collapsed.

Courtney was never able to piece together what happened after that. People, she remembered, gathered around Cara in an effort to offer words of comfort. But Cara, who had been destroyed with guilt over the stealing of Courtney and Clint's baby, now lifted her cinder-blackened face in a strange pride—something ethereal in her expression. Bravely, she gathered her flock close without tears.

"You child'run kin be proud uv yore papa. He proved to hisself he wasn't no no-good man—'n th' Good Book sez dyin' fer each other's th' greatest love uv all."

* * *

Courtney looked around her numbly, trying to deny the scene, stuff it into the unconscious and make believe it never happened. But this is dangerous. Grief and pain have a way of sneaking back. Ignored, they are violent and filled with vengeance. The canker had begun.

How did it all happen? And WHY?

She must have asked the first question aloud. Fragmented answers came from all directions. The men met somewhere . . . sad, sad, but they had failed to find the baby . . . and they saw the savage creatures hurtling from the woods and heard their bloodcurdling war cries . . . lancing the darkness with their torches.

Darkness? Indians did not attack at night, something buried deep in Courtney's heart wanted to protest. Instead, she listened in horrible fascination, the way one reads a history book. Her heart could not accept that all she knew and loved was swept away.

How many? Who knew? The cowards fled when Roberta fired the old musket into the air—Roberta? Yes, Mrs. Glamora herself. Oh, she was a brave one all right. A body got the feeling that if the leader hadn't given the high sign after setting fire to the Mansion, that little lady they had thought so gentle and shy would have separated the chief's skull from his shoulders. The renegades had scattered by the time the men made it home, but the fire-arrows had down their job. The only target was the Mansion, far as they knew, but the devil winds spread the fire . . . yes, it ricocheted like a stone skipping across the creek—burned the Laughtens' out-buildings and completely destroyed the two cabins Miss Arabella, God rest her soul, had so kindly lent to the newcomers from the East. No ma'am, no survivors.

Here the half-crazed mourners had to stop and sob uncontrollably in unison, their burden being too much to bear. Coldly, her heart having turned to stone, Courtney prepared her next question.

"How many perished?" she asked as any spectator might.

"Miz Bella," somebody sobbed, " 'n now John Laughten—oh, what's t'come o'them chil'lens and th' widder? Nobody's fer sure jest how many in them cabins—and thar wuz one doctor, not t'mention what's-his-name, th' hawg raiser what raised Cain likewise with neighbors 'bout them beasts a-rootin'—but we're powerful sorry now—saddest thang ever hit th' valley—oh, whar's Brother Jim? We gotta pray—"

An emotion akin to none she had ever known churned within Courtney—a poisoning that coursed through every artery and capillary. A man in a sooty white coat, unmistakably a doctor, was scribbling identifications on shingles that had blown from somebody's roof and laying them atop the victims, swathed in sheets and laid, like mummies, along the sidelines of the confusion. Another doctor worked among the injured. His face, even with its mask of cinders, was vaguely familiar. Oh yes, the doctor who once—a thousand years ago—had told her that she would be unable to bear a child—

Child! Where were her children in all this carnage? Still numb, but driven by instinct, she shouldered her way toward the smoldering acreage of fiery ruins which tried to die down only to be fanned into flames again by the winds to become a roaring furnace. Which of the wells? And where were Clint . . . Efraim . . . *Donolar*? Donolar would know.

It was Roberta, sobbing—her eyes ringed in red from the smoke—who restrained her, read her mind. "They are safe, darling—*all* of them. Donolar, love his soul, remembered his history—the story of a family's lowering themselves into an abandoned well. He is bringing them up now—all of them, yes, even my Yada. I let go because I had to. We never expected to live through it—*Courtney, are you listening?* Oh, my darling, I am sorry... the fire... Cousin Bella... the others—and that your darling baby is still missing. Oh, Court—"

But Courtney had pulled away and was running wildly toward the old well which had caved in and was boarded over years ago. And there, like mud balls, were her children talking excitedly then running toward her in childish abandon that recognized no tragedy once they were united with their parents. She scooped the three of them up with superhuman strength in an embrace expressing all her pent-up emotions, causing them to squeal with delight.

"Oh, thank God you are safe! Thank God for *children!*"

"We were very good," Jordan said stoutly. "We did not make a sound no matter what happened."

"Well, we whispered—huh, Jordan? Whispered real quiet," Jonda added.

"Just loud enough for God to hear," her twin brother answered.

It was Little Kenney's turn. "I hungry," he said.

* * *

Somebody brought coffee. Courtney drank the steaming amber gratefully, hardly feeling the scalding in her throat. Somebody else brought her a shingle. In the red glow of the coals that once were Mansion-in-the-Wild, she read the names scribbled with a piece of charcoal. Names of those for whose deaths she was indirectly responsible. To be added to the others she had allowed to die...Doc George...Rose Wind...and undoubtedly, there would be others.

She, the mistress of Mansion-in-the-Wild, had been negligent. Why, then, was she unable to weep? The historical house was gone. She would take its place, shackle herself to the painful past. Did she deserve so severe a punishment when she had not wanted the responsibility? Forget, others would tell her—only the pain went too deep, lodging in her heart. The wound was too severe to be healed—unless—

Yes, that was it. Unless there was justice. *Justice*.

"We have to find them—punish—make them pay," she muttered to nobody in particular.

"Nobody ever gets even in the pain game, my darling." The words were Clint's. *Oh, Clint!* She fell into his arms. "What's done is done—there is no getting even with pain. It is futile—"

His voice broke. She must try to realize how he had suffered—was suffering. And she had been partially responsible for that, too. Amid all this, Clint had no idea where she was—or if she was alive. She had left no note, just recorded it in her journal. Now it, too, was ashes— dead along with Cousin Bella, John Laughten, and the others.

But sympathy, even for Clint, seemed to have died, too. The hurts and self-doubts had gone on too long to avoid a backlash. She had failed to forgive herself. How could she forgive others—the guilty ones? Or sympathize with the innocent? Once the future had lain in her hands.

"We will erect headstones," she said dully and could have added "*in memory of my failures*." "But first comes justice—we *have* to find them, those who committed this heinous crime—"

That is when somebody quoted: "Vengeance is mine, saith the Lord."

Oh, how blind they were! Not vengeance. *Justice!*

Clint was talking, telling her where he was sending the children before resuming the search for their baby. But Courtney did not hear. She was only dimly aware when Efraim brought someone with him, embraced her, and whispered, "Oh, little sister, my darling, my darling, we have lost the only mother we ever knew. We will never forget, but forgive we must—and forgiving is love's toughest assignment. We will find them—look, we have something here already. Doctor—"

Doctor? Courtney disengaged herself and stood face to face with Dr. Freeman. "I wanted you to know, my dear," he said softly, "that one of the attackers lies among the dead," his head tilted to the heartbreaking line of those who had not survived, "was shot. He was not Indian."

Not Indian. Then it was possible that the whole thing was a hoax. That the kidnappers, too, were subhuman whites? *Why* they would have taken her baby as a helpless pawn in their filthy game—or what prize the winner was to receive—was unimportant. Somebody could have bribed the old squaw, promising her food and Rose Wind's baby, if she would participate in the dangerous game.

"Find Clint, Efraim! We have to go—*now!* Cousin Bella would want it that way—*please*—"

"Clint is saddling a fresh horse, but you are staying—"

"Oh no I'm not! I am the only one who knows—come on, we have no time to spare." She shuddered. "We will make it right for Cousin Bella."

"Your sister is right," the doctor said in his usual low voice. "I, too, will join you. I am an anthropologist and will recognize—"

Perhaps there was more talk. Courtney failed to recall. It seemed to her that no time elapsed before she, Clint, Efraim, and Dr. Freeman were heading, according to her directions, into the deep woods where she had seen the old squaw. In a low voice, Courtney related the events that led her here with a calm that surprised her. Probably because she was able to feel nothing but white-hot anger—so akin to hatred that it frightened her. But that, too, must be dealt with later.

For now, she was slowing Peaches and motioning the men to stop. "Be careful—oh, be careful," she whispered. "Whoever he is—or they are—will be crazed with hatred else this sordid thing would never have happened." Squaring her shoulders and inhaling deeply, she whispered, "I must go alone."

"No!" It was Dr. Freeman who objected with more emotion than she would have supposed him capable of. And with that, he forged ahead on foot. In a sense, he was the logical one. Nothing the kind man had done would put him in jeopardy, but the rest of them were involved. On the other hand, it was she who had received the ransom note. Yes, it was she who must go first. The men would try to stop her, but—

"Stand in the shadows," she ordered. And, before the men could object, she had shoved past like a female animal whose young is threatened. Holding her breath, she parted the low-hanging branches of the willow. Then, cautiously, she pushed aside the fir boughs serving as a door. And there sat the old squaw, a baby cradled to her bosom.

Every fiber of her being urged Courtney to spring forward and snatch the child from the withered arms. But instinct held her back. Sensing rather than seeing, she knew there was another presence in the green gloom. The baby whimpered, telling Courtney what she already knew. It was Blessing! One chubby fist reached out—

But something else moved at the same time. Her eyes had grown accustomed to the dark and, with a bit of imagination, she could make out the form of a man— his back to her—standing against the trunk of the ancient willow. His body was bare except for a narrow loincloth circling his middle and curving between his thighs. His dark, tangled hair almost reached his bare buttocks. Careful. She must be very, very careful. Oh, for an inspired tactic! But time was against it.

A wild "Ay-*eee*!" split the world in half and a slender form sprang out of the dark. Swift Arrow! And before Courtney could react, the young brave had grasped the long hair of the other man and jerked.

To her horror, the long tresses fell to the ground and, for a terrifying moment, she was sure he was scalped. As Samson lost physical prowess when his locks were shorn, the man in the shadows apparently lost the power of his senses. With a curse of rage, he whirled and fired, missing Swift Arrow who had jumped astride his back. And on the floor lay a *wig*!

But the shot, fired aimlessly, had struck another victim. Dr. Freeman, who had never harmed anybody, lay prostrate, his face deathly white, blood flowing from his limp body in the area of his heart.

Shock, nature's way of protecting the human mind, pulled a curtain over the awful reality. Someday, Courtney knew, she would awaken and feel something which for now was beyond her grasp. At present, she could only add another death to her conscience. How could God forgive her?

Somewhere out of the impersonal darkness there came a confusion of sounds. Hoofbeats. Voices. And Donolar's whistle. Help was on the way. Of course. Donolar would have watched and reported.

They circled the scene and had a full view of the anonymous man attempting to flip the Indian boy from his back. The man turned, making the mistake of his life. In an effort to pick up the disguising wig, he dropped his gun. And Brother Jim made a seven-league leap to recover it.

"Well, I'll be—*Isaac Jacobson*, the solid citizen, the keeper of the law, the iconoclast whose holiness created a holocaust!"

Courtney sprang forward and hungrily grabbed Blessing, holding her so hard that the baby cried out. Her cry brought the frightened woman Swift Arrow had called Grandmother Old to her feet, a strange emotion wrinkling the weathered face even more. It was kindness Courtney saw in the watery eyes. She had been good to the baby.

Impetuously, Courtney touched the gnarled hand. "She *is* my child—"

The woman nodded. "Not child of sorrow. But I no would hurt child—or that of Rose Wind, who was of royal blood—not Indian—"

"I know, I know. Now, go to your people—and tell them that we will get food to you. Swift Arrow is a true friend of us all."

The woman, obviously grateful that she was to receive no punishment, turned to flee. Then she stopped and, face filled with fear, pointed to Isaac Jacobson. "More gun," she whispered.

Brother Jim had seen, too. He saw, also, the banker's snake eyes turn toward the limb on which the firearm was propped.

"Touch it and you're a goner!" Brother Jim bellowed. He fingered and leveled the gun he had recovered when Jacobson dropped it. "Get them money-grabbin' hands in the air—*higher*! You're comin' with us. One false move and I'll blast you right where your britches belong, sendin' you to the sweatbox the Almighty's got waiting!"

Isaac Jacobson cowered. "Higher!" Brother Jim bellowed again. Up went the shaking hands another three inches. "You—you don't understand—she—it was a matter of honor—family name—"

The blubbering made no sense. None of this whole crazy thing did. And yet, Courtney's rage formed a red halo about the kidnapper's face. She ran at him, hands extended like claws as if to tear him to shreds. "You could hang for this, you, you *slime*! But that would be too easy—"

Clint grabbed her, held her securely. "It's all right, darling. The law is here. Give me the baby—is she all right?"

Gently he was steering her away as she handed the gurgling bundle to her husband. "The squaw took care— she and Swift Arrow. There were no other Indians involved." Fiercely, she wrenched free and resumed the attack. "There never *was* any Indian trouble, was there? It was you—you and your other demons. You would have killed Rose Wind, Swift Arrow, and Grandmother Old. Of course," she spoke slowly, the revealing light of truth filling her being, "your partner in crime took the wrong baby, the other being the son of your *niece*! She was Jewish—married in the eyes of God to her own kind, the father of her child—*and you killed him!*"

Two officers were moving forward, handcuffs in hand. "There's a matter of extortion as well as kidnapping and murder," one said.

"I only wanted what was my own—my blood relative—and money that was rightfully mine until the unfair Lovelace will—" whined Jacobson.

The second officer joined the first. But Brother Jim moved between them. "Leave him be, kind sirs, let the lady finish, I beg. *Higher*, Jacobson, you yellow-bellied sapsucker!"

Clint and Efraim were moving toward Courtney after handing a cooing Blessing to Donolar. From the corner of her eye, Courtney saw the doctor leaning over Dr. Freeman, shaking his head. And again the red curtain closed around her. Outdistancing her husband and brother, she stood so close to Isaac Jacobson she could feel his foul breath on her face.

"I am surprised," she said, each word sheeted in ice, "that you forgot your manners. I would have expected you to say, 'Why, if it isn't Mrs. Desmond!' I would like to hear those words again."

"I—I—" The man cringed, his insufferable arrogance gone.

"Say it!" Brother Jim ordered in a voice that set the willow leaves trembling. "It's up to you whether you go out with a whimper or a blast. *Say it, you coward!*"

"Why, if—it—isn't Mrs. Desmond," he muttered in shame, as the men of the law cuffed him and dragged the near-naked body to the horse that was waiting. But Courtney could feel no remorse. No pity. Just a certain satisfaction that she had forced him to crawl. She hoped Rose Wind knew. . . .

"Wrap the blanket around the baby's face, please, Donolar," she said calmly. "I must say *good-bye* to a loyal friend."

Courtney leaned down to touch Dr. Freeman. "He's breathing," the doctor smiled. It was then that she collapsed in her husband's arms. . . .

CHAPTER 43
As We Forgive

🍂

Tomorrow dedication of the new church would take place in the first public gathering since disease and lawlessness had changed the lifestyle of the valley. Until now, thought of celebration in face of the fiery catastrophe that changed the course of history was a mockery. To Courtney it would have been like receiving a black valentine.

At first, there was chaos and, although the coals of fury and guilt—in alternating currents—lay smoldering within, outwardly she functioned. There was the business of sifting through the ashes, comforting others, and living life by the day. She was unable to see beyond that for now. How Donolar's sacred "Innisfree" had come through safely (while the fire had destroyed the more-distant Rambling Gate) was a miracle. The moat surrounding it, perhaps—or the fanning of the butterflies' wings (his version, which the children loved). Now the immaculate little cabin served as temporary quarters for the twins and the older Laughten children. Cara welcomed company. Courtney and Clint, Roberta and Efraim, with their babies, moved in until other arrangements could be made.

"Iffen you'd be kind enough, Mr. Clint, t'fix a shelf fer displayin' Doc George's fiddle—it would make my John mighty happy knowin' th' bossman hisself done it—" Cara's voice quivered, but she held her head high. Her husband had done a noble deed and his sacrifice had

served to purge his widow of remorse for her "negli-
gence." His self-abasement was the balm of penance for
them both.

Neighbors brought food and comfort. Efraim and
Roberta made a trip to town to shop for a few pieces of
wearing apparel and returned with enough for all to be
clothed—but, more importantly, the news that Isaac
Jacobson and his accessories to crime had received a
speedy trial by a local jury and were now to be tried for
further sentencing by the government. Under cover of
darkness, the militia escorted the scalawags out of town
as talk of a lynching filled the saloons.

"It would serve them right," Courtney said through
clenched teeth. Hardly aware that she had spoken, she
was remembering the neighbors' well-meant attempts
to bring comfort, the pity that coated every word. "Don't
pity *me*—pity *them*," she had said. Justice, blindfolded
and without partiality, had been served. Why, then,
could she feel no release? It was as if she, not they, were
the prisoner. Oh, to be free again—

"Courtney, *yoo-hoo!*" She realized then that Clint was
speaking to her, had been for some time. It was good to
hear a slightly teasing lilt in his voice again, although she
was unable to respond to it.

"Let's go for a walk," Clint said. "We need to check on
Mandy and Mrs. Rueben. Mrs. Ebberlee is thinking of
extending her boardinghouse and may have work for
them—that's where Miss Lizzie is staying, you know—"

"But fer goo'ness sake don't tell th' young'uns. They'd
go pesterin'—oh, did y'all know Brother Jim wuz stayin'
thereabouts, too?" Cara asked.

The conversation hardly registered, but Courtney welcomed the walk. And, thank goodness, the path led the
opposite direction of the cemetery. She was not ready to
look upon the new mounds again. It was too soon for
scar tissue to form over the wounds in her heart.

The service had been simple. Simple and in the best of taste. A manner which would have been pleasing to all those who now slept in the little country churchyard. Here, Brother Jim had said in a quiet, subdued tone (his own heart aching), there was weeping for these dear ones were much loved. But over *there* angels were singing 'round the throne. Heaven overflowed with songs of praise. Once again love had conquered, the lost had been found. And from that lofty place of heavenly joy came back the echo for earth below—making them one family now and forevermore. "We have John's word for it," he ended, "as he quoted the Master: 'I ascend unto My Father and your Father; and to My God and your God.' He lives—and they live—let us be comforted." Dear, dear Brother Jim. What would he do now?

How still the world was. So still that their footsteps echoed on the grasses which, like those she loved so much, had completed their work. But the air was sweet with pine and cedar, their eternal green begging to be an inspiration. Their fragrance sparked a memory. Soon it would be Christmas, a time of joy. A sob caught in her throat.

"Let's open up and talk about it, darling. We hurt—all of us."

"I know," Courtney said, taking the hand Clint offered. "I just have no idea where to begin—my transgressions are too many."

"You are not on trial, Courtney darling. I refuse to let you go on torturing yourself. It began with your becoming mistress of Mansion-in-the-Wild—and you have felt responsible for everything that took place within those walls. Am I right?"

Courtney nodded. "I caused Doc George's death—let in the germ—"

"Keep walking—you need it. And breathe deeply—good girl. Would it help to know that the doctor who was such a help at the fire had attended Doc George—and that he had outlived his life expectancy? There was a hole in his heart the size of a quarter. He knew and chose to keep going, the way we all must—and in so doing left a legacy more precious than the shares for Efraim. A case history which very well may lead to a breakthrough in treatments of such cases. Someday there will be medications—maybe even repair—"

"How does one repair a heart?" Courtney's voice was sad.

"With the help of brave men like him, some kind of surgical miracle such as they did on my eyes may come. But repairing a *broken* heart...oh, would to God that I knew! You see, Courtney, I am living with guilt, too! I— I—let Aunt Bella die—"

"Oh Clint, no! No, *no*, NO!" Courtney stopped in horror. She had let her husband suffer loss of their baby alone—and now this! Cold which no blizzard could spawn held her in its icy fingers. Even the scene changed from somber November to winter—beautiful, but treacherous. The river stood motionless, a white ribbon which wound back into the dark woods. How like her heart. She grabbed at the warm reality of him to restore her sanity.

And there, clasped in his arms, Courtney listened to her husband's tortured story. Crazed with fear for her safety, faced by the awful possibility that their baby had been harmed, and exhausted by the futility of endless searching, he had smelled smoke and headed home alone. Alone to find hysterical women attempting to dash water on the blazing Mansion. The children could be inside...and certainly his aunt...and so he had covered his head with a wet blanket and taken the stairs three at a time. Only to find Arabella Lovelace's door locked from the inside. He called. He pounded. He tried to break down the door which, like other doors throughout the house, was massive. Once Clint thought he heard a call for help. Desperately, he tried harder. And then the words he would never forget: "Go back to safety—back to your family, your pride and joy—and mine. Respect my wishes—let me go with the Mansion—to—be—with my George Washington . . ." A flaming beam had fallen against the door then and Clint, knowing he had failed, stumbled down the stairway just as it caved in. And then the whole upstairs collapsed and he had to be dragged from the scene by the other men who had arrived.

"But you tried, darling. You did all that was humanly possible."

"Did I? John Laughten went in after that—" Clint, holding her tighter, broke into the kind of dry sobs that break one's heart because they come from a man who gives comfort instead of seeking it.

"Darling, darling," Courtney soothed, reaching high to comb his hair with loving fingers. "We must do what Cousin Bella asked. It was her last will and testament—that we go on, raise our family. Ours is the only family she had—Clint, we gave her what she wanted. And now," Courtney raised her chin, wondering where the words were coming from (certainly not herself!), "we must stop heaping ashes on our heads."

*   *   *

The belfry crowning the new church fingered the sky and boasted a bell which could be heard from one of the "twin cities" to the other. And it seemed as if every soul from them both heard and accepted the invitation on the day of dedication. The very ribs of the building appeared to bulge. Ahab, the smithy, and Tony Bronson, proprietor of the Company Store, passed a collection plate with great pomp—while eyeing each hand that reached at the collection plate in a way that encouraged a reputation-making offering and *dis*couraged any sticky fingers from a few "high rollers" they recognized from the pool halls.

The pews had upright backs instead of the benches of yesteryear—and yes, that was an honest-to-goodness stained glass window right above the pulpit. But the center of interest was an organ, full-size and constructed of black walnut. As if that were not distinction enough, Miss Lizzie, the schoolmarm (nothing priggish-like about that fine lady)—who had made the donation—could tickle those ivories until they sang right along with her! And her voice was sweeter than wine—well, all right (after a nudge from their wives), make it honey, the men said. Rumor had it that the reverend was captivated with the musician. Well, a man needed a wife for nudging him, they said good-naturedly. "Jest joshing," the men grinned.

But the "joshing" stopped when the sermon began. Brother Jim's opening question, "Is it well with thee?" was omitted. The bulky man whose physique still looked as if he were "in the pink" for the next boxing bout, was blessed with a surprisingly sensitive nature. He knew the heartbreak that prevailed—and addressed it.

After the prayer of dedication, Brother Jim—his voice choked with emotion—summed up the tragedies and misfortunes which had besieged the valley. Wounds the devil had inflicted and left God to heal. But God was All-faithful. More than up to the job. And, as always, the victor because He and He alone had purchased mankind. He had paid the ransom. Unless, God forbid, mankind refused to be freed by His Son and chose to remain captives living out the years with unforgiving hearts. Forgive hurts slowly, one transgression at a time.

Courtney listened with tight lips, her handkerchief wadded in her lap. Petty annoyances, yes, she could handle with a flair—even a smidge of humor. Certainly, she could be tolerant with those whose ideas differed in philosophy and ways of life. But was she penny-wise and pound-foolish when it came to the bigger injustices? Could even God help her—as Doc George used to phrase it—perform "spiritual surgery," carving away the malignant growth of hate the way doctors removed decayed tissue before it destroyed the patient?

Clint's concerned eyes watched her. Courtney could feel them. It occurred to her, also, that the other women— including Roberta and Cara—were looking to her for leadership as they had so long ago.

And then Brother Jim, who had lost his lifelong friends to the enemy—so unjustly, so cruelly, so senselessly— caught and held her gaze imploringly. *Turn away*, she told herself. And could not.

"Not one of us—*not one*—can pass through this vale of tears without unexplainable pain to the body and the heart. Let's prove to the Deluder we can pray our way out of his sinful net. *Now!*"

In the pin-drop quiet, heads bowed one by one. Strong men and weak men. Protestant and Jew. Red, yellow, black, and white. All seeking forgiveness.

Clint gripped her clenched hands and then, gently— one by one—released her fingers, stroking each to renew the circulation. Courtney felt the warm blood course through them. She closed her eyes—and waited.

"I am unable to pray," she mouthed without voice.

Clint read her wooden lips and pressed his own against her ear. "Tell God, darling. He understands. Tell Him— He knows anyway—"

The words came slowly from her heart, each letting out a vial of poison. *I—cannot—pray—forgive—my— unbelief—*

"Now! See, Satan, you're licked. Your back's to the mat and the count of ten is over! We have ground you with our heel. No squealin' for we're not listenin'! Stop sneakin' back to tempt us into rememberin' what God's forgot! Stop tellin' us we don't deserve to be hurt and our enemies don't deserve forgiveness. We got you there, Satan. The Almighty has told us we deserve to be healed. It won't be easy, but the Great Physician holds the healin' secret in His hand—and you don't know the formula! God will bring us through!"

The *Amens* came then. And the congregation burst into song:

> By and by, when the morning comes,
> With the Saints in Glory,
> We'll be gathered home,
> In that land where Saints never die,
> We'll sing hallelujah,
> Sing hallelujah...by and by...

Courtney raised tearful eyes to meet Clint's, the flow of hurt reversed to pour out silently into the past. For them, morning had come.

Finale
And Backward to the Future
❦

The valley had reason to be proud of what its people accomplished in the next five years. They had hacked their way through a wilderness and, with all the tragedies and heartbreaks—amid seemingly impossible odds—had carved out an empire. They had taken God's extended hand, tackled the job which "couldn't be done," and done it!

With all its rich natural resources, Washington was destined to become one of the richest, if not the wealthiest, state in the expanding Union. And certainly it was among the most beautiful. Where else could a man bring his family, hungry and empty-handed, and (if willing to bend his back, put his hand to the plow, get down on his knees, and yes, "beat sword into plowshares") regroup with neighbors to protect one another and ward off the enemy, rebuild their lives, their homes, their cities, and replenish their larders until their tables and those who sat around them groaned with the plenty of it all? Here they found their Innisfree, their El Dorado, their "piece of heaven on earth." Here—in this corner of the world—where the mountains supported the sky, they had found the fulfillment of a dream, the answer to a prayer. . . .

But, it was always wise to look back before traveling on. For surely the past shaped the future, just as the prophecies of the Old Testament planted the seeds for the New Testament's harvest of love. Not so different, after all, from their planting wheat and civilization. And look back, they did—with pride and praise.

A white-robed January dismissed the old year and welcomed the new following the tragedy at Mansion-in-the-Wild. All in all, people on both sides of the creek dividing the two growing cities were accepting the inevitable merger. Reports had it that a good many eyes were blackened, teeth removed prematurely, and ribs "busted" (along with some friendships). But guns had been put away. Saloons, while still operating, were no longer a battleground, and no man died from "shooting off his mouth." Both towns were what one might loosely call decent. And the church—oh my, what the church had become! In small ways and large, Brother Jim had demonstrated that love was a stronger weapon than violence. Everywhere folks seemed to be reaching out for beauty and light, for dawn after a long, dark night. Even on the reservation the Cayuse, Klikitats, Yakimas, Spokanes, Palouses, and Coeur d'Alenes were smoking the peace pipe with the Nez Perces, Flatheads, Bannocks, and Shoshones. Swift Arrow and Dr. Freeman came and went, carrying food, arranging for educational classes, and distributing Bibles. Eventually, Brother Jim would be welcomed. He was—one year later.

Closer to home, matters were in a state of flux for Efraim and Roberta. The newspaper was flourishing—even though some said a nickel was a trifle high for cheap pulp. Efraim agreed and changed to "white rag"—easier to read and less apt to leave fingers inky. The newspaper was instrumental in helping with the merger undoubtedly since he was at liberty to editorialize, and Roberta managed to insert a bit of politics into the "Women Involved" ladies' page. Even so, voters had to march to the polls no less than four times before the measure passed. Circulation increased when actual campaigning began for the representative to Washington, and the paper began turning a profit. *The Territorial*

Gazette carried stories of the business boom—hardware stores, livery stables, general merchandising, hotels, jewelers, and more—and, of course, carried the flamboyant ads of the braggarts who operated them. And, reading the stories, more newcomers poured in.

One day they would have to select a name for the unified city. Columbia, Twin Cities, and Washington Town were among the suggestions. Added to them were Cabrillo and Gray (for the explorers), as well as Fremont and Vancouver (for military men by those names). And there came one suggestion for Forty-Ninth Parallel, for the historical division back in 1853 between Great Britain and the States.

"What's in a name? A rose by any other name would smell as sweet," Donolar quoted Shakespeare. His great eyes showed no emotion, but there was weeping in his voice. Rose Wind—someday his roses would bloom again for her.

Yes, looking back was painful—in a beautiful sort of way. Courtney and Clint marveled at decisions they had made and how aborted plans had opened new passages. Take Roberta and Efraim...

"Strange," Clint said, shaking his head as he looked out over his shining green fields of wheat which brightened their view—and their viewpoint. "Yes, very strange how Roberta was so bent on building a cabin, 'away from it all,' only to end up having this one constructed so close to Donolar's—"

"Yes," Courtney said slowly as she glanced with pride at the frilly curtains, pots and pans, she had added to make the Glamora house into a temporary home while their own was under construction. "But no stranger, I suppose, than our decision to build—where—well, it will be vastly different though—the cabin we will have and the Mansion—"

Her throat still betrayed her when there was mention of the great, sprawling house that once was "home" to so many. Clint heard and turned the conversation tactfully. "I doubt if they ever occupy this place, as Efraim is sure to win the election—and you know he would go nowhere without Roberta and Yada."

He was right on both counts. Efraim undoubtedly would have won the election thumbs down, but by a strange twist of fate, he was appointed by Governor John McGraw instead. With his input and the will of the Washington populace, the constitution was adopted and ratified. *The Territorial Gazette*, left in the hands of an able staff, published colorful accounts of the ripple in society Representative and Mrs. Efraim Glamora were making in Washington D.C.'s somewhat discriminating social circles.

Brother Jim had formed a fast friendship with one Rabbi Tobias Epstern, who had tutored Rose Wind. The two engaged in many a serious difference that rivaled the famous Lincoln-Douglas debates, but agreed that they were not "a house divided." The rabbi was simply a temple—all right, then, *synagogue*—in need of windows! It was through Tobias that Brother Jim gathered the missing pieces of the puzzle surrounding Rose Wind. It was true that the girl was orphaned. But she was *not* stolen. Her parents left the infant a sizable inheritance, unfortunately with her father's brother, Isaac Jacobson, as guardian. He had betrayed their trust...hidden the child away with the Indians...threatening to deal harshly with the few who knew, should they reveal the secret. Jacobson placed the six-pointed star on the wall as a warning whenever rumblings threatened Rose Wind's finding out the whole truth. How did she know? The rabbi massaged the line around his dark skullcap before admitting that it was through himself. Yes, he had told the child as much as he dared. She needed to know her heritage. The money? Oh, that capable pair of lawyers—God bless them—who had taken the beautiful

Yada to their hearts were handling it with care. The youngest Glamora would have the finest of educations.

The deep friendship deepened. Somehow the valley folk, who had come to accept others (if not their ideas), were not surprised when Rabbi Tobias Epstern performed the ceremoney for Brother Jim's marriage to the "brilliant" Miss Lizzie. After all, the good man was bound to be struck down like Paul one of these days—and then, oh what joy would come to this valley! And the man was "real human," they discovered—didn't seem a whit bothered by some of the guests being tipplers ... take old Jed Higginbotham, the town rabble who'd been smoking corn-silk cigarettes since before he could button his pants (and now was on the "hard stuff"), cussed like a sailor, too, except on Sundays, well, that Jew-preacher wasn't one bit blue-nosed—no sir!

Where would the newlyweds live? Why, likely as not, in the Glamora cabin. Yeah, sure the bossman was at the still-producing mine (when it had a mind to). He was also the wheat farmer, the lumberman ("th' butcher, th' baker, th' can'lestick maker," they called him affectionately), and he and his just-beautiful wife were apt to be doing something else. Just you wait and see. They were destined to keep Miss Arabella's dream alive.

So five years had passed. And now, with their beautiful children tucked in, all four of whom were like wildflowers tamed and domesticated by the most-loving parents in the world (by their own acknowledgment), Courtney and Clint watched a solitary star as if it were their very own in the vault of night's blue sky. "The strangest thoughts are circling in my head, Clint."

"I know, darling—about our blessings, one of which is the ability to forgive."

Courtney moved to stand in the shelter of his arms. "I think we confuse forgiving with forgetting. We can never forget the past—nor should we—just its wrongs."

Clint's arms tightened. "We have to surrender our 'right to hurt' to God—"

They were silent for a long time. And then they talked as if there were no stopping place. About the foundation of their home rising on the very spot where the ashes of the Mansion lay. About the headstones erected for all but Arabella Lovelace and John Laughten. Cara and her sewing machine were in great demand now, but something was missing before the story could close. It was as if the spirit of Arabella Lovelace stood between Courtney and peace.

"Clint," Courtney's voice trembled. "I am thinking of memorials—"

"Yes darling?" his voice trembled also, as if he knew in advance what she was about to propose.

"A thousand years ago, or so it seems, I wanted a cabin all our own. I was afraid—so afraid of being different from other people. A cabin represented what I had missed—a loving home."

"And now?"

"It is unfair. Two made a supreme sacrifice—and a cabin is so small—"

"Yes."

"Even out-of-place," Courtney's words were tumbling out now. "A cabin looks so alone, so lonely surrounded by vast wheat fields and giant trees—lonely and inhospitable. Where have the valley folk to go for the big gatherings we need so much for fellowship and love?"

"Nowhere." Clint had pulled her to face him and she could feel his heart thudding near her own, keeping time as if it were one heart. "But it is a beginning."

"We could extend—build on—add on as needed— bring Mandy and Mrs. Rueben back."

Clint let out a joyous whoop which she was afraid would awaken the children. And paraphrasing, he said, " 'If all the houses were one great house, what a house of love that would be!' "

"You mean—"

"I mean!"

Strange. But true. Their star—which likely began as the evening star—had become the morning star. Somewhere a bird called to announce the dawn. "Cousin Bella, we will do it—and we will live out the future rooted in the beautiful past you gave us. Then we will tell you all about it when God calls us home and your morning comes again."

"Well, darling," Courtney whispered softly to Clint, "I guess this could be called love's happy ending."

"Wrong!" Clint laughed joyously. "Love like ours knows no end at all."

HARVEST HOUSE PUBLISHERS

For The Best In Inspirational Fiction

RUTH LIVINGSTON HILL CLASSICS

Bright Conquest
The Homecoming
The Jeweled Sword

Morning Is For Joy
This Side of Tomorrow
The South Wind Blew Softly

June Masters Bacher
PIONEER ROMANCE NOVELS

Series 1

1. Love Is a Gentle Stranger
2. Love's Silent Song
3. Diary of a Loving Heart

4. Love Leads Home
5. Love Follows the Heart
6. Love's Enduring Hope

Series 2

1. Journey To Love
2. Dreams Beyond Tomorrow
3. Seasons of Love

4. My Heart's Desire
5. The Heart Remembers
   (Coming Spring 1991)

Series 3

1. Love's Soft Whisper
2. Love's Beautiful Dream
3. When Hearts Awaken
4. When Hearts Awaken

5. When Morning Comes
   Again
6. Gently Love Beckons

MYSTERY/ROMANCE NOVELS

Echoes From the Past, *Bacher*

PIONEER ROMANCE NOVELS

Sweetbriar, *Wilbee*
The Sweetbriar Bride, *Wilbee*
Sweetbriar Spring, *Wilbee*

Available at your local Christian bookstore

Other Good
Harvest House Reading

LOVE'S SOFT WHISPER
by *June Masters Bacher*

In just seconds Courtney Glamora's world split in half. Her mother was sending her away again—and this time far away to the Columbia Territory. Now the shy 16-year-old finds herself caught in the center of a lingering family feud. Through a special relationship Courtney learns to trust God and uncovers long-hidden secrets.

LOVE'S BEAUTIFUL DREAM
by *June Masters Bacher*

In this anxiously awaited sequel to *Love's Soft Whisper*, Clint Desmond and Courtney Glamora deepen their relationship with the Lord and with each other as they face and overcome Clint's tragic accident, their broken engagement, and the fear and regret that threaten their life together.

WHEN HEARTS AWAKEN
by *June Masters Bacher*

Clint and Courtney's love triumphs at last in *When Hearts Awaken*, and they are married in a beautiful Christmas Eve wedding. But the ensuing days of deepening love are soon torn asunder by Courtney's struggle between the mother who tries to control her and her love for her husband, for whom she has pledged to "forsake all others."

But it is the mysterious secrets of Rambling Gate that pose a dangerous threat to Courtney and Clint. It is there that Courtney's world explodes, robbing her of the promise of motherhood.

In the face of growing sorrow and the widening gulf between herself and her beloved husband, Courtney must find renewed hope and the courage to once again believe in God's faithfulness.

ANOTHER SPRING
by *June Masters Bacher*

This is the fourth book in the *Love's Soft Whisper* series and the sequel to *When Hearts Awaken* by bestselling Pioneer Romance novelist June Masters Bacher. The romantic saga of life in the beautiful Columbia Valley continues as Courtney and Clint and the pioneer families struggle to settle the Northwest Territory and overcome adversity caused by the uncontrollable forces of nature and the foolishness of man. Old family rivalries resurface, as tragedy entangles Courtney and Clint in a custody battle for her sister's young twins. As spring returns, miraculous events prove to Courtney that God's promises to the faithful are fulfilled far beyond human dreams. There are over 1 million Bacher Pioneer Romance novels in print.

Dear Reader:

We would appreciate hearing from you regarding the June Masters Bacher Love's Soft Whisper Series. It will enable us to continue to give you the best in inspirational romance fiction.

Mail to: Love's Soft Whisper Editors
Harvest House Publishers, 1075 Arrowsmith
Eugene, OR 97402

1. What most influenced you to purchase *When Morning Comes Again?*
   - ☐ The Christian story
   - ☐ Cover
   - ☐ Backcover copy
   - ☐ _____
   - ☐ Recommendations
   - ☐ Other June Masters Bacher Pioneer Romances you've read

2. Where did you purchase *When Morning Comes Again?*
   - ☐ Christian bookstore
   - ☐ General bookstore
   - ☐ Other
   - ☐ Grocery store
   - ☐ Department store

3. Your overall rating of this book:
   - ☐ Excellent ☐ Very good ☐ Good ☐ Fair ☐ Poor

4. How many Bacher Love's Soft Whisper Romances have you read altogether?
   (Choose one) ☐ 1 ☐ 2 ☐ 3 ☐ Over 3

5. How likely would you be to purchase other Bacher Love's Soft Whisper Romances?
   - ☐ Very likely
   - ☐ Somewhat likely
   - ☐ Not very likely
   - ☐ Not at all

6. Please check the box next to your age group.
   - ☐ Under 18
   - ☐ 18-24
   - ☐ 25-34
   - ☐ 35-39
   - ☐ 40-55
   - ☐ Over 55

Name _____

Address _____

City _____ State _____ Zip _____